COLLATERAL CASUALTIES

A Kate Huntington Mystery

Kassandra Lamb

Collateral Casualties
A Kate Huntington Mystery

Published in the United States of America by *misterio press*,
a Florida limited liability company
www.misteriopress.com

First Edition

Collateral Casualties is a work of fiction. Names, characters, and events are all products of the author's imagination. Any resemblance to actual events or people, living or dead, is entirely coincidental. Some real places may be used fictitiously.

~~~~~~~

Edited by Marcy Kennedy

Cover design by Martina Dalton
Print cover and interior design by Melinda VanLone,
Book Cover Corner

ISBN 13: 978-0-9913208-6-8 (misterio press LLC)

ISBN 10: 0991320867

*This book is dedicated to all my clients
who worked so hard in therapy to transform
themselves and their lives;*

*and to the people of Colombia,
who have suffered too much for too long.*

PROLOGUE

The man ran through the wooded park. Despite the cooler than normal day, his hair was plastered to his sweating skull. Adrenaline surged through his system.

He felt himself sliding into the zone, the rhythm of his feet slapping against the hardened dirt, in sync with his breathing–inhale, slap, slap, exhale, slap, slap.

He glanced ahead. This was his favorite stretch of trail, looping through the untamed western-most section of Patapsco State Park. The narrow path was carved out of the side of a ridge, a wall of slate and clay to his left and the embankment down to the river on his right. His foot kicked a small stone. It flew over the edge and rattled down through dry weeds. He was several steps further along before he heard it hit the water below with a soft plop.

He was considering picking up his pace on the straightaway–maybe he could beat his personal best–when he glanced up again. The decision was taken out of his hands. A man on a mountain bike was headed his way, helmeted head down, pumping hard.

Slowing his pace, the runner moved to the right side of the path to give him room to pass. The cyclist kept coming full tilt down the center of the trail.

Doesn't he see me?

"Hey," he yelled with as much breath as he could muster.

The cyclist, head still down, seemed to pedal faster.

Now slowed to a jog, the runner moved onto the strip of scraggly grass between the path and the drop-off. "Hey!" he yelled louder.

The cyclist, less than thirty feet away and closing fast, finally looked up. Aviator sunglasses covered most of his face.

Hope he doesn't wipe out when he hits the brakes.

There was a quick flash of white across the cyclist's lower face, then he ducked his head and kept pedaling.

What the hell?

Survival instinct overrode confusion. The runner dove off the bank.

~~~~~~~~~

He had no idea how long he'd been out. His training kicked in, despite his fuzzy brain and the years that had intervened since he'd last used that training.

Lie still. Assess the damage. Locate the enemy before you give away your position.

His head hurt like hell. Something warm and sticky oozed down his cheek. His body ached in multiple places, but there was no screaming pain. Probably no broken bones or major lacerations. Just the sting of many smaller cuts and scrapes.

It took a moment for him to realize that his feet were higher than his head. Water lapped against his left arm, flung out to his side. Something slithered along his wrist. He fought the urge to flinch away.

There were no sounds other than those made by the river. Either the creatures of the woods were still reacting to his swan dive off the cliff or his assailant was nearby.

Opening one eye a slit, he gave his brain a moment to process what he saw. A trail of flattened weeds, crushed underbrush and scraped earth, punctuated by a few jutting rocks, marked the path of his descent. Almost at the top of the image being projected into his brain were the toes of white sneakers, hanging slightly over the edge of the embankment.

He slowly opened his eye a bit further, until he could see the owner of the sneakers. Black track suit, fingerless black biking gloves, the sunglasses and red helmet still in place.

A flash of white teeth against darker skin, then the man turned away.

Lying still as death, the runner watched the top of the bank through one slitted eye until the bushes began to rustle and a bird chirped in one of the trees along the riverbank.

CHAPTER ONE

Kate was annoyed.

She'd been looking forward to this evening all day. Not that she was happy about her husband working on a Sunday night, but an evening all to herself was a rare treat.

Once the kids were tucked into bed and Maria had retreated to her third-floor apartment, Kate had put on her old chenille robe and stretched out on the bed to read, a glass of wine within easy reach on the nightstand. She'd added her sigh to the soft moans and creaks of the old Victorian house settling down for the night.

But she couldn't concentrate on the damn book. She kept thinking about the man she was having lunch with the next day. Pursing her lips, she gave up and put the book down. She took a sip of wine and let her mind wander where it was determined to go anyway.

After all, it wasn't as if her memories of the man were unpleasant. Well, one of them wasn't totally pleasant. Miller Dawson had scared the crap out of her during his first session at the trauma recovery center where she'd worked.

Just two years out of grad school, she hadn't always felt the confidence in her skills that she pretended to have. But her boss, Sally Ford, had told her repeatedly, "You have to *act* like you know what you're doing. About twenty five percent of the effectiveness of therapy is due to the client's *belief* that it's going to work and their trust in you, the therapist."

Another fifty percent, according to Sally, depended on the

client's own motivation to change. Only about twenty percent was due to the therapist's skill level. Sally's advice had both reassured and humbled Kate. In other words, she didn't have nearly as much to do with whether or not her clients got better as she thought she did.

Novice Kate hadn't had the nerve to ask about the remaining five percent, but the more experienced Kate of today knew what Sally's answer would have been. That last five percent was due to dumb luck. Or one might prefer to think of it as divine intervention.

In Miller's case, Kate knew his success was eighty percent his own determination, with a healthy dose of dumb luck/divine intervention thrown in. *Maybe* two percent had been due to her actual skill at the time as a therapist.

His Aryan good looks and suave charm had thrown her a bit, during that first session, as she tried to figure out if he was coming on to her.

He'd just had another romance fall apart and wanted to figure out what he was doing wrong. So far, so good. That was a common enough reason for people to seek therapy.

His most recent ex had accused him of being insufferably overbearing, egotistical and sometimes downright verbally abusive. Oh, and by the way, he informed his new therapist, he was awaiting trial on stalking charges for harassing this same ex-girlfriend.

Kate had gulped a little. "Have past girlfriends said anything like that?"

She'd expected a denial but instead he casually replied, "Oh yeah. Especially the egotistical part. But I figure if you've got it, flaunt it."

Oookkaay, bolstering self-esteem apparently didn't need to be on their list of therapeutic goals. Or was this just narcissistic bluster to cover up self-doubt?

"And what exactly do you feel you have to flaunt?" Kate hoped her tone sounded neither sarcastic nor flirtatious.

Miller held out his arms, as if to say, *Just look at me*. "And I'm very successful at what I do."

"And what is it that you do?" Kate had asked, thankful for the segue into the next part of the intake interview, getting a personal and family history. With men, starting with their work history was often a good way to get them talking.

Miller grinned. "I could tell ya, but then I'd have ta kill ya."

Kate let out a nervous laugh.

"I'm not completely joking. My work's classified. Currently I'm attached to an office at NSA. You know what that is?"

Kate nodded. Most Marylanders knew that the National Security Agency was housed at Fort Meade, and that the intelligence-gathering organization was quite hush-hush about what it did and how it did it. "You said 'currently.' What have you done in the past?"

"Well, I'm a lieutenant in the Army Reserves. I was on active duty during Desert Storm. Saw my share of action there. Before that I was... I guess you could say a 'consultant'." Miller made quotation marks in the air. "Worked for a government agency that I definitely can't tell you about unless I'm willing to kill you. They paid very well if you did good work for them. And I did good work. I took out some bad guys in several places I can't admit I've ever visited."

Kate had tried not to stutter. "What do you mean by 'took out'?"

He looked at her as if she didn't speak English. "I killed them."

She gasped. "You were a paid assassin for the government?"

He'd given her a mock-insulted look. "*Assassin* is such an ugly word. I prefer *operative*. And yes, I was a mercenary for the good ole U.S.A. But make no mistake, the guys I took out were evil. We're sitting here today enjoying our freedom because they never got a chance to do the things they were planning to do."

Kate took another sip of wine and smiled at her naiveté back then. She had literally run to Sally's office as soon as Miller's heels cleared the center's outer door. As she told her boss about this new client, she *had* actually stuttered. "I th-think he's a-a psychopath, S-Sally."

"Maybe, or possibly just a narcissist with a capital N." Then Sally had suggested a question Kate could ask Mr. Dawson the next time he came in, to assess if the man had a conscience.

She'd begged her boss to take over the case.

"Not yet. See what he says when you ask him that. And try to be a bit subtle, so he doesn't catch on to the reason you're asking."

"And how am I going to do that? How do you *subtly* ask a guy, 'If you found a wallet on the ground, would you try to find its owner or would you just take out any cash and throw it away?'"

Sally chuckled. "Make up some other random questions and tell him it's a psychological test you're required to give to all clients. Then watch his body language. Is he sincere, or does he just *seem* to be sincere? But keep in mind that psychopaths are excellent liars. You know what to look for when someone is lying?"

Kate nodded.

"Forget it in this case. This guy may very well lie without batting an eye."

"Great."

Sally graced her with one of her rare smiles that lit up her chocolate brown face. "Just pay close attention and trust your instincts." Then she offered an additional reassurance. "By the way, I'll believe he's Army Reserves and was in Desert Storm. He's the right age and that's too easy for us to check out. But secret assassin for the CIA? Come on!"

"He didn't say the CIA, but I guess that's who it had to be. They're the ones who do that kind of stuff, aren't they?"

"Oh, I believe it of the CIA but, honey child, I don't believe for a minute that this guy was one of their operatives. For one thing he wouldn't be talking about it so casually."

Kate reached for her wine again. *Hmm, almost gone.* Did she want another glass? She normally only had one in the evenings, as part of her wind-down routine, unless they were celebrating something. Or unless her husband seduced her before she got around to the wine. Giving in to said seductions was another excellent way to wind down in the evening.

Grinning, she shuffled out to the kitchen in her slippers to refill her glass. She reached up to push a stray dark curl out of her eyes, then grabbed the curl and pulled it back around to get a good look at it. *Three gray hairs!*

Well, what did she expect at forty-four.

Taking her refreshed wineglass over to the living room sofa, she sat down and fast-forwarded her memory to the next session with Miller.

In response to the wallet question, the man had looked her right in the eye, then smiled. "Depends on how much cash was in it. No point in being an ass over chump change. But if I looked in there and saw a fifty or more staring back at me, I'd probably take out the money, then mail the wallet to the poor schmuck. I've lost my own a couple times. Royal pain to replace everything."

"Would you put a return address on the envelope?" Kate asked.

That question he'd thought about for a moment. "Probably. Too important to risk it getting lost in the mail."

"What if he contacted you and asked about the money?"

"I'd lie and say it was empty when I found it."

"Would you feel guilty?"

"Not very." Miller sat forward, his expression serious. "Honestly, I've got a lot bigger stuff than that to feel guilty about."

"Such as killing people for hire?" Her voice was gentle. She was actually starting to warm up to this guy.

"Them, not particularly. I thought of it as a necessary evil. They... well, I don't want to say they deserved to die. But I knew the world would be a safer and better place without them.

"But there's other things I feel guilty about. Such as the Iraqis I had to kill in Desert Storm. Most of them were kids, even younger than I was at the time. And they were draftees. Had no choice in the matter."

Kate waited a beat. "I'm sorry for them but also for you, Miller, that you had to deal with that. I can't even begin to imagine how soldiers do what they do."

He looked away. "Bad memories."

Kate couldn't recall how she'd segued into finishing the personal history, but she remembered Miller saying, "More bad memories. That's why I'm here. I know my problems with women have to do with my childhood. I just don't know how to fix it."

"Hopefully I can help you figure that out," she replied softly.

His story was one of the saddest she had ever heard, before or since. The only child of an Army sergeant and a stay-at-home mom, he had seen more heartache by the time he was ten than most people have to face in a lifetime. His father, when he was home from a tour of duty, was a binge drinker. He'd never hit his pretty wife but he had, in Miller's words, "torn her to shreds verbally." Miller's mother got back at her husband by bringing a string of men into her bed whenever he was away. One of her most frequent lovers was her husband's best friend, a man Miller thought of as family.

At that point in the story, Miller had paused and looked up at the ceiling, swallowing hard. "Not ready to go there yet." Three sessions later, he'd told her that the man hadn't confined his sexual exploits to his mother's bed. He'd molested Miller on a regular basis, and his mother knew what was going on.

But in that second session, Miller had said, "Kate, I know this is gonna be rough, going back and dealing with all that sh... uh, crap. I'm gonna try real hard to be honest with you, 'cause I really want to get married and have a family. I love kids. I want to have the good family, the happy family we should've been back then." It was a common desire of people who had grown up in severely dysfunctional families, but Kate had never heard it expressed quite so earnestly before.

"And time's running out on me. I'm thirty-six years old. If I don't get my act together soon..." He stopped and shook his head.

Miller's parting shot, that second session, was to point out he'd known exactly why Kate was asking about hypothetical lost wallets. "Believe it or not, and despite all I've done, I try to be a moral man. I don't want to be like my parents."

By the end of that session, Kate had known this man was not a psychopath, but he was a textbook case of narcissistic personality disorder. His boastful arrogance was a defense mechanism against low self-esteem, not surprising considering his history. Personality disorders, by definition, were almost impossible to cure; they were too ingrained in the person's basic make-up. She'd decided to give it her best shot, though. She liked this guy, a sentiment she didn't always experience when dealing with narcissists.

Fast-forward another three years. She was now Kate Huntington, having married her first husband, Eddie. And Miller Dawson resembled the man who had first walked into her office in appearance only. He had completely reinvented himself and was now a kind, thoughtful and, indeed, extremely moral man.

Sally had read her one-page summary of Miller's final session. Then she'd looked up, dark eyes narrowed. "Is this for real, Kate?"

"Yes, ma'am, it is."

"Is this the same guy you thought was a psychopath when he first started with you?"

"Yup, same guy. Well, not the same guy really, but still lives in the same body and goes by the same name. He's changed more dramatically than I ever thought anyone could."

Sally's brilliant smile split her face. "Sweet Jesus, you've cured a personality disorder."

"Correction. I guided the man down the path. He cured himself."

"But still..."

"Yeah, I'm feeling an extreme natural high at the moment. As a matter of fact, I'm resisting the urge to grab you and dance around the office."

"Don't you *dare,* girl!" Sally was the quintessential professional, always fastidiously dressed and dignified. She would no more dance around her office than she would moon someone.

Kate had just grinned and floated back to her office two inches off the ground.

What she hadn't shared with her boss was that she'd taken a risk with Miller. When female clients cried in her office, she usually leaned forward in her chair to hold their hand or pat a knee or an arm. It was considered unethical to make such gestures across genders, however. Even if the therapist didn't mean anything but comfort by the gesture, the client could take it the wrong way.

But the second time this tough guy had broken down in her office, talking about how his mother had failed to protect him, Kate couldn't help herself. She reached out and gently touched the back of Miller's hand, resting on the arm of his chair. The next thing she knew he was kneeling in front of her, head in her lap, sobbing like a baby. She patted him on the back, like one would a crying child.

At the end of that session, he asked for a hug.

Kate hesitated. "Okay, but I have to open the door first, so it can't be construed as anything other than a friendly hug."

He gave her a puzzled look. "Construed by who?" She knew then that there was no sexual agenda here. He just wanted a damn hug!

After that, they'd ended every session with a hug, with Kate praying that Sally wouldn't find out and make her stop. She knew Miller needed those hugs, the first non-sexual affection he'd had in his entire life.

Kate had learned two very valuable lessons from her work with Miller Dawson. One was that her clients needed more than just her support and guidance to heal the wounds of the past. They needed a good mommy. Transference, as Freud had dubbed the phenomenon, was not always a bad thing. Two years after Miller's last session, Kate attended a workshop called "Reparenting the Inner Child" and discovered that other therapists in the trauma recovery field had come to the same conclusion.

The other thing she'd learned from Miller's case was that one *could* cure a personality disorder. But only if the client was willing to dig deep enough into the pain to undo the traumatic experiences that had distorted their personality development in the first place.

Miller was one of the few clients who felt the need to stay in touch once they left therapy. Every year, he sent her a Christmas card, with a long note catching her up on his life. A little over a year after finishing therapy, he'd married Jill Thompson.

After his kids were born, he ended each yearly missive with the words, "Without you, Kate, my children wouldn't exist, and I wouldn't have the wonderful wife and family I've always wanted."

She always sent a short note back, closing with the comment that he deserved the credit for his success in therapy and in his life. He had changed himself. She had just walked the path beside him.

Kate hadn't thought to notify him when she'd left Sally's agency to go into private practice. She hadn't thought about him at all, until she received an e-mail from him the following January. She'd never given him her e-mail address.

He'd asked if it was okay to contact her that way, then he gave his yearly update and attached recent pictures of his children. She responded that e-mail contact was fine and apologized for disappearing on him.

"You weren't that hard to track down," he'd replied. "Remember who I used to work for." This was followed by a winking smiley face. Maybe he'd been with the CIA after all. She'd always assumed that was just narcissistic bragging, especially when he'd never mentioned it again after the second session.

She'd received one or two e-mails a year after that. Then, this past Friday, he'd called out of the blue, asking if he could meet with her, but not at her office. He tried to make it sound like he just wanted to have a friendly catch-up chat but the whole conversation had been a little strange.

She'd gently pointed out that it wasn't appropriate for her to go to lunch with him and suggested he come to the office instead, quickly reassuring him she wouldn't charge for the time.

But he kept insisting that he really wanted to take her to lunch. When she finally agreed, he asked her to meet him at the food court in Columbia Mall, a rather strange place to take someone to lunch. Then the conversation had gone from weird to weirder. "If you get there before me, go ahead and get what you want to eat and I'll pay you back." Before she could respond, he'd disconnected.

Kate reached for her wineglass on the coffee table and realized it was empty. She glanced at her watch. Ten o'clock. She needed to get to bed. Long day tomorrow. Was she wound down enough to go to sleep? Not really, since she was now ruminating again about why Miller wanted to meet for lunch, and in such a strange place.

She thought about another glass of wine but decided against it. Two glasses was her limit on a weeknight.

Then she heard a key in the front door lock. A grin spread across her face. Skip was home. She was fairly sure she'd be able to get to sleep just fine, in a little while.

CHAPTER TWO

Kate stood beside the fountain that dominated the center of Columbia Mall, scanning the lunchtime crowd. She spotted a man who might be Miller–right height, slim, blond hair. It no doubt had a good bit of gray in it now. He'd be in his early fifties.

She raised her hand to wave but the man turned away. He fell into step with a group of people walking past him. Nope, not Miller. He was probably fat and bald by now. She'd mistaken the stranger for him because he looked like Miller had in his thirties.

She walked into the food court itself. An array of fragrances assailed her, dominated by that of hot grease. Her stomach rumbled.

She didn't see anyone who resembled an aging Miller. Would they even recognize each other after thirteen years?

He'd said to go ahead and get her food so she ordered a turkey wrap and fruit smoothie. She was standing at the counter waiting for her food when someone tapped her on the shoulder. Turning, she found the stranger she had thought was Miller standing behind her.

He wasn't a particularly tall man, just a few inches over her five-seven, but he was trim and fit. There was indeed considerable gray mixed in with the blond hair. His tanned face had several wrinkles. They just made him look more rugged rather than old.

She still wasn't sure it was Miller until he grinned at her. She cocked her head. *Why'd he pretend not to see me when I waved?*

With a mental shrug, she moved to give him a hug. But he grabbed her hand instead and shook it vigorously. "It's so good to see you, Kate. You haven't changed a bit."

She smiled. "I thought you always tried to tell the truth, Miller. You know that's a barefaced lie."

The surly teenager behind the counter plopped the tray with Kate's food in front of them. Before she could demand payment, Miller said, "Could you get the same for me, please?" The girl grimaced and walked away.

While they waited for his food, they chatted a bit about their kids. It was obvious the man was incredibly proud of his young daughter and preteen son. "Johnny's getting a little rebellious now," he said. "But they're both good kids."

Food received and paid for, they walked toward the tables. Miller took Kate's elbow and steered her to one that was some distance from the other diners.

Once seated, he said, "I know I sent you a condolence card, but I've got to tell you again how sorry I was when I heard about your husband's death. It was like a fist in the gut. Here you'd helped me get healthy enough to find a wonderful woman and have the family I'd always wanted. And then you lost the man you loved, before you could even have kids."

"Thank you. It was a horrible time, but I did have his child. I discovered I was pregnant a month after he died. And I'm happily remarried now. I have a wonderful family, so you don't need to feel bad for me."

"I assumed both your children were your second husband's."

"Well, they are in his heart. Edie knows about her biological father but Skip is the only father she's ever known. When she asks me about Eddie, I tell her to imagine Skip, only six inches shorter and a bit skinnier, with the same easy-going personality."

Instead of the smile Kate was expecting, Miller's expression turned serious. He dropped his gaze for a second. When he raised his eyes again, she saw anxiety and determination in them.

"I have an ulterior motive for this get-together and you've just given me the best opening I'm gonna get. I want to hire your husband's detective agency, but I can't tell him exactly why."

Taken aback, Kate didn't know what to say.

"I can tell you because you already know my past, or at least some of it. And I know you'll keep it confidential. I was hoping you could ask him to do the little assignment I need done, without asking any questions."

Kate stared at him, struggling to keep her expression neutral.

"Take a bite of your food, please," Miller said. "I'm trying to make this look like a lunch interview between a businessman and a potential employee."

She shook her head slightly. *What the hell?* But she obediently took a bite of her wrap.

"I know I'm sounding a little crazy but it'll all make sense in a minute." Miller kept his voice low. "A month ago, new people moved in down the block from us. Another neighbor threw them a welcome-to-the-neighborhood party. When this one couple arrived, the hostess led them around the room, introducing them to everyone. They got to me and Jill and the man was introduced as the ambassador of a South American country. I didn't recognize his name but as I shook the man's hand, I realized I was looking into the eyes of a man I killed thirty-two years ago."

Kate choked on a sip of her smoothie. Her heart kicked into overdrive as her brain scrambled to process what Miller was saying.

"He'd had some plastic surgery but I knew who he was. The problem is I didn't cover up that fact fast enough. He knew I'd recognized him. He said he hadn't caught my name. The hostess repeated it, then he said it over to himself, like he was memorizing it."

Kate gasped. "My God, Miller!"

"Yeah, not good. Finally I got my wits about me and said, 'So is this lovely lady your wife?' He introduced her. Then I said, 'You know, when I was a young man I did some wild and crazy things, but now I'm so happy to be married and settled down. No man wants to do anything to jeopardize his wife and family.'"

"Wasn't that telling him just how to get to you?" Kate whispered.

"Yes, but Jill was standing right next to me. She'd been introduced as my wife. I figured that was the best way to convey to him that I was out of that life and wasn't going to jeopardize what I had by telling anybody about his new identity. There was a threat in there too. That I'd go after his family if he messed with me. I gave him a slight nod and he nodded back. Message received, or so I thought. But since then I've had some things happen. I think he's trying to kill me, but make it look like an accident."

Miller glanced at his watch, doing a credible imitation of a busy executive a little annoyed that his companion was taking so long to eat. Kate took another bite of her neglected wrap. It tasted like cardboard. She finally managed to swallow it.

"What does all this have to do with Skip?" she whispered. "He's a private investigator, not a spy."

"I'm getting to that. I'm about to hand you a folder, inside is a letter. Don't take it out of the folder. It's on distinctive stationery so if he's watching he'd probably recognize what it is. Make it look like I'm showing you a job description."

Miller handed her the folder. She opened it carefully. On cream-colored stationery, that looked like it was only one step away from pure linen, was a typed note. *I am hoping you will do me the honor of your presence on Friday, 16 September, 2011, for a short chat. I believe you will find the discussion worth your time. I will contact you by Wednesday next with further details. In the meantime, please take care of yourself. A Concerned Friend.*

"That came in the mail last Wednesday. No return address," Miller said.

"How do you know this note is even from this ambassador?"

"I'm pretty sure it is."

Kate narrowed her eyes at him. "And what exactly did you want to hire my husband to do?"

"He doesn't have to hurt anybody and it's not dangerous, I swear. I just need to get another look at this guy. I still have some contacts. Had them do some checking on the ambassador without telling them why." Miller's voice was still low but he was talking fast. "They got back to me Friday morning. They think they've located the residence of the man's mistress. He goes there every Monday, Wednesday and Friday, for several hours in the late afternoon. If I show up near there and he spots me, that wouldn't be good. I need somebody he won't recognize to go to the door with some excuse, like he's delivering a pizza and got the wrong address. I'll give him a fake pen. It's really a small camera. I just need a decent head shot of the man, a close-up."

"You're not sure it's that same guy, based on his reaction? And I'd think an ambassador would have his picture in the newspaper at times."

Miller shook his head. "My gut says it's him but I don't have any proof. I don't want to... take action unless I'm sure. I did a search on him, of course. There's no official photo on the embassy's website. And in the newspapers, he's always standing behind someone or has his head turned away."

That *was* a bit strange. "Why can't one of your contacts get the photo for you?"

Miller rubbed his hand up and down his face, then stopped suddenly, as if remembering his role as a busy executive interviewing an applicant. He looked at his watch, then put on a polite listening look. "I've been doing too much of the talking. Can you act like you're talking while I try to explain?"

"I'm not a very good actress, Miller."

"Okay, just whenever I pause, say something–the alphabet, the first line of a nursery rhyme, whatever."

"Eeny, meeney, miny moe. Hickory, dickory dock... This is ridiculous."

"You're doing great."

"Gee, thanks. Did I just pass Spying 101?"

He smiled at her. "The first test at least. I haven't told my contacts who I think this guy is because then... uh, they would do something. I need to be sure first. Before I do anything."

Kate's stomach clenched. Bile rose in her throat. She pushed her plate away.

"You're going to kill him, aren't you?" she said so quietly she wasn't sure he could hear her over the noise from the mall and other diners.

His expression said he'd heard her, but he didn't respond right away. "Not exactly," he finally said. "I'll tell my contacts who he really is, and he'll be deported."

"And then?"

Miller hesitated again. "He'll probably end up being executed for treason by his government. That's why I've got to be sure he's the man I think he is."

The horror Kate felt must have shown on her face because he quickly added, "I have no choice. It's not just about me. I'm terrified he'll go after Jill or the kids if I don't show up for this meeting on Friday."

"Why is he waiting so long to have that meeting?"

Miller shrugged. "He could be buying time while he sets up another hit on me. Or he might be watching to see what I do in the meantime."

"Oh, good, so here you sit talking to me."

"He won't think you're anybody important to me. When we're done here, we'll stand up, shake hands and I'll say, 'Thank you for your time, Ms. Smith. I'll get back to you soon.' Then you thank me, using my real name, and we part company. I'm being very careful to make it look like I'm not worried, that I'm just going about my business as usual."

"And do you usually interview applicants over lunch in the mall?"

"Actually, yes. I work out of my home now, as a consultant on engineering projects. I don't like to bring strangers to the house so I often meet with customers, or potential temporary employees I might need for a certain job, over a meal out in public."

His failure to acknowledge her wave now made sense. He'd apparently been a good spy. Either that or he was having a psychotic breakdown and this was all an elaborate delusion.

"Have you seen the movie, *A Beautiful Mind*?" Kate asked.

Miller let out a short bark of laughter. "I'm not crazy. You saw the letter. This is all horribly real."

Yeah, *if* the letter was really from this ambassador and not some kind of weird sales pitch or scam that had become part of his delusion.

"I'm sorry. I'm not going to involve my husband in this. It's too dangerous. And you don't even know that this guy means you harm. If he's an ambassador now he's probably one of the good guys, in his new identity at least."

"I seriously doubt it. Three decades ago, this man was part of a movement to overthrow the government of his country, and they used some pretty nasty tactics to try to accomplish that goal."

Kate frowned.

Miller leaned forward. She thought for a moment that he was going to take her hand, but then he caught himself. "I understand that you don't want to jeopardize your husband's safety, but I really don't think there's much risk. I wouldn't even ask just for my own sake, but like I said, I'm scared for my family."

"I feel for you, Miller. I really do. But this is totally out of Skip's league. And I just couldn't handle it if anything happened to him, not after losing Eddie. I'd... I'd be the one who would be crazy, and I've got kids who need me, need their father. I'm sorry."

Miller sat back in his chair. "No, I'm sorry. I should've realized it was too much to ask. I just thought... I don't know what I was thinking. I'll find another way."

"Let me ask Skip for some referrals of other detectives. People he knows are good." *And a little crazy.*

"You can't tell him any of this, Kate. I really shouldn't be telling you. I could be prosecuted for treason for breaching security, if it got out that I'm talking about this."

"I'll think of a way to get some names without telling him anything specific. How can I get in touch with you? Should I just e-mail–"

"No. Don't make any contact with me in a way that can be traced. I called you Friday from a throwaway cell phone." He took out a business card and slid it across the table to her, while retrieving the folder with his other hand. "Number on the back is another throwaway. After I hear from you, I'll toss it. Don't say your name when you call, just leave the info on the voicemail."

Kate shook her head. "This is unreal."

"I wish it were. Oh how I wish it were."

He stood up and extended his hand. She rose and took it. As they shook, he said his lines in a slightly louder than normal voice.

She gave his hand a small squeeze before letting it go. "Take care of yourself, Miller," she whispered. Then in a normal voice she said, "Thank you, Mr. Dawson. I'll look forward to hearing from you."

Kate picked up her purse, turned and walked away. If Ambassador What's-His-Face was watching, she hoped he wasn't close enough to see that she was blinking back tears.

~~~~~~~~

When Kate got back to her office, she had a few minutes before her first afternoon client was due. She called Skip and asked him for some names of detectives for a client.

"It isn't something I can help with?" he asked.

"It's not your kind of case." She suspected he was dying of curiosity, but he knew better than to ask for an explanation once she'd told him it was related to a client.

"Hang on a sec." She heard paper rustling. "Okay, you got a pencil?"

"Yes."

He said a name, spelled it, gave her a phone number. "This guy's done some subcontracting for us, when we were short-handed. Smart, discreet, won't ask questions. From the few minimal, minuscule details you've given me..." Kate could hear the grin in his voice. "I'd say he should be able to handle the job."

"Two referrals would be good."

A pause, then Skip gave her another name and number. "He's a sleaze ball, will do anything for a buck. But he usually dances with the gal who brung him. He won't double cross your client."

Kate thought the second guy was the better bet. "Thanks, sweetheart. I love you so much."

"Gee, I get that for some lousy referrals. What do I get if I actually do some detecting for you?"

"Oh, I think we can come up with a fitting reward," Kate said, her voice a bit husky. "And you don't have to do *anything* more. You've done just enough."

Skip laughed and disconnected.

Kate closed her eyes for a moment. Could she do this? Could she help Miller indirectly sign a man's death warrant? Then she saw in her mind's eye the last pictures Miller had sent of his kids. His daughter in a riding habit hugging a pony, horse-crazy like her little Edie was. His son with an impish grin on his face.

She pulled out the card he had given her and called the number.

CHAPTER THREE

Skip looked down at his wife sitting next to him on the sofa. The preoccupied expression, that had been coming and going all evening, was back. "Hello. Earth to Kate," he said gently.

Her eyes lost the faraway look as she turned toward him, but they were still the washed-out gray they became when she was worried or stressed.

"I'm sorry, sweetheart. What were you saying?"

"I was telling you about seeing Janice today. She wants me to do background checks on the witnesses for one of her criminal cases," he repeated. "She jokingly called me Paul Drake and I pretended to not know who that was."

Kate snorted. "What'd she say?"

"She spluttered and faked being insulted, until I called her Perry."

"You know, it's going to be really sad when all those old TV classics have faded so far into history that the younger generation truly doesn't know who Perry Mason and Paul Drake are."

"Oh, speaking of age," Skip said, "she's invited us to her fiftieth birthday party. I told her I'd have to check with you, make sure we're free that night."

"Richard isn't even bothering to make it a surprise party?"

He shook his head. "She's planning it herself. Said she didn't trust Richard not to just invite his cronies and talk shop all evening."

"Oh, yeah, that would be a blast," Kate said. "A whole room full of estate lawyers."

Skip faked a loud snore and let his chin drop forward onto his chest. She laughed and reached over to brush back the hair that flopped down on his forehead.

His skin tingled where she'd touched it. He was tempted to sweep her up and carry her off to bed. But it was a little early yet, and he was hoping eventually she'd open up about whatever was bothering her.

"I guess we shouldn't be stereotyping like that," Kate said. "They may not all be as dull as Richard."

"I hope not." Skip draped an arm across her shoulders. They sat in comfortable silence for a few moments.

He glanced down. The preoccupied expression was back. "What's the matter, darlin'?"

Kate looked away. "Unfortunately I can't talk about it. It has to do with a client, a former client actually."

"Can't you talk about it in general terms, without violating confidentiality?" Skip had learned that his woman often needed to process things out loud to get them out of her system.

"Not this time. It's too sensitive a situation. My client's in physical danger, until certain things get resolved. That's making it harder to put aside."

Physical danger? He didn't like the sound of that.

He tightened his arm around her. "Is this the client you needed PI referrals for?"

"Yes, but let's not talk about it anymore. I might slip and say more than I should. So about this party, what night is it?"

Reluctantly he allowed the subject to be changed. "Saturday, October first."

"I don't think we have anything on the calendar, but I'll have to check with Maria. See if she's willing to watch the kids."

"You know she won't let us pay her overtime," Skip said. They tried not to take advantage of their live-in nanny and housekeeper who was normally off duty on weekends. But the daughters of their closest friends, Rob and Liz Franklin, were now grown and they hadn't found any other babysitters they trusted.

"I've learned to just put it in her next check without discussion."

Kate was smiling, but her eyes were clouded with worry again. This time he found out the cause right away.

"Sweetheart, do you ever get the sense that Janice is coming on to you?"

He grinned down at her. "Nope. Apparently tall, dark and Texan isn't her type."

She smiled back.

"Seriously," he said, "I wonder what the hell she sees in Richard."

"My best guess would be transference."

"Meaning what?" He vaguely remembered the term from Psych 101 in college.

"Richard unconsciously reminds her of her father," Kate said.

"She never talks about her father, just her mother and grandmother. I don't think he was around much."

"There you go."

Skip decided to offer a little extra reassurance. "She teases a lot, but she doesn't flirt. It's not her style."

Kate smiled up at him. "I really do like her, sweetheart. We've become friends in our own right. And since I have a platonic friendship with a man, I can hardly complain. I just wish I could warm up to Richard more."

Skip suppressed the urge to say, *Why? The man's a jerk.*

They sat in silence for another moment, then Kate let out a sigh. He suspected she was thinking about her client again. Well, if he couldn't help her with that problem, he could at least distract her from it.

He picked up her hand and gently kissed her palm. She sucked in her breath. Pulling her tight against him, he lowered his lips to hers. She parted them and invited him in.

He never grew tired of exploring her mouth. A sensation like sweet, warm liquid flowed through him. Quite a few body parts were tingling now. For a second, his throat closed at the flash of memory from the year before, when he'd almost lost her. He pushed the thought aside.

Eventually, Kate leaned back, gasping for air.

Skip stood, pulling her to her feet with him. Then he swung her up in his arms.

She snuggled her head against his chest. "You know, someday we're gonna get too old for this sweep-me-off-my-feet routine."

"Not for a while yet," he murmured, as he nuzzled her neck.

~~~~~~~~~~

Her husband's loving attentions sufficiently distracted and relaxed Kate that she fell into a sound sleep.

But at four in the morning, she woke up gasping, her cheeks wet with tears. Skip rustled next to her but didn't wake up. Kate stared at the ceiling, trying to get her breathing under control.

She couldn't remember most of the nightmare. But each time she began to drift off again, her mind flashed to the one image she did remember. Miller Dawson falling forward with a knife in his back.

At five-thirty, she gave up and slipped out of bed. Might as well go to the *dojo* and get in some extra *aikido* practice. She knew the owner would be there. He always arrived early.

In the bathroom, she pulled on the loose pants of her martial arts uniform and tied her green belt around the jacket of the *gi*. She froze for a moment, realizing part of the significance of the dream. A little over a year ago, she had almost been killed. She'd been a bit phobic regarding knives ever since.

That event had spurred her to research self-defense training. She'd wanted to know she could protect herself should she ever end up in such a situation again. *Aikido* had the most appeal because it was purely defensive. You used your opponent's energy and momentum against them. An assailant comes at you, you step aside at the last moment and they go flying past. They lunge and grab for your arm, you grab theirs and dip your shoulder. Their momentum carries them right over your back.

Kate drove into the empty parking lot of the Towson *dojo*. Apparently she had beat Brad there after all. She parked, then cranked her seat back a notch and closed her eyes.

When she'd first enrolled at the *dojo*, she'd been informed that the instructor, referred to as *sensei*, required an in-person interview to determine each new student's goals. She'd been surprised when the *sensei* had turned out not to be the wizened Japanese gentleman she had imagined but a buff, thirty-something, blue-eyed blond named Brad. After hearing her reasons for wanting to refresh her self-defense skills, he had bluntly told her that training once a week would produce only a false confidence in her ability to protect herself.

She'd thought he was just trying to promote his program, but after being thrown about unceremoniously by her classmates, she'd realized he was right. Unfortunately with her busy schedule, twice a week was the best she'd been able to accomplish, but she had managed to earn her green belt.

Kate jumped at the sound of knuckles against glass. Brad had arrived.

A half hour into their practice session, he caught her around the waist and set her back on her feet. "That's the third time you've started into a roll off balance. You're distracted."

"Sorry, *Sensei*. I didn't sleep well."

Brad cocked an eyebrow at her.

Kate grimaced. For a young man who made his living throwing people around on mats, this guy had a disconcerting level of psychological astuteness. "Okay, yes, I'm distracted. I was hoping a hard workout would help me get grounded."

Brad shook his head. "Not workin', and you're gonna get hurt. Go home."

"But class starts soon."

Brad pointed toward the door of the *dojo*. "Come back tomorrow."

She sighed. The man might be a decade younger, but in the world of *aikido* one does not argue with one's *sensei*.

Kate dragged through the morning, struggling against fatigue and preoccupation to focus on her clients' needs. By lunchtime, she'd realized she wasn't going to be able to let go of her worries about Miller until she talked it out with somebody.

And the most logical person was Rob Franklin, her lawyer and her closest friend after Skip. She and Rob usually had lunch together on Wednesdays, a tradition started years ago when their consultations on mutual cases had first blossomed into a friendship.

Kate called Rob's cell phone. The call went to voicemail. "Hey, can you come to the house tomorrow for lunch, instead of going to Mac's Place. I've got something I need to bounce off you that I don't want anybody to overhear."

~~~~~~~~

When Rob arrived the next day, there was a dollar bill sitting next to his plate on the oak table that dominated one end of Kate's kitchen. He lowered his big frame into a chair and tapped the money.

"What's this?" he asked, running meaty fingers through thick hair that was already, at fifty-two, more gray than its original dark brown.

He had a strong suspicion what her answer would be.

"That's your yearly retainer. I believe it's overdue."

Rob reached out to snag a sandwich from the platter she placed in the middle of the table. "So what you need to talk about is confidential."

"Extremely so. It's so sensitive I can't talk to Skip about it, even in general terms. But you, as my lawyer... Well, I probably shouldn't tell you either, but I've got to talk to somebody."

Rob pocketed the dollar bill and smiled at her. "As your lawyer, I will go to my death with your secrets intact."

"Don't joke about that. This really is a matter of life or death." It took fifteen minutes for her to spell out the gist of her client's situation, leaving out names and other identifying information.

After the first few minutes, Rob put his sandwich down. He was used to hearing some pretty wild stories from his clients, but this was mind-boggling. Kate had worked with *a spy*? And now somebody was trying to kill the guy.

Holy crap!

"I feel bad," Kate said. "He wanted Skip's help and I said no."

"You did the right thing. There's no way you all should get involved in this."

"I know, but I still feel bad. What if something happens to him or his family?"

Rob was a little afraid to ask the question hovering in the back of his mind. Kate tended to be protective of her clients. He chose his words carefully so he wouldn't sound like he was putting the man down. "How sure are you that this guy isn't having some kind of mental breakdown?"

"Trust me, that thought has crossed my mind a dozen times since Monday. But I'm about ninety percent sure he's as sane as you or me, and what he told me is all too true."

"I feel for the guy, but I still say leave it alone. And stay as far away from him as you can get."

Rob picked up a sandwich from the platter and put it on Kate's empty plate. She ignored it. Not a good sign. She normally had a voracious appetite.

"That didn't help you feel better, huh?" he said.

"Yes and no. You've validated my own reaction, but there's more. I got him some names of other private investigators from Skip–"

"Then you've definitely done all that you should."

Kate shook her head. "He needed a detective to help him verify this ambassador's identity. Then he's going to report the guy to the CIA. The man will be shipped home to be executed as a traitor. So no matter how this mess turns out, somebody's going to die."

Before Rob could point out that this wasn't her fault, she jumped up and paced around the room. "Then I come back around to thinking he's crazy. But I know he's not. I worked with him for three years, walked with him down into the bowels of emotional hell, and he never cracked, not even a little bit."

She stopped and turned toward Rob. Her eyes were shiny with unshed tears. "All he ever wanted was to have a loving family. Be the guy with the white picket fence and the mini-van full of kids."

Rob grabbed for her hand before she could start pacing again. He pulled her down onto the chair next to him. "And he's had that. Years of happiness he wouldn't have had without your help. But now his past has caught up with him, and there's nothing you can do about that. Nothing you *should* do about that. It's sad. It's horrible. But it's not your problem. You're a therapist, not a spy!

And as for the ambassador, he made his bed as well. He's had three decades of the good life but now his past has come back to bite him."

"Okay, that helps." She wrapped both her hands around his big paw and hung on tight. "Dear God in Heaven, please keep him safe. Keep his family safe."

Rob knew she didn't mean the ambassador. He stood and pulled her up to give her a hug. "Try to let it go, sweetheart."

~~~~~~~~

Kate found it somewhat easier to put aside her worries about Miller on Thursday. Her talk with Rob had helped. After a day of focusing on her clients' various issues, she was packing up her briefcase and looking forward to dinner and a relaxing evening with Skip and the kids.

When the phone on her desk rang, she toyed with the temptation to let it go to voicemail. Finally the responsible part of her overrode the tired part and she picked up the receiver. "Kate Huntington," she said, giving the name she still used for professional purposes.

"Kate, if you have a few minutes," Miller said without identifying himself. "I could really use a sounding board."

Kate was struggling to get her tired mind back into therapist mode. When she didn't respond right away, he said, "Oh, man, I'd forgotten how lonely it gets when you can't tell anyone what's going on."

Her heart ached for him. She cleared her throat. "I'll be happy to be your sounding board, Miller. I was just a bit surprised for a second. I hadn't expected to hear from you again, after all the cloak and dagger stuff on Monday."

"I'm on another throwaway cell. Bought it for cash, no way to trace it back to me."

"I didn't mean it that way, although I appreciate your concern for my safety. What do you need to sort out?"

"I got the confirmation I needed. Thanks for your help with that. But I also got another communication from the party in question, with reassurances that he means me no harm. Indeed, he says he's trying to keep me from harm. A little hard to believe since I harmed him, but still..."

Kate waited patiently for him to continue.

"I'm just not that guy anymore." She heard anguish in his voice. "I can't stop thinking about the look of horror on your face when you realized what would happen to–"

"Don't let that stop you from protecting yourself and your family. This stuff is so far out of my league, I don't even know how to react." She stopped, made herself take a calming breath. "Please don't let my reactions influence your decisions about what's best for you."

He chuckled. "Spoken like a true therapist."

"No! I'm not talking as a therapist here. I have no clue how to advise you." She softened her tone. "I'm speaking as someone who cares about you, who knows you're in a terrible bind. I can't see the way out of that bind any better than you can."

Silence on the line for a moment. "Thank you for caring so much, Kate." Another pause. "I don't know why but my instincts are telling me to trust... Well, maybe trust is too strong a word. Let's say I'm inclined to give him the benefit of the doubt. He's practically begging me to meet with him tomorrow."

"You haven't told anyone who you think he is?" Kate realized she'd picked up a pencil from her desk and was jabbing the point repeatedly into the note pad she kept by the phone. She made herself put the pencil down.

"No, by the time the detective got back to me I'd already gotten this letter and was having second thoughts. He implies that someone else is involved. That he's trying to protect me from that someone."

"So what are you planning to do?"

"That's what I need to figure out. The place he wants to meet me, it's a place where I would normally go. He's not asking me to break my routine, do something unusual. Which fits with the idea that someone else might be watching me. It's possible he's telling the truth, that he isn't the one who's been trying to kill me."

"Isn't it dangerous though, to meet him?" Kate picked up the pencil again. "Can't you take one of your, uh, former friends?"

"I don't think I should. I've already made them suspicious enough. That's another thing, another reason why my gut says he may be telling the truth. He didn't say anything about coming alone."

"Maybe he realizes you'd just ignore such a request."

"Maybe." Miller paused. "You may not hear from me again, but know that you've helped tremendously, just as you did years ago."

The pencil snapped in two and fell from her fingers. But she managed to keep her voice calm. "No, it's not the same at all. Then I knew what to advise, how to steer you."

"Still, you've helped, just by being somebody I could talk to about all this." Another pause. "Please don't feel guilty if... if things don't go the way I hope they do."

Kate was very glad he couldn't see her face. "You're going to meet with him then?"

"I think so. I think I need to hear what he has to say. I couldn't live with myself if I condemned him, and he wasn't really a threat." His voice was thick with emotion.

Kate clutched the phone receiver. "Dear God, be careful!"

In typical excruciatingly-honest-Miller fashion, he didn't jump right in and reassure her that he would be. "I'm gonna do my best to take care of myself," he said after a moment. "But at least if this doesn't turn out good for me, he'll probably leave my family alone. And you still can't tell anybody, Kate, no matter what happens. I don't want you getting caught up in this and getting hurt."

"Miller..." Her throat closed with fear for him. She swallowed hard. "I've never told you this, not in so many words, but you are the most remarkable person I've ever known. The world would be... a darker place without you."

She wasn't sure but she thought she heard a sob. After a long pause, he cleared his throat. She could see him, in her mind's eye, pulling himself together, squaring his shoulders, sitting up straight, ready to do what a man has to do.

Part of her wanted to tell him all that was crap. He should just take his family and run! But it wasn't her call.

"Please, please, be careful!"

"I will be, as careful as I can be." His way of saying there was no way to do this without putting himself at risk.

"Miller, I think you'll know how I mean this. I love you."

Another long pause. "I love you too, Kate. Thank you for being there for me, again."

This time the silence was different. She held the phone receiver in numb fingers, staring sightlessly across the room, until a recorded voice started squawking in her ear, "If you'd like to make a call, please hang up and try again..."

~~~~~~~~

Three days later she read the obituary in the paper.

CHAPTER FOUR

It took every ounce of Kate's energy to pretend to be interested in four-year-old Billy's description, over Sunday dinner, of the friend's birthday party he'd attended that afternoon. She had been severely depressed ever since she'd read the headline in the morning paper, *Sykesville Man Found Dead on Hiking Trail*.

The paper had honored Miller with a longer than normal obituary, detailing his volunteer work in the community and the supposed accident that had taken his life while doing one of the things he loved most, running on the trails of Patapsco State Park.

Skip kept watching her, worry in his eyes. Twice he'd asked her what was wrong, but she just shook her head.

By the time the kids' baths were done, she was so tired she could hardly stand upright. When Skip took over for story time, she trudged downstairs and into the master bathroom to brush her teeth.

Skip found her already getting ready for bed. He looped an arm around her waist and dragged her over to sit next to him on the bed. "Come on, talk to me. What's the matter, darlin'?"

Kate shook her head, struggling not to cry. "I can't tell you. It has to do with that case. And tomorrow I won't be home for dinner. I have to go somewhere after work."

"You said the client's in danger." There was alarm in his voice. "You're not going to meet her, are you?"

"The danger's over now," Kate said, not bothering to correct his assumption about the client's gender. "Sweetheart, I wish I could talk to you about this, but I can't. Confidentiality..." She caught herself. She'd been about to say, *Confidentiality doesn't die with the client.* Skip was an investigator. She dared not give him any hints about what had happened or he might start poking around in this hornet's nest. Kate shuddered at that thought.

"Confidentiality doesn't allow me to say anything more, but I need to go somewhere tomorrow evening. It's important to me." She prayed he would stop asking questions she couldn't answer.

"Okay, but the suspense is killing me."

Better suspense than foreign agents, Kate thought as Skip pulled her onto his lap. She closed her eyes and relaxed against him.

He touched his lips to each of her eyelids and wrapped his arms more snugly around her. She was grateful for the warmth of his embrace, but it didn't completely ease the hollow feeling in her chest.

~~~~~~~~~

Kate arrived at the funeral home Monday evening shortly after the viewing had begun. She planned to hover in the background until she could discreetly approach the coffin to say goodbye, and then offer her condolences to Jill Dawson as a friend Miller used to work with. It wasn't a lie. He had worked with her, very hard in fact, in therapy.

But things did not go according to plan. Stepping into the funeral home brought back a flood of memories from Eddie's memorial service. The low voice of the funeral director as he greeted her at the door, the cloying fragrance of the flower arrangements, the murmur of conversations... It was all she could do not to turn and run.

She hid in the cloak room for a few minutes, actively struggling to find the delicate balance between warm caring and clinical detachment that came so naturally in her therapy office.

Still a bit shaky, she stepped out into the main room. But she couldn't make herself go up to the coffin. One glimpse of Miller's immobile face from ten feet away told her she would burst into tears if she got any nearer. That would make the other mourners far too curious about who she was.

When there was a lull in the line of people trickling past the widow, Kate approached, her hand extended. "I'm Kate Canfield. Miller and I worked together years ago. I'm so sorry for your loss. He was a wonderful man."

Kate's use of Canfield did not fool Jill Dawson. Her red-rimmed eyes went wide. "You're Kate. Oh, thank you, Lord!" She grabbed Kate's arm and hustled her to a far corner of the room.

An older man started to approach but Jill shook her head slightly in his direction. "That's my father. The kids are home with my mom. They were here earlier but I couldn't put them through this again." Her voice broke on a sob but she quickly got herself under control.

"You're the Kate he saw, the therapist that helped him, right?"

Kate nodded. Out of the corner of her eye, she saw the elderly gentleman discreetly steering people away from where they were sitting.

"I need to talk to you. I know he met with you recently." Jill's words tumbled out. "He told me not to contact you, but whoever killed him wouldn't suspect anything from this. I mean it's only natural that you would come here to pay your respects, and that I would talk to you for comfort, right?"

Kate looked around nervously but no one was within earshot. What could she say to this woman to convince her that Miller had died of natural causes, or at least get her to let it go? There was nothing to be gained from the truth now. He was dead, and if Jill pursued his murderer it would just put her and their kids in danger.

"The paper said it was an accident but I just overheard someone say that Miller had a heart attack. That must've caused his fall."

Jill snorted. "He didn't have a heart attack. He was only fifty-two years old and healthy as a horse!"

"I know it's hard to believe but seemingly healthy people do have heart attacks. I know of at least two cases. One was an acquaintance of my first husband. The man was a runner, like Miller–"

"Stop! I appreciate what you're trying to do." Jill paused and looked around herself. She lowered her voice. "But you and I both know that Miller was murdered."

What the hell could she say to that, without flat out lying?

"I need your advice," Jill said, "but we can't talk here. Can I come to your office tomorrow? Do you think that would be safe? For you, I mean."

"You know what's going on then?" Kate whispered.

"Some of it. I need to figure out what to do."

Kate pulled one of her cards out of her wallet and slipped it to Jill. "Can you come at noon?"

Jill nodded. "The funeral's in the morning. When we get home, I'll tell people I want to lie down. My folks'll cover for me and watch the kids." She stood up and took Kate's hand. Kate rose and they walked back toward the coffin.

Kate suddenly stopped, shaking her head. "I'm sorry. I can't..."

Jill squeezed her hand. "I understand," she said under her breath, then in a normal voice added, "Thank you so much for coming. It really helps to know that Miller touched so many people's lives."

Kate squeezed her hand back. "Be careful, Jill," she whispered.

~~~~~~~~

At noon the next day, Jill Dawson perched on the edge of the loveseat in the corner of Kate's office. Kate sat in an armchair facing her. Jill dispensed with the niceties. "I found an envelope in Miller's best suit when I took it out of the closet to take to the funeral home. Writing on the outside said, 'Jill, only open this if I don't come home Friday evening.' There were two anonymous letters inside along with a rather vague explanation of what they meant." She handed Kate two sheets of expensive stationery, one of which she had seen before.

"I was hoping you could fill in some of the blanks and help me decide what to do," Jill said.

"Knowing Miller, he told you what to do," Kate said softly.

Jill dropped her gaze to her lap. "There were instructions on how to access a bank account in the Caymans, and how to establish new identities. He said to take the kids and go away. Start over somewhere else."

She raised her eyes to meet Kate's. "So my first question is, was my husband losing his mind?"

"No," Kate said. "I had my doubts, but not now. Did he say who the letters were from?"

"No, just that someone from his past had, quote, 'come back to haunt him.' And that he couldn't say more in writing, and maybe the less I knew the better."

Kate sat back in her chair, mentally putting herself in Jill's shoes. She'd want to know what the hell was going on, so she could best decide how to protect herself and her kids. "I'm not sure I agree with that," she said out loud. "You need to know what you're up against. But I think you should go away, at least for a while." She filled Jill in on what Miller had told her.

"He said there were some attempts on his life, things that would have looked like accidents. Do you know what he was talking about?"

Jill gazed at the ceiling as she thought about that. "A few times he seemed preoccupied. One of them was the day after that party. Then, a couple weeks ago, I came home and he was all scraped up. He said he'd been running and slipped and fell down an embankment. He kept changing the subject when I asked for details. I wish I could remember that ambassador's name. I could ask my neighbor."

"No! Miller would not want you to investigate. Anything you do that lets on that you know he was killed and why, then you're in jeopardy."

Jill's mouth was set in a stubborn line. In a much gentler voice, Kate said, "One of the last things he said to me was that if things went wrong on Friday, at least *they* would leave his family alone. If you try to investigate and get yourself killed, his death will be for nothing, and your kids will be orphans."

Tears streamed down Jill's face. Kate handed her the box of tissues she kept close at hand. "Is there someplace safe you can go?"

Jill dabbed at her eyes. "I've been giving that some thought. I have a friend in Colorado. We've lost touch the last few years so there's no record of recent contact, but I know she wouldn't move without telling me. It's the kind of friendship where we just pick up wherever we left off, no matter how long it's been. If I show up on her doorstep, she'll take me in."

"Can you give me her address and phone number?" Kate asked.

"I didn't think to bring them with me."

"Okay, here's what I suggest. Go home and pack. Do you have a garage?"

Jill nodded.

"Pull your car in there so no one can see you loading it up. Just clothes and your most precious small mementos. Nothing more than will fit in your trunk. When you pull out of there tonight, it should look like you're taking the kids to McDonald's for dinner."

Kate's brain was scrambling for a way to safely get the contact information from her. Wait, she could have Rose pick it up.

"Write down your friend's address and phone number, then take with you or destroy anything that might lead someone to her, old Christmas cards, anything. Give me your address. A friend of mine will come by this afternoon. A short Hispanic woman with her hair tied back in a bun. She'll pretend to be taking a survey or have a fake petition to sign. Slip her the contact information."

Jill nodded again as she pulled a small pad out of her purse to write down her address.

"I'll be in touch in a week or so, after the dust settles some," Kate said, leaning forward to take the slip of paper. "It might be a good idea for your parents to leave town as well. If you have to call me, use a prepaid cell phone, then destroy it after we talk."

Jill let out a short humorless laugh. "We sound like a bad spy movie. How did this happen? How did my life end up in this place?" She started to cry again.

Kate gave her a moment, then softly said, "You know Miller never imagined this would happen. He thought all of that was well behind him. A different lifetime."

"He only mentioned it a couple times, and then rather vaguely. He said he'd done some things he wasn't proud of, but that were necessary."

They talked for a few more minutes, Kate doing the best she could to be supportive in a situation that was totally beyond either of their experiences.

After Jill left, Kate used her cell phone to call her friend and the co-owner of her husband's private investigations agency.

"Hernandez," Rose answered brusquely.

"It's Kate. I have a big favor to ask. Are you willing to do something for me, no questions asked, and you can't tell your partner about it?"

Silence for a beat. "Yes to the favor, but I do have to ask why I can't tell Skip?"

"It has to do with a client, and if he knew what was going on he wouldn't be able to resist investigating."

"Okay, one more question which you can refuse to answer," Rose said. "Why would that be a bad thing?"

"Because it would probably get him killed."

~~~~~~~~~

Kate came out of her last session of the day to find a stocky man with swarthy skin sitting in her waiting room. She stifled a gasp. For a moment, she considered walking right out the door with her client.

The man stood up, holding his hands out, palms up. "I assure you, Mrs. Huntington, I mean you no harm. I was hoping to talk to you about my grief regarding the death of a friend."

Kate's client gave her an apprehensive look.

"It's okay, Amanda." Kate ushered her to the outer door.

Turning back to the man, she said, "How can I help you?"

"May we go into your office?"

Good idea! In her desk was the .32 revolver her friend, Mac Reilly, had purchased for her when she went into private practice, insisting that a woman in an office by herself needed some means of protection. Kate locked the outer door of the waiting room, just in case this guy had a few henchmen out in the hall. She made an after-you gesture toward her office.

Pointing to the chair in front of her desk, she moved around it and sat in her own chair. Heart in her throat, she casually rested a sweaty palm on the handle of the desk drawer containing her gun. At least, she hoped the gesture looked casual.

"I assume the person you're referring to is M–"

He held up his hand. "No names, please." He took out a cloth handkerchief and wiped his brow.

Kate waited in silence. Her heart was pounding, but anger was starting to override her fear.

"I am deeply grieved by our mutual friend's death," the man said. "I wanted to personally reassure you that I was not responsible for it. I believe that I have identified the person who was responsible and I have dealt with him accordingly."

"And why, Mr. No Name, should I believe that?" Despite herself, the anger crept into her voice.

He gave her a sad smile. "You have every reason to be angry. Even though I did not kill the gentleman, he died because of his acquaintance with me. I had great respect for him and it saddens me that his young children are now fatherless."

"You had respect for him? He tried to–" Kate caught herself.

The man shrugged. "He was just doing his job, and quite frankly his agenda at the time was more noble than my own."

Kate raised an eyebrow at him.

"Let me tell you a story, Mrs. Huntington. Once upon a time, a young boy, just sixteen years old, left his parents' farm to become part of a group that was attempting to overthrow the corrupt government of his country, a government that cared nothing about the poor.

"This young boy fought for their cause for several years, until he was twenty. By then he was not quite so naive. He had come to realize this group was corrupt in its own way. They had begun to take money from those who grew crops that would then be exported to the United States and turned into addictive drugs. The leaders justified this by saying that the drugs would happen anyway. At least this way, a good cause was being financed, and when we had taken over the country we would help the farmers learn how to grow more respectable crops.

"Then they made this young man a lieutenant and put him in charge of those responsible for collecting the *fees* from the farmers. He was not at all comfortable with that role. He was shamed by the looks of terror and hatred on the poor people's faces, people like his parents. But this was an army, a war. Soldiers are not allowed to question or complain. They are expected to follow orders."

"And anyone attempting to leave would be treated as a deserter," Kate said, drawn into the man's story despite herself.

"Exactly." The man leaned forward and looked her in the eye. "Our mutual friend did that young man a great favor. He woke up in a hospital, with no papers, no identity, his face scarred by the fire in which his body was supposed to have been consumed."

Leaning back again, he scratched his chin through his beard. The coarse black hairs didn't completely conceal the shiny surface of old burn scars.

"That young man pretended to have amnesia. A doctor took pity on him and did some rudimentary reconstructive surgery. When he was released from the hospital, he made his way to a place where he had been burying most of his wages for years, intending to someday go back to his village and buy his parents a better farm.

"Instead he bought himself a new identity and, through bribery, got a job with the very police force he had once fought against. He had an uncanny ability to know where the rebels were hiding and where they might strike next. This helped him advance through the ranks. His contributions to establishing relative peace in his country eventually earned him a place in the government he had once despised."

"So why should I believe that you wouldn't see... my friend's recognition of you as a threat?" Kate asked.

"Oh, I did, for a moment or two, until he reassured me, indirectly, that he had no more desire to dredge up the past than I did."

"Then how did anyone else even know that he'd recognized you?"

"That is what I so deeply regret, Mrs. Huntington. I discussed the matter with my wife, and apparently a member of my household staff was eavesdropping. I am as mystified as you are as to why that person felt the need to protect my current identity. If anything, I would have expected him to turn me in to our country's authorities, hoping for a reward. But instead, he eliminated what he perceived to be a threat to his employer."

"What happened to him?"

"Do you really want an answer to that question?"

"I guess not." Kate already knew the answer, but there was no sense of justice, only sadness that yet another person had died because Miller and this man happened to run into each other at a party.

"There is another reason I have come to see you this evening," the man said. "I wanted to warn you to leave all of this very much alone. Do not ask any questions, make any phone calls. Don't even look up anything related to me, my country or our friend on the internet. I am not at all sure that the killer was working alone. It has crossed my mind that members of the group to which I once belonged might attempt to blackmail me with exposure, in order to use my influence within the government to their own ends. I am currently investigating that possibility. Until I know for sure that my employee acted alone, there is indeed some reason for concern and caution."

"So you have come here, drawing attention to me," Kate said, fury in her voice.

"I assure you that I know how to enter a building without being seen, and I did not tell anyone, not even my driver who is my most trusted employee, where I was going. He thinks I am getting a massage at a spa five blocks from here."

The man stood up. "I have taken enough of your time, Mrs. Huntington. I will communicate with you when I am convinced the situation is completely resolved. In the meantime, I trust your discretion."

She followed him out of her office. Without looking back, he crossed the waiting room. He turned the lock on the knob as he exited so the door locked behind him.

Kate started shaking. Heart pounding, she ran back into her office and reached for the phone, then thought better of it. What if this man had planted a bug in her office?

She quickly gathered her things. After a moment's hesitation, she pulled the pistol from her desk drawer and dropped it into her purse. Racing out of the building and down the sidewalk, she waited until she was a block away before pulling out her cell phone. She hit the speed dial number for Mac Reilly, her friend since childhood and Rose Hernandez's fiancé.

"Reilly," Mac barked in her ear.

Kate's voice came out as a squeak when she tried to talk. She cleared her throat. "Hi, Mac. Is Rose home yet?"

"Sure, sweet pea," Mac said, using his childhood nickname for her.

"Uh, Mac, before you go, do you have anything that can tell if a place is bugged?" She thought that he might, since he had been a Green Beret in his younger years.

"You mean with listening devices?"

"Yeah, my office and my car probably ought to be checked and maybe for anything else that might be attached that shouldn't be there."

"What the hell's this about?" Mac growled.

"I can't tell you. It's related to a client. There's probably no threat, but just to be on the safe side."

"Where are you?"

"A block from my office, headed to my car."

"I'm on my way. Here's Rose."

After reassuring Kate that her mission to Jill Dawson's house had been completed without incident, Rose echoed her fiancé's words. "What the hell's going on?"

"I wish I could tell you, but I can't. I just need you guys to..." Kate stopped, unsure how to end the sentence.

After the briefest of pauses, Rose said, "We've got your back."

"Thank you." Kate was tempted to tell Rose she loved her, but she knew that would far exceed her brusque friend's mush tolerance threshold.

As she disconnected, Kate remembered Miller's comment about loneliness.

CHAPTER FIVE

After a restless night, Kate called Rob on Wednesday morning. When his admin assistant put her through, she told him that she would come to his office at lunchtime, rather than meet him at their usual restaurant.

"I need to talk to you again, confidentially."

"Same topic?"

"Yeah, but it's gotten a lot more complicated."

"Okay, I'll ask Fran to get us sandwiches from the deli. You okay with ham and cheese?"

"Whatever. I haven't had much appetite lately."

After a beat, Rob said, "Okay, see you then."

At noon, Kate drove around for fifteen minutes, one eye glued to her rearview mirror, before heading for Rob's office.

Once settled in his visitor's chair, she opened her mouth. A sob came out instead of words, surprising both of them. Rob jumped up and moved around his desk. She waved him off as she struggled for control.

"My God, Kate, what's happened?"

"My client's dead."

Rob muttered a curse under his breath. He perched on the corner of his desk while she told him about the obituary, her discussions with Jill Dawson, and the visit from the swarthy gentleman who was no doubt the mystery ambassador of Miller's story.

"Why didn't you call me sooner?" Rob said gently as she wound down.

"I was afraid to. I had Mac sweep my office and car for bugs last night. He's going through the house today while Skip's at work. And I drove around for a while to make sure I wasn't being followed before coming here. I'm terrified that I'm going to give these thugs, whoever they are, reason to believe I've told someone something and they'll kill somebody I love."

Rob reached over and took her hand. "I'd like to say that you're over-reacting, but I'm not sure that's true. So you told Mac what's going on?"

"No, although maybe I should. He's hinted about being involved in secret operations, back when he was a Green Beret."

"I'd feel a lot better if somebody who knew how all this works was looking out for you," Rob said.

He let go of her hand and reached into a brown paper bag. Pulling out a wrapped sandwich, he tried to hand it to her.

The thought of eating made Kate nauseous. She shook her head. He put it down on the desk in front of her.

"I don't know what to do. Anybody I tell, I'm putting them in danger. I've already put you in danger."

"It's not about who you tell," Rob said. "It's about who these people *perceive* that you've told. I can call Mac now. If he's free, he can come here. He'll just be another client coming into a busy law firm."

Luck was with them. Mac was available and said he would be right over.

Rob nudged her sandwich.

Kate slumped back in her chair. "I can't eat. I'm afraid I'll get sick all over your carpet. As a matter of fact, I think I need to cancel my afternoon sessions. Nobody's in crisis at the moment, and I know I won't be able to concentrate. I have no clue what I said to my clients this morning but I seriously doubt they got their money's worth." She dug her appointment book out of her briefcase and made calls while they waited for Mac.

Fran ushered in the short, wiry man, who as usual looked like he'd slept in his clothes. He was not alone. His fiancé, neatly dressed in a crisp white shirt and khaki slacks, followed him in.

"Things are a little slow today," Rose said. "Thought I'd tag along." She tilted her head toward the door. "I'll sit out there and shoot the breeze with Fran, if you want."

Kate hesitated.

"No one knows they're here to see you," Rob reminded her.

"Yeah, but there's the whole client confidentiality thing."

"Do you really think your client would care about that now?" Rob said. "He'd want you to do what you need to do to stay safe."

Kate heaved a sigh. Miller had specifically said she shouldn't tell anyone, even if he was killed, but that was because he didn't want her involved. Now, it was looking like she was already involved.

"Sit down, guys. This is top secret, for two reasons. One, it's about a client and confidentiality doesn't die with the client. And two, I'm not sure I want to tell Skip what's going on. I'd like your input on that, Rose, once you hear the whole story."

Without using Miller's name, Kate filled them in. When she got to the obituary, Mac, who was one part Greek Orthodox and three parts Irish Catholic, crossed himself. Rose followed suit.

When Kate had finished, they were silent for a moment. "First order of business is bodyguards," Rose finally said.

"No! If someone's watching me that will give it away that I've told others."

"Not necessarily," Rose said. "You could've just hired some guards on your own."

Kate shook her head. "I've got my gun on me, and I know enough *aikido* now to put up a good fight. I think it's important that it look like I'm not worried about anything."

Mac rubbed his stubbled chin. "She's got a point."

"What do you think the risk is?" Rob asked him.

After a moment, Mac said, "We got two options here. Tell the authorities the ambassador's secret. Then Kate's no longer a threat. Or sit tight and act normal. See what happens."

Kate noted that Mac hadn't answered Rob's question about the degree of risk. She suppressed another wave of nausea. "I'm not comfortable telling the authorities. That's condemning the man to death. I don't completely buy his story. I'm sure he's cleaned it up some to make himself sound more innocent than he was, but I think he's sincerely turned over a new leaf. Either that or he's the best pathological liar I've ever seen, and I've seen quite a few through the years."

"So we go with act normal for now," Mac said.

"Now the other big question," Kate said. "Do I tell Skip?" Her husband was as laid-back and level-headed as anyone she knew, but they'd all seen him blow before, when something threatened his family.

Rose sat still, a thoughtful look on her face. Then she shrugged one shoulder. "I honestly don't know what to tell you."

"He's gotta know 'bout it eventually," Mac said. "And he's gonna be royally pissed when he finds out you kept it from him."

"That boat's already sailed, I'm afraid," Kate said. "He's gonna be royally pissed now or later. The question is whether he'll go off half-cocked and try to investigate the situation, or worse yet, confront this ambassador."

"He's not normally an impulsive man," Rose said.

Kate arched an eyebrow at her. "Key word is *normally*." She rubbed her temple. "I can't think straight. I haven't slept well in over a week."

"You know you need to tell him," Rob said. "But you don't have to figure out how to handle that conversation just now. Why don't you go home and relax for a while, get your head clear. Then look for an opening to tell him this evening."

Kate gave him a slight nod. Her stomach churned again at the thought of that conversation.

Mac stood up. "Gotta get going. Try not to worry, sweet pea."

Overwhelmed by a wave of gratitude, Kate jumped up and pulled him into a hug. He squirmed and patted her awkwardly on the back. Letting him go, Kate turned toward his fiancée.

Rose jumped out of her chair and backed away.

Kate grinned for the first time in days. "Thank you both so much. This is above and beyond the call of friendship. You two are—"

Mac cut her off. "I don't know 'bout you, honey bun, but I'm insulted. We're not friends, Kate. We're family."

"He calls you *honey bun*?" Rob said, a chuckle in his voice.

Rose glared at him and marched out the door.

~~~~~~~~

When Skip spotted his lunch date entering the restaurant, he stood up and pulled out a chair for her.

"You're not hard to find in a crowded room." Janice stood on tiptoe to peck him on the cheek, then sank onto the chair with a sigh. "Sorry I'm late. I was in court. Judges get cranky if you get up and leave. You got some good dirt for me so I can put this miserable case to rest?"

Skip grinned. "The plaintiff's got a rap sheet as long as his arm, under several different aliases."

"Say what?"

"William Dunning is not who he says he is. He's served time in three states for scams similar to the one he pulled on your client's mother."

"Son of a bitch. My client's actually telling the truth."

"Yup," Skip said. "He may have beat the crap out of Dunning but any jury worth its salt is likely to give him a medal after they hear Dunning's history."

The waiter approached to take their drink orders. "Champagne," Janice told him. "Your best bottle."

"Uh, I don't usually drink at lunch," Skip said. "Makes me too groggy to get through the rest of the day."

"That's okay." Janice crossed her arms over her chest. "I may drink the whole bottle myself."

Skip thought her tone rather morose considering the news she'd just received. He cocked an inquisitive eyebrow at her.

"I'm divorcing Richard."

He struggled to keep his mouth from falling open.

"I probably shouldn't be telling you this, since it'll make things awkward at the party Saturday night, but I had to tell somebody. I've had it in the back of my mind ever since I made up the guest list and I realized how many of my friends he's alienated through the years.

"But the main reason I'm divorcing the jerk is no children. And he let me believe all these years that the problem was with me. Well guess what I found out?" Anger flashed in her eyes. "The S.O.B. had a vasectomy three years before we got married. Never bothered to tell me."

Skip resisted the temptation to stick his fingers in his ears. This was way too much information.

"I was thirty-two when we got married and I told him I wanted to have children right away, before it was too late. He agreed. 'Oh, yes, dear, I want a family too. We'll have two point three kids, blah, blah'."

The waiter arrived with the champagne and two flutes. "I think I'm the designated driver," Skip told him. "Just half a glass, please."

The man nodded, then presented the bottle to the lady for her approval before popping the cork and pouring. He propped the bottle in an ice bucket.

Janice tasted the wine, then took another sip before they ordered their food. After the waiter left, she sat up straighter in her chair. "Sorry. I'm being totally inappropriate here."

"It's okay. That's one hell of a secret he was keeping. When did you find out?"

"Last night. He insisted I meet him and one of his boring clients for cocktails after work. The guy let it slip that Richard had the snip-snip operation, as he called it. The son-of-a-bitch told his client, but he didn't bother to tell his wife that he was *incapable of breeding*."

"Do you really want to go through with the party Saturday?" Skip asked.

After a beat, Janice replied, "No, actually. Best case scenario, it would be a farce."

"Worst case, you'd deck him in front of dozens of witnesses."

Janice gave him a wicked smile. "Oh, what a lovely fantasy."

"Hey, after the dust settles, Kate and I'll have you over for dinner, and we'll celebrate your birthday in style. I'll make my six-alarm chili and we'll drink margaritas 'til dawn. You can stay in the guest room upstairs so no worries about driving home."

"Sounds delightful." Janice took a large gulp of champagne. "You know what's really pissing me off is the betrayal. If he'd told me up front he'd had a vasectomy, we could have discussed it. At that point, I was madly in love with him. I would have still married him, but I wouldn't have gone through years of longing and wondering, hoping against hope that this would be the month when I got pregnant."

Skip shook his head. "That was pretty damn cruel of him."

"Cruel. Yes, that's the word for it. I always knew he was self-centered, but back when I still adored him that didn't seem to matter, because he was the center of my universe too. But watching me suffer all those childless years. That wasn't just self-centered."

"Are you sure you want to go home tonight? Do you want to come stay with us for a few days?"

"That's really sweet of you to offer, but no, thank you. I don't want to tip my hand just yet. I'm meeting with a divorce lawyer tomorrow. Then I'll decide when to tell Richard I'm dumping his sorry ass. In the meantime, I might call my girlfriend out in Arizona and see about flying out there for the weekend."

"That's an excellent idea." Skip lifted his glass and touched hers lightly.

"To friendship." She drained her glass, then pointed it toward the ice bucket.

Skip hesitated, not at all sure that more champagne before she'd eaten anything was a good idea.

"Come on, Handsome Man. Pour me some more bubbly."

"I think I like Paul Drake better as a pet name."

"Nope, I like Handsome Man better."

"Um, you might not want to call me that in front of Kate."

Janice's expression sobered. "I'd have never pegged her for the jealous type."

"She's not really," Skip said. "But, uh... Okay, there's no way to say this without sounding incredibly obnoxious–"

"But you're drop dead gorgeous so she can't help but worry some," Janice said.

Skip felt the heat creeping up his cheeks. He squirmed in his seat.

"Oh my God, he's blushing." Janice clapped her hands. "Skip Canfield is blushing!"

"Why don't you say it a little louder? I'm not sure the kitchen staff heard you."

Janice chuckled. "I'm sorry."

"No you're not. You're enjoying every moment of my humiliation."

She laughed out loud and grabbed the bottle to pour herself another glass of champagne. "Thank you, Skip, for being you. You've reminded me that not all men are bastards."

Their food arrived and they applied themselves to it. After a few minutes, Janice said, "So tell me about the latest little dramas in the Canfield household. Let me live vicariously."

Skip grimaced.

"Seriously, Skip. I love your kids. Don't feel like you can't talk about them because I told you about the whole childlessness thing."

"It's not that," Skip said, then wished he hadn't. Today was not a good day to mention his concerns about his wife.

But there was a reason why he was attracted to Janice as a friend. Despite all her bluster, she was a very astute lady. "Then what is it?" she asked.

"Nothing," he said.

"Bullshit."

Skip poked at his half-eaten steak, then took a bite of baked potato.

"Come on, Tex, 'fess up. What's bothering you?"

"You do love to invent nicknames. Now I'm Tex?"

"Yeah, I think I like that one best. So what is it, Tex? What's bothering you?"

"You know, Janice, I'm not sure about this whole platonic friendship thing," he said, half teasing, half serious. "I'm not sure I can handle two women trying to get inside my head."

"Sorry. You don't have to tell me."

"I'm making more of it than it deserves." He poked again at

his steak, trying to decide how much to say. "I'm just worried about Kate. She's upset about a client who's in a bad situation. It's got her depressed and preoccupied, but because of confidentiality she can't tell me about it. It's frustrating to see her unhappy and there's nothing I can do."

"See, that wasn't so painful," Janice said with a small grin, then her expression sobered. "My dear Skip, your wife does not need you to *do* anything about it. She just needs to know you're there for her."

~~~~~~~

Skip managed to get home a little early that evening. Kate's Prius was parked in front of the house. She had apparently gotten home even earlier.

Inside, the house was quiet, except for the faint sound of children's voices. He walked through the laundry room and out the back door. Billy was kicking a ball around the yard. Maria sat at the picnic table with Edie, who was laboriously writing on a pad of paper.

"Edie learn to write her letters in school," Maria proudly announced when she saw Skip.

"They've got homework in kindergarten?"

"It's *real* school, Daddy," his daughter said, with a touch of disdain for the preschool she had so recently attended.

Skip hid a grin. "Where's Kate?" he asked Maria.

"She take a nap. I bring kids out here so dey not disturb her."

"What time did she get home?"

"One-tirty."

Skip's stomach clenched with worry. Kate didn't cancel her clients' appointments without good reason. Was she sick?

"Look, I'm going to fix something for the kids," he said. "Then could you do their baths and bedtime routine?"

~~~~~~~

Kate woke to the fragrance of chicken frying. Her stomach rumbled. She looked at the clock beside the bed. Seven-ten. She'd almost slept past the children's bedtime.

She went into the bathroom and splashed water on her face,

then straightened her rumpled clothing.

Out in the living room, the kids were playing on the floor, already in their pajamas. Skip came out of the kitchen, spatula in hand. "Kiss 'em goodnight, darlin'. Maria's doing story time."

After goodnight kisses all around, Skip led Kate into the kitchen. On the table were a platter of chicken, a green salad and a covered dish of wild rice. "You feel up to eating something?" he asked.

"Yeah, I'm okay. I just needed to catch up on some sleep." She knew this was as good an opening as she was likely to get... But he'd fixed this nice dinner. It wouldn't be right to let it get cold.

They ate in silence for several minutes.

"Darlin'–"

"Sweetheart–"

"What?" Skip asked.

"No, you go first. What were you going to say?"

He told her what Janice had found out and that she'd decided to divorce Richard.

"I figured it was only a matter of time." Kate shook her head. "Why do people even get married if they care so little about the other person's feelings or goals?"

"I offered to let her stay here for a few days, but she said she was going to a friend's in Arizona for a long weekend."

"I take it that means the party is off."

"Oh yeah."

As they finished their food, Kate worked on screwing up her courage again. She put her fork down and took a deep breath.

But before she could say anything, Skip took her hand. Tilting it to kiss the tender skin on the inside of her wrist, he whispered, "I love you."

She sucked in her breath. And lost her nerve.

~~~~~~~~

Thursday afternoon, Kate's last client canceled on her. She headed home, vowing she would tell Skip what was going on before dinner.

She arrived just as Maria and the children were returning

from Edie's riding lesson. Maria whispered to her that the little girl had been upset because the teacher had let another child ride Fiddlesticks, the pony Edie normally rode. "Teacher give her yellow horse to ride instead. She seem okay by end of de lesson."

Kate went into the living room. Edie had settled on the floor and was drawing yet another picture of a horse.

"Mommy, when I get my own horse, I want a pal'mino."

Kate hid a smile. "*If* you get your own horse, its personality will be more important than the color of its coat." When she saw the stubborn look on her daughter's face, she added, "But we can look for a palomino, *if and when* the time comes."

Edie vigorously nodded her head, making the dark curls that matched her mother's bounce up and down. She apparently considered herself victorious in that exchange.

Her mother stifled a sigh. They were trying to put off the purchase of a horse until Edie was a few years older, but the little girl was a very persistent lobbyist.

Kate was too nervous to sit still. She started tidying the living room. She picked up the State and Local section of the morning paper from the end table and headed for the recycle bin in the kitchen.

She was halfway there before the headline registered, *Arson Suspected in Sykesville House Fire*. With a sick sense of foreboding, Kate skimmed the article under the picture of a raging fire. *Arson is suspected in the early morning fire that claimed this Sykesville home while the family was away.* The family wasn't named and the specific address wasn't given, but her eyes froze on the last paragraph. *The owner of the house has had more than her share of tragedy lately. She recently lost her husband in an accident in Patapsco State Park.*

The burning house in the picture was the Dawsons' home.

CHAPTER SIX

Kate raced to the phone in the kitchen and punched in Mac's cell number. "I need to talk to you," she said when he picked up.

"Be there in a minute."

A minute? Kate went to the back door and pulled the curtain aside to look out. She didn't see him but she knew Mac was out there, slipping through the shadows under the trees.

Anger battled with gratitude. She and Mac had grown up together. Their parents had been best friends. Mac was an only child, a year older than Kate, and he'd always treated her like a little sister.

Leaving the back door unlocked, she made a pass through the living room to check on the kids, then sat down at the kitchen table to wait for him.

When Mac walked in, he looked even scruffier than usual. She suspected he'd spent the night in the back alley watching the house. "What happened to acting normal?"

He gave her an offended look. "Ain't nobody gonna see me when I don't wanna be seen."

Kate decided to let it go. She handed him the newspaper. "That's my client's house. I need to call his wife but I'm not sure how to do that safely."

Mac pulled a cell phone from the pocket of the jeans hanging from his skinny hips. "Pre-paid throwaway. Lemme do another sweep of the house first." He produced what looked like a small radio with an oversized antenna from another pocket.

When Mac had finished, Kate placed the call. A mechanical voice invited her to leave a message. "I'm calling for your house guest. Tell her to stay gone for now–"

"Kate, is that you?" a voice in her ear interrupted.

Kate filled Jill in on the house fire and her visit from the mystery ambassador.

"Dear God! I'm so sorry I involved you in this."

"I think this guy had already figured out my connection to Miller, before you and I spoke," Kate said. "But the house fire doesn't fit with what he said, so either he's lying through his teeth or he's still got a loose cannon on his staff."

She gave Jill the number of the disposable cell phone. "Use that instead of the number I gave you, and I think you need to stay out there for a while longer."

"I've already enrolled the kids in school here. I think we'll be staying for good," Jill replied. "But I'm just worried about you. It sounds like the killer is tying up loose ends."

"The ambassador said that no one knew he was coming to my office, so whoever it is probably doesn't know I exist," Kate said, giving the ambassador's reassurance more credence than she believed it deserved. She figured Jill had enough on her plate without worrying about her. "And I have help now. A friend of mine has experience with these things. I'll be okay. I'll call you if anything else happens."

"Thank you. Be careful, Kate!"

"I will. You, too."

After Kate disconnected, Mac said, "I think we need some insurance. Let's go talk to Rob."

"I don't want to involve him any more than I already have."

"Don't worry, sweet pea. I'll get us there without anybody following."

~~~~~~~~

Mac had called Rose to ask her to join them. When they were all gathered around Rob's desk, Kate summarized the latest developments.

"The ambassador may be behind the arson or he may not even

know about it," she said. "He may think he's stopped whoever's doing this."

"But he hasn't," Rob said.

"We need an insurance policy," Mac growled.

"Some surefire way to blow the whistle," Rose said, "if anything happens to Kate."

"Or to anyone else," Kate said.

Rob started flipping through the old-fashioned Rolodex on his desk. He pulled out several cards as he went. "I can send the information about the ambassador's true identity, in sealed envelopes, to several colleagues, with instructions to go to the FBI with them if I fail to contact them at given times."

"That'll work," Rose said.

Rob reached over and hit the power button on his computer to boot it up. "The question is, how do we let the ambassador know we've done that?" He opened his word processing program, then flexed his thick fingers and started to hunt and peck on the keyboard.

Rose rolled her eyes. She walked over and nudged Rob's shoulder, then made a shooing motion. "If we wait for you to type out the whole sorry story, we'll be here 'til midnight."

Rob vacated his desk chair and Rose sat down. Her fingers flew over the keys. "Do you know how to get in touch with this ambassador?" she asked Kate without missing a stroke.

"No, I don't know his name, or even what country he's from. Mill... uh, my client knew where his mistress lived. That's where he sent the PI to get a picture."

"I'm going to need to put your client's name in here." Rose nodded toward the computer monitor. "If someone has to eventually give this information to the authorities, they'll need to know the connection to his death."

Kate hesitated, then sighed. Miller would want her to do what she had to do to protect herself and her loved ones, not to mention his own family. "It's Miller Dawson."

Rose hit the page up key and filled in the name.

"Miller was going to turn the ambassador in. Until he got the second letter. He called me, all torn up..." Kate's throat tightened as she remembered that wrenching conversation. "He decided to go to the meeting. But either the ambassador wasn't as sincere as he sounded, or someone else got to Miller first."

"This ambassador won't know we don't know his name," Mac said. "We just need to figure out how to contact him, so's we can tell him 'bout the insurance."

Rose clicked the mouse and pages started spewing out of Rob's printer. Then she opened the computer's browser. "I can find out who he is."

"No!" Kate reached across the desk and grabbed Rose's arm. "The ambassador warned me not to do an internet search or do anything to find out about him."

"They can't be monitoring every search engine out there," Rob said.

Rose sat back in the desk chair. "No, but they could be monitoring the hits on the embassy site. Once I find him, they'll know it. And they might be able to track it back to this computer. I'll have to get Dolph to work on it."

Kate thought about that for a moment. Dolph Randolph, a retired police detective, was the oldest member of the Canfield and Hernandez staff, but he was by far the most computer savvy of them all, with the exception of Rob's wife, Liz. But still...

"I don't want to involve anybody else," she said, shaking her head. "The private detective would have the mistress's address. Miller said the ambassador goes there several times a week."

"Who was the PI?" Rose asked.

"Skip gave me two referrals, but I can't remember their names. I shredded the paper with the information on it once I passed it on to Miller. The guy he most likely used was the one Skip said was a little sleazy."

"Howie Kaplan?"

"Yeah, that's it."

"Will this Howie character tell you the address?" Mac asked. "That'd be violatin' client confidentiality."

Rose snorted. "He will if I offer him enough money."

"Whatever it takes," Kate said. She had a sizeable investment account thanks to a life insurance policy Eddie had taken out a couple years before he died. Normally she didn't touch it, except in emergencies. If this wasn't an emergency, she didn't know what was.

Rose raised an eloquent eyebrow at Kate. "Since my partner's conspicuously absent, I'm assuming you haven't told him yet."

Kate dropped her eyes. "I chickened out."

"I'm going home with you."

Kate shook her head. She didn't want to put Rose at risk, and she doubted Skip would enjoy having an audience for this particular conversation.

"Nobody'll think twice about my coming to visit Maria," Rose said. "I'll be nearby, just in case you need reinforcements."

Kate's heart sank. *She thinks Skip's gonna blow up.*

Kate decided not to argue. Rose had a point. She was Maria's cousin and she often stopped by the house.

"I'll send a follow-up letter when we find out the ambassador's name," Rob said. "We're sending these out today." He picked up some of the papers from the printer tray. "In sealed envelopes, with a cover letter saying the recipient should take it to the nearest FBI office if they don't hear from me at least once a day."

"Dictate your cover letter," Rose said. "Mac should mail them, just in case someone's watching you." She typed almost as fast as Rob dictated.

She instructed the computer to print, then opened a new document. "Next, the letter to the ambassador."

"Dear Mr. Ambassador," Rob said. "I have taken out an insurance policy on behalf of the acquaintance you have in common with the late Mr. Dawson. Sealed envelopes containing all relevant information have been delivered to various people around the country, with instructions to take the envelope to the nearest FBI office should they not receive a telephone call once a day. If anything should happen to the mutual acquaintance or any of her friends or family, that call will not be made. We bear you no ill will and have no intention of revealing any information about you, unless you give us no choice. Sincerely, A Concerned Friend."

"Add something about the fire," Kate said.

Rob and Rose both nodded. She typed as he dictated. "P.S. It may interest you to know that Mr. Dawson's house burned down. The fire marshal has concluded it was arson."

Once the insurance packets were put together and addressed, Mac picked them up. He nodded at Kate. "Rose'll take you home, sweet pea. Try to relax now. This should put it to rest."

"Easy for you to say. You don't have to face Skip."

~~~~~~~~

On the way to the house, Rose used her hands-free car phone to call Howie Kaplan. She got his voicemail. "Rose Hernandez here, Kaplan. I need some info from you asap. There's a fifty in it for you."

Rose rattled off her cell number and disconnected.

"Only fifty," Kate said. "Are you sure he'll tell you the address for that?"

"Hell, no. That's just where we're starting the negotiations."

Skip was home when they got there. "Hey, Rose, I landed a new account this afternoon with another insurance company."

Rose expressed an appropriate level of enthusiasm for this news, then excused herself to go visit with her cousin and the kids. "Hey, you two, it's nice out," Kate heard her say. "Let's go out back and play catch."

As the pounding of little feet receded, Kate turned to Skip. He gathered her to him and kissed the top of her head. She wrapped her arms around his waist and squeezed, savoring the warmth of his embrace since she knew he would be furious with her in just a few minutes.

Get to it before you lose your nerve again. She leaned back in his arms. "Sit down, sweetheart, I need to tell you something."

Once they were seated at the table, Kate took a deep breath. "The client I was worried about is dead. In his youth, he was an operative for the CIA. A little over a month ago, he ran into someone he knew from back then, someone who had changed his identity and is now an ambassador to the U.S. for his country."

She quickly summarized the encounter at the party. "My client–Miller is, was his name–thought everything was okay, but then there were several attempts made on his life."

Skip had been listening patiently up to this point. Now his body tensed and his eyes went wide. "Shit, Kate! What the hell have you gotten yourself into?"

"Sh, keep your voice down, or the kids'll be in here wanting to know what's going on. There's no reason to be... Well, let me put it this way, we should be safe soon. It's being taken care of."

"What's being taken care of? And by whom?" Skip's face was calm on the surface, but she noted the telltale tightness in his jaw.

"Please, sweetheart, let me finish," she said, trying to keep her voice steady. "Miller made every effort to keep me out of it, but he needed a sounding board. He was going to turn the ambassador in, to protect himself and his family, but then he got a letter, assuring him that the ambassador meant him no harm and wanted to meet to warn him about something."

"And your client fell for that?"

"Not exactly. He was very conflicted about it. He called me." She could hear Skip's teeth grinding together. "From a disposable cell phone. This man used to be a spy, sweetheart. He knew what he was doing."

"Oh yeah, then why is he dead and my wife's in danger?"

"I'm getting to that. The ambassador may or may not have been on the up-and-up. He claims the killer was someone on his staff who got wind of what was going on–"

"Wait! He claims? You talked to this guy?"

"I'm getting to that. Let me tell it in sequence. Miller had left a letter for his wife to find. She came to see me."

Skip grabbed the hair on the sides of his head and pulled.

"Sweetheart, please calm down. She's the grieving widow of my former client. Why wouldn't she come to see me for a counseling session? I've tried to be careful every step of the way with this."

"My God, Kate, do you have any idea how far in over your head you are? Why didn't you come to me about this right away–"

Pressure built in her chest as her own temper flared. "Yes, I'm fully aware of how far over my head I am. And there's nothing you could've done without putting yourself at risk, and *increasing* the risk to me." She struggled to rein in her anger and soften her voice. She had to get the rest out so he'd know things were already under control. "That is exactly why I *didn't* tell you. Not to mention the whole confidentiality thing."

She took another deep breath. "The ambassador came to my office on Tuesday to reassure me–"

Skip jumped up, paced across the room, then turned and stared at her.

"Yes, he somehow figured out my connection to Miller. But he was there to reassure me that he'd identified the killer and had dealt with him. He also told me that no one, not even his most trusted employees, knew he was at my office or knew anything about me."

"Come on, and you believe him? You know a secret that could destroy him and you think he's not going to do anything about it?"

"I didn't say I believe him. But to his credit, we were alone in my office and he could have very easily tried to kill or kidnap me and he didn't."

"No, he wouldn't have tried, he would have succeeded. He killed a trained CIA operative."

"We don't know that," Kate said. "What we do know is that whoever killed Miller is still cleaning up loose ends because Miller's house burned down–"

Skip narrowed his eyes. "*We?*"

Kate ignored the implied question. "To be on the safe side, we've taken out an insurance policy." She rushed through a description of what they had done, trying to get the rest out before he exploded. "Rob sent out the packets with instructions to take them to the FBI if they don't hear–"

This time Kate was stopped by the stony look on Skip's face. She stood up and took a step toward him. "I'm sorry I didn't tell you sooner, but I really couldn't."

"No, but you could tell all your friends, apparently."

"I just told Mac and Rose yesterday, to get their input. I was going to tell you last night, but..."

He was glaring at her, his hazel eyes the flat muddy brown they became when he was angry. "How long has Rob known?"

"I needed a sounding board, and I could justify telling him because of the whole lawyer confidentiality thing."

"How long?"

"A week."

Skip turned and walked out of the room. A few seconds later, she heard the bedroom door slam.

~~~~~~~~

Rose stepped into the kitchen doorway. "That could've gone worse."

"It could've gone better too." Kate sat back down at the table and dropped her head into her hands.

Rose caught movement in her peripheral vision. She turned and saw the bedroom door opening. Her partner closed the distance to the study in a few long strides.

"Uh oh, spoke too soon."

After a moment, the gun safe door slammed with a metal clang. Kate winced. Rose spotted Skip's keys lying on the kitchen counter and snatched them up.

"I'm going out. Don't wait dinner," Skip growled from behind her. He leaned over Rose's shoulder to look around on the counter. "Where are my damn keys?"

Rose used her elbow to not so gently move him out of her way. She headed for the front door. "I've got them, partner. Come on, we're going for a drive."

Skip was a lot bigger but Rose was quick and agile. She made it to the curb before he caught up with her. He held out his hand for his keys. She gestured toward her car instead.

"Stay out of this, Rose. It's none of your business. Now give me my damn keys!"

Rose narrowed her eyes. She was surprised by how much the none-of-your-business comment stung, even though there was truth to it. "Get in my car! We're going to talk."

He turned on his heel and walked away from her down the block. "Or, we could go for a walk," she muttered.

She jogged to catch up with him. "I told your wife you're not an impulsive man. Thanks for making a liar out of me."

Skip ignored her. He continued down the sidewalk in long strides that kept her jogging beside him. As they neared the corner, she veered across somebody's front lawn to cut him off. "Damn it, Skip, take a deep breath and settle down."

"I told you this is not your business," he repeated through clenched teeth.

"Normally I would agree with you, but the stakes are too high here. And Kate did what she thought was best. If the shoe were on the other foot, you would've kept it from her. Considered it agency business that was your responsibility to deal with."

Skip didn't say anything. Rose continued in a quieter voice. "This was a matter related to *her* work. A confidential matter that she didn't have the right to tell you about. But she could consult with Rob for advice, her attorney who is also sworn to keep such things confidential."

"So how come she told you and Mac?" Skip's voice was still angry.

"That was Rob's suggestion. Because of Mac's background." Rose looked around to make sure no one was in earshot. "He's worked undercover in Special Forces. He's even been on black ops. He's the best person to deal with this."

"And you just happened to be tagging along yesterday?" Skip said, his tone now sarcastic.

Rose tamped down her own temper. She understood his anger. "Yeah, on purpose. I knew something was up with her."

Skip sucked in air, then blew it out again. "Okay, I'll buy the confidentiality issue initially. But as soon as things started to unravel, she should've told me."

"Come on, let's walk." Rose turned and started down the sidewalk. Skip fell in beside her.

She was trying to sort out what to say. She knew in her gut why Kate had handled things the way she did but how to explain it to Skip? She hit on an idea. "Who'd you have for psychology at Towson University?" They'd both studied criminal justice there, but at different times.

Skip looked startled by the abrupt change of subject. "Can't remember her name right now," he said after a beat, "but she was one of the best profs I had."

"Dark hair, reading glasses perched on the end of her nose?"

"Sounds like her."

"I had her too. One time in class, she talked about differences between men and women. It stuck with me, 'cause it had me wondering for a while if I was really a guy. Doctor... Damn, I can't remember her name either. Anyway, she said that men are all about action, while women are into emotions. Men want to just fix the problem. Women want to talk it to death, figure out how they *feel*." Rose dragged out the last word as she rolled her eyes.

Skip actually chuckled. "Boy, ain't that the truth." Then he stopped walking and turned to face her. "This isn't about Kate's feelings, though. It's about the possibility that she could end up dead because she knew a man who used to be a spy."

"You're missing my point, partner. Kate was afraid that if she told you what was going on, you'd feel you had to take action. She asked my advice yesterday, about telling you." Rose knew she was risking Skip turning his anger on her but she forged ahead anyway. "I told her I honestly didn't know what to suggest. 'Cause I wasn't sure you wouldn't go off half-cocked, like you almost did today."

Skip just shook his head. "I was mostly pissed about her not telling me."

Rose looked up at him. She cocked one eyebrow at a forty-five degree angle. "If Kate had told you right after her client was killed, what would you have done? Think about that for a minute before you answer." She started strolling down the sidewalk again.

They rounded the next corner. "I would have discreetly tried to find out who the ambassador was," Skip finally said, with a touch of chagrin.

"And if Kate asked you not to get involved?"

Skip thought for a few seconds. "I probably still would've done it. I just wouldn't have told her I did it."

"And if the shoe were on the other foot. You had a situation with a case that got dangerous, and... well, you wouldn't tell her 'cause you wouldn't want to worry her, but suppose you did tell her about it. What would you expect her to do?"

Skip stopped in his tracks. "I'd expect her just to listen, let me vent. It would never even occur to her to get involved. She'd just beg me to be careful."

Rose grinned up at him. "A rather large double standard ya got goin' there, don't ya think?"

Skip shook his head, then gave her a small grin back. "Next time I see you doling out rope, I'm gonna know you're about to hang me with it."

~~~~~~~~

As they rounded the corner back to his own block, Skip said, "How'd you get so smart about men and women, Rosie?" He intentionally used the nickname she hated.

She punched him in the arm. He winced. Rose was one of the few women who could hit him hard enough to hurt.

"Usually I'm as baffled by other women as men are, but I get where Kate's coming from, most of the time at least. She's..." Rose paused.

"A straight shooter," Skip finished for her.

Rose nodded, stopping beside her car. She pulled his keys out of her pocket and handed them to him. "Go make up with her, Skippy. She needs you. She's been terrified by all this."

Guilt tugged at Skip's heart. Why was it he suddenly needed other women to tell him to be there for his wife? He used to believe he was a sensitive man.

Rose had beeped her car unlocked and opened the driver's door. "Where you going, partner?" he asked.

"Kaplan got back to me, while you and Kate were talking. I've got the mistress's address. Gonna do some reconnaissance. Ambassador should be there tomorrow afternoon. That's when me and Mac'll deliver our little insurance policy. I'm putting him in charge of this case." She arched an eyebrow at him again. "So you and I *both* take orders from him."

Skip started to protest, then thought better of it. Rose was in charge of allocation of personnel, and she was right. He was too close to the situation. Mac was the best person for the job.

"How much did Kaplan soak us for the mistress's address?" he said instead.

"Only a hundred."

Skip snorted. "The man has the morals of a toad."

"Please, that's insulting to the poor innocent toads."

Skip found Maria in the kitchen. The children were playing on the floor around her as she scrubbed the already spotless counter tops. Skip pulled a twenty-dollar bill out of his wallet. "Could you take the kids to McDonald's for dinner?" he whispered so they wouldn't overhear him.

Maria answered him with her own eloquent Hernandez eyebrow.

"I know. I've got some fences to mend," Skip said.

"Lez jist hope you no burn no bridges," she replied tartly, taking the money from him. "Come on, *mis niños*, we go out."

Skip opted to be amused rather than annoyed by Maria's fierce loyalty to Kate. He went in search of his wife.

And couldn't find her. After a thorough ground-to-attic search, he opened the back door. And there she was, sitting in the Adirondack chair at the end of the tree-shaded yard. They never used that chair, but she'd resisted getting rid of it. He'd sat in it once, and had a hell of a time getting out of it again, because of its tilted back.

He walked down the yard. The sight of tear tracks on Kate's face tugged at his heart. He squatted down beside her chair. "Why are you sitting way back here?"

"It's where I sat when I was grieving for Eddie," she whispered.

She might as well have stabbed him in the chest with a knife. "I'm so sorry," he managed to get past the guilt and fear clogging his throat.

Her eyes went wide. "I'm the one who screwed up. I should've told you sooner."

"No, you didn't screw up. Rose made me realize I would've handled it exactly the same, if the shoe'd been on the other foot." He tried to gather her up in his arms, but the weird slant of the chair made that impossible.

He stood up, then pulled her to her feet and wrapped his arms around her. "I'm sorry I stormed out, darlin'," he said into her hair. He breathed in the floral scent of her shampoo.

She shook her head against his chest. Her muffled voice said, "You had every right to be furious."

He held her slightly away from him so he could look into her eyes. "Sometimes life gets messy, and there is no clear-cut way to handle it."

Kate's mouth twitched. It looked like she was trying to smile but couldn't quite get the muscles coordinated. "Have I ever told you how much I admire your astuteness, Mr. Canfield?"

"Yup, as a matter of fact, you have, darlin'. But it's okay with me if you repeat yourself now an' again." He pulled her snug against him and rocked gently back and forth.

When he felt her body relax, he bent his head down to whisper in her ear. "Maria took the kids to Mickey D's for dinner." He bent a little further, nudging aside the collar of her shirt to kiss the sweet spot where shoulder curved up into neck. She shivered and let out a soft gasp. "You up for a little make-up sex?"

She leaned back in his arms. "Is that a rhetorical question?" This time her mouth muscles remembered how to smile.

CHAPTER SEVEN

Friday at three-fifteen, Mac pulled a rented car, its license plates obscured with mud, up behind a black limousine parked on a side street in Bethesda, Maryland. Skip, having convinced Mac and Rose to let him be their back-up, was a block further back hunched down in his own truck, watching the action through binoculars.

The limo driver had lowered his windows to enjoy the mild autumn day. He had his head tilted back, eyes closed, listening to a Spanish radio station.

His eyes flew open when Mac touched the cold end of his Glock's barrel against the man's temple.

"Move a muscle and your brain's history." Mac growled from his position crouched down beside the car.

The man stared straight ahead. To his credit, he was neither shaking nor sweating.

Lot more than just a driver, Mac thought. "What's your name?"

"Raul." The voice was flat.

"Okay, Raul. Nice and slow, put your hands on the steering wheel. No sudden moves or my finger might get twitchy."

Without moving his head, Raul's eyes flicked to the right, toward the townhouse his boss had entered ten minutes ago. Rose was blocking his view, leaning slightly in the passenger-side window as if she were having a conversation with him.

Mac could make out the rectangular bulge of a cell phone in the outer, right pocket of the man's uniform jacket. "Take your phone out, real slow."

Raul´s right hand moved toward the inside pocket of his jacket.

Mac jabbed him with the gun barrel. "Other pocket, asshole. Wouldn't want my finger to slip, now would we?"

Raul froze, then reached into the appropriate pocket.

"Hands back on the wheel." When Raul had complied, the cell phone now in his left palm, Mac reached inside the man's jacket and removed his pistol.

"Nobody gets hurt if ya do what we say." Mac nodded to Rose. She handed Raul a sheet of paper.

"My partner's goin' to the door," Mac said. "If your boss calls, ya tell him what's on that paper and only what's on that paper."

Typed on the sheet, in Spanish, was *She says she means you no harm, but she needs to talk to you about a mutual friend who has died. She's not armed.* The last sentence was a lie.

"Ya say anything else and your brains'll be splattered all over the ambassador's nice leather seat."

Mac looked over at Rose. Her jacket showed a comforting bulge where her hand was wrapped around the .32 inside her pocket. Mac nodded.

Turning, she walked to the front door of the townhouse and rang the bell.

Thirty seconds later, Raul's cell phone rang. He answered it. "*Hola.*"

After five years of living with Rose, Mac had picked up enough Spanish to know the man was sticking to the script. Raul disconnected.

"Hands back on the wheel," Mac said from his crouched position.

Raul complied.

Another few seconds went by. A stocky, middle-aged man opened the door of the townhouse. His tie was loosened and the sleeves of his white dress shirt were rolled partway up tan arms. Scratching his bearded chin, the man looked over at the limousine.

"Eyes straight ahead," Mac growled at Raul.

~~~~~~~~

Inside the house, a slender, fair-skinned woman, with long shiny dark hair and perfect posture, was standing in the middle of a tile-floored room. She wore a simple black, floor-length dress. The man in the doorway stepped back and gestured toward a brown leather armchair.

"Have a seat, Miss...?" he said, as he sat down on the matching loveseat and draped his arm across the back. A slight sheen of perspiration on his forehead belied the casualness of the gesture.

Rose remained standing. Her eyes quickly scanned the room for places a person could hide. The big potted plant in the corner maybe, but she doubted it. She was more concerned that there might be other employees elsewhere in the house.

"*¿Ella habla español?*"

The ambassador shook his head. "Annabelle, leave us, please," he said in English.

The young woman glided from the room, the sound of the black slippers on her feet almost imperceptible on the tiles.

"Anybody else here?" Rose asked.

The man arched an eyebrow at her, then shook his head again.

Her right hand still on the gun inside her pocket, she pulled Rob's letter out with her left. "I have a message from a friend of a friend." Taking a step toward the ambassador, she stretched out her arm and handed the letter to him.

He took his time reading it, then nodded. "I understand."

"If anything happens to any of my friends," Rose said, "in addition to the consequences mentioned in that letter, *te rastreo y te pongo en una brocheta como si fueras un puerco relleno.*"

The ambassador's expression didn't change as she threatened to track him down and skewer him like a stuffed pig. Rose begrudgingly admitted to herself that she was impressed.

"I understand," he said again.

"*Bueno.*" She turned on her heel and moved quickly out the door.

Back in the rental, as Mac pulled away from the curb, Rose called the driver of the Ford Expedition parked further down the street. "Message delivered and received." She heard an audible sigh from her partner.

~~~~~~~~

By Sunday afternoon, Kate was convinced that Mac's insurance plan was working. She knew she would grieve for Miller for a while, but she was happy to get her life back to normal.

At a little after four, Skip was taking a nap and she was reading to the children when the doorbell rang. She got up and went to look out the peephole in the front door.

At first Kate didn't recognize the middle-aged woman in a rumpled lime-green pantsuit standing with her back to the door. The woman was staring off across the lawn. She ran a hand through short silver hair as she turned to ring the doorbell again.

The dramatic streak of black above Janice Browning's right temple was unmistakable. Kate threw open the door. "Janice–"

"Sorry to barge in unannounced, Kate."

"Not a problem. Come in." Kate studied her friend's face with concern. Janice's brown eyes were red-rimmed. Her mouth was set in a grim line that accentuated the wrinkles around it.

"Skip's taking a nap. I'll wake him."

"Oh, don't," Janice protested feebly.

"It's okay. If he naps much longer, he won't be able to sleep tonight." Kate pointed toward the living room. "Entertain the rug rats for a minute, would you?"

Kate headed toward the bedroom. The door opened just as she reached for the knob.

"I thought I heard the doorbell," Skip said.

"You did. It's Janice."

"Say what? What's she doing here?"

As Kate and Skip entered the living room, Janice was finishing up the storybook Kate had abandoned. Kate went over to the television and picked out a video she knew was a favorite. She didn't like using the TV as a babysitter but sometimes it was a necessary evil. "Here, guys, how about you watch this while the grown-ups talk in the kitchen." She put the DVD in the player.

"*Toy Story 3!*" Billy yelled.

"Inside voice please, son."

In the kitchen, Kate put the kettle on the stove and got out tea bags and mugs. Skip gestured toward the table.

Janice sat down. "Bastard changed the locks while I was in Flagstaff."

"You're more than welcome to stay here tonight," Kate said.

"I was going to go to a hotel. But I need some help with something first."

Kate shook her head. "No way you're staying in a lonely hotel room. Not when we've got a guest suite upstairs. That's ridiculous."

Janice gave her a small smile. "Thanks, I'll take you up on that offer then. But I was hoping Tex here knew someone who can pick locks. I want to get my personal belongings out of the condo before Richard decides to destroy them, if he hasn't already."

"He's not home?" Skip asked.

"Wasn't when I got there, but he might be by the time I get back... Thanks," Janice said as Kate handed her a mug of tea.

"Sugar? Milk?"

"This is fine. I like my tea straight up." Janice blew on the steaming liquid, then took a sip.

"Are your things worth a showdown with Richard?" Kate asked. The woman looked done in.

"My photo albums. Things that belonged to my mother and grandmother. Oh, yeah, they're worth it. He took away my chance of having children. He's not getting my childhood, too." Her voice broke. She cleared her throat. "Sorry."

"No need to apologize," Kate said as she took the portable phone from its charger on the counter. She punched in a number.

"Hey Mac," she said when he answered. "Do you know Janice Browning?"

"Yeah, I've worked a couple of her cases with Skip."

"She's got a problem you could help with. Are you busy right now?"

"Nothin' can't wait 'til later. What's up?"

"We'll explain when you get here. Bring your lock picks, please."

"Okay if Rose tags along?"

"Sure. She may be able to help as well."

Kate disconnected and turned to Skip. "There are some broken-down boxes in the basement. Could you get them, sweetheart?"

"She don't mess around, does she?" Janice said to Skip.

He grinned as he headed out of the room. "I think she was a drill sergeant in a previous life."

Kate pulled a roll of plastic trash bags out from under the kitchen sink. "These'll work for your clothes."

"You all don't need to help. I just need the services of your lock-picker."

Kate sat down again. In a gentle voice, she said, "You look exhausted. What kind of friends would we be if we didn't help you deal with this?"

Janice's upper lip trembled. A couple tears broke loose. "Now see what you've done. You've got me blubbering like a baby."

Resisting the urge to point out it was okay to cry, especially under the circumstances, Kate got up to get a box of tissues off the counter. "Why don't you get your things from the car."

Janice just nodded as she wiped her eyes.

Kate went upstairs to check the guestroom. She put fresh towels in the adjoining bathroom. When she came back down, Janice was standing near the front door looking lost, a wheeled carry-on at her feet. Kate's heart ached for her. She'd walked the path of divorce with clients enough times to know that things were going to get worse before they got better.

The kids' giggling at the antics of the animated toys on the TV brought Janice out of her reverie. "Where am I hangin' my hat tonight?" she asked Kate.

"I'll take that up for you. Why don't you finish your tea?"

When Kate came downstairs again, Mac and Rose were now gathered around the kitchen table with Janice and Skip. The latter had cobwebs in his hair. A half dozen flattened boxes were leaning against the wall.

"What lock we pickin'?" Mac asked.

"The one my son-of-a-bitch husband put on my home while I was out of town," Janice answered.

"Is hubby likely to be home?"

"Don't know. Is that a problem for you?"

"Not really," Mac said. "Just like to scope out the job ahead of time."

"It's not illegal, by the way, to break into your own home."

"Rose, would you mind watching the kids," Kate asked, "so I can go and help Janice pack her things?"

"Kate, you really don't need to–"

"No problem," Rose said.

"Let's get this show on the road." Kate stood up before Janice could protest further. Rose followed her into the living room. "Aunt Rose is going to watch the movie with you. Be good. Daddy and I'll be home soon."

"Okay, Mommy," Edie said.

"Can we have ice cream after the movie, Aunt Rose?" Billy wheedled.

Rose rolled her eyes. "Do I look like I was born yesterday, kiddo? You haven't even had your dinner yet."

Kate hid a smile and turned toward the door. "Leftovers in the fridge," she said back over her shoulder.

"You owe me, Kate," Rose called after her.

"What does she mean?" Janice whispered to Kate. "*I'm* the one who owes her, all of you."

"That's not what she means," Kate whispered back. "She'd rather be going with us than babysitting. She's annoyed 'cause she's missing out on the action."

CHAPTER EIGHT

Janice and her helpers were almost to the elevators in the lobby of her building when Mac glanced back over his shoulder. Skip followed his line of vision. An average-sized, middle-aged man, dark hair too uniform to be anything but dyed, had come through the entrance. He was wearing an expensive business suit and a tanning-salon tan.

"Uh, oh. Here comes Richard," Skip said in a low voice.

They hustled the rest of the way to the elevators. Janice slipped a key into a keyhole in the middle of the metal plate next to one of them. The door slid open. "Quick, everybody in." She put the same key into a slot where the floor buttons normally would be. The door closed just as her husband got to them.

When the elevator reached the top floor, Janice turned the key in the slot again. "That locks it up here, but that only buys us a few minutes. He'll take the regular elevator to the floor below and hoof it up the fire stairs."

They raced down the hall. There were four doors, two on each side. "Which one?" Mac asked.

"Last one on the left."

Mac popped the lock just as the fire door at the other end of the hallway flew open. Richard Browning stormed through it, cell phone in hand. "I've already called the police. I'm having all of you arrested for breaking and entering."

Janice let out a short bark of laughter. "Richard, you are just too amusing sometimes." She entered the apartment and pointed Kate toward the master bedroom. "Closet on the right is mine."

Richard puffed out his chest. "I suggest you all get out of my home right now, or you'll be spending the night in jail."

"Oh shut up, Richard. The cat here knows more about criminal law than you do." Janice leaned over and scooped up an orange tabby. "This is my condo too and these folks are here as my guests." Ignoring her husband's spluttering, she headed down the hall to her study.

Richard started to follow her. Skip stepped into his path. "Settle down, man. She just wants her things."

The shorter man took a step backward. An awkward silence reigned in the living room for a few minutes. Then Richard sneered, "I should've known Janice's pet private dick would come to the rescue."

Kate had just come out of the bedroom, carrying a lumpy plastic bag. Skip caught the flash of anger in her eyes. He gave her a slight shake of his head. The goal here was *not* to escalate the situation.

Janice came out of the study, the cat in its carrier in one hand, a bulging briefcase in the other. She put both down on the floor near the door and pulled a clump of papers out of the briefcase. Handing them to Skip, she said, "Deed of trust to the condo, in both names. Be a love and wave it at the cops when they show up."

Skip hid a smile. Janice seemed to be getting a second wind. Nothing like a little anger to get the old adrenaline pumping.

Janice turned to Kate. Pointing to the carrier in which the cat was meowing miserably, she said, "I can take Peaches to a kennel if you all don't want her at the house."

"She's welcome too, but the kids may not give her back when you leave."

"Cops coming," Mac said from his post by the open door.

They all turned toward him just as two uniformed police officers appeared in the doorway. Richard started across the room but Skip cut him off, blocking his path long enough for Janice to get there first.

"Good evening, officers. What we have here is a minor domestic issue. The jerk standing behind my friend over there is my soon-to-be-ex-husband." Janice stepped over and took the papers from Skip's hand. "Deed to the condo, both our names on it. But the asshole can have it. Let him try to pay the mortgage on what he makes. I'm just clearing out my belongings."

The older of the two officers took the papers from Janice and started to look them over. Kate headed back to the bedroom.

"Mac, there's a box of papers in the study. Would you mind getting it, please?" Janice asked. Mac headed down the hall.

"Can I see some ID, ma'am?" the senior officer said.

"Sure thing." Janice dug her wallet out of her purse and handed over her driver's license.

Skip's attention was on the officers when he felt a flutter of movement behind him. In the next instant, his hand was wrapped around Richard's wrist. "What the hell do you think you're doing?"

"He's got a gun," Richard squeaked.

The officers tensed, their hands flying to their holsters. Kate had just stepped out of the bedroom, another bag of clothes in her arms. "He's a licensed investigator!" she shouted.

Skip let go of Richard and raised his hands in the air. "I've got a license to carry concealed." He cocked his head in Mac's direction as the latter came out of the study. "He's carrying too. Also a PI, duly licensed."

Mac stopped and slowly lowered the box he was carrying to the floor. He straightened, keeping his hands well away from his body.

"Gentlemen, I need to see your weapons and your licenses to carry," the older officer said, his hand still on the butt of his gun. "Please remove them slowly, one at a time."

Skip turned to the side so the officers could watch as he used two fingers to remove his granddaddy's pearl-handled .38 from its waistband holster. He was praying the officers wouldn't decide to confiscate it. Laying it on an end table well out of Richard's reach, he then slowly extracted the thin leather wallet that held his PI and carry licenses from his back pocket.

Mimicking Skip's slow movements, Mac handed over his wallet, then pulled his Glock out of its waistband holster.

"How the hell does he keep his pants up carrying that thing around?" Janice said *sotto voce*.

No one laughed, but the tension in the room eased as the officers examined Mac's and Skip's credentials. The senior officer nodded, handing the wallets back, and the men retrieved their guns. Mac picked up the box of papers and went out the door.

Richard pointed at Skip. "Arrest that man, officers. I'm pressing charges for assault."

Skip's jaw tightened. Was this guy for real? "I grabbed your wrist because you were reaching for my gun." *Asshole!* he mentally added.

"I was just going to point it out to the officers. How dare you bring a gun into my home." Richard's attempt at the irate innocent party fell flat. Janice was glaring at him.

Kate dropped the bag of clothes by the door. "My husband is a former police officer," she said, exasperation in her voice. "Mr. Reilly is ex-military. They rarely leave their homes unarmed."

That explanation seemed to satisfy the officers. Off-duty police were expected to carry, just in case they ran into a bad situation. It was a hard habit to break.

A flash of movement caught Skip's attention. He and Kate both lunged for Janice but they weren't fast enough.

She launched herself at Richard. Planting her hand flat against his chest, she shoved him. He stumbled backward until his legs hit the edge of the sofa. He sat down hard. Janice loomed over him, full-blown fury on her face. "I can't believe I married an idiot!"

The police officers moved quickly. The younger cop grabbed Janice's arm and pulled her away from Richard. "Mrs. Browning," the senior officer said in a calming voice. "Please, let us handle this."

As the officer turned back toward the sofa, Skip caught the hard look in his eyes. His mouth was set in a grim line.

Skip wasn't sure who the cop was pissed at, but he soon found out.

"Arrest her! Assault and bat..." Richard's voice trailed off as the officer's expression registered.

"Mr. Browning, if you wish to press charges, you are welcome to come down to the precinct tomorrow and do so." The officer's voice was low and even. "In the meantime, I'd suggest you avoid further provocation, until your wife has finished removing her belongings."

Doing a poor job of hiding a smirk, Janice turned to Kate. "Help me pack my mother's china, would you?"

~~~~~~~~

Back at the house, they hauled the poor cat and the bags of clothes up onto the porch. The men took the truck around to the alley to put the boxes in the small garage on the back of the property.

Kate led the way inside. "I'll take the cat up and get her settled," Janice said, heading for the stairs with the carrier.

Kate recapped the events of the evening to Rose as they stashed Janice's clothes temporarily in the study.

Then Kate headed for the refrigerator. She was famished, but first things first. She was pulling out a bottle of Chardonnay when Janice came into the kitchen.

Kate brought the bottle and a fistful of wineglasses to the table. "Have a seat. I'll get some dinner started and then we can relax for a bit." She headed back to the refrigerator.

Rose shook her head vehemently. "Janice, first rule of survival around here. Never eat anything Kate cooks." She walked over and nudged Kate out of the way with her hip. "I'll cook."

"Hey, even I can heat up leftovers," Kate said with mock indignation.

Rose just arched an eyebrow at her. "And there are so many leftovers, why? Because Maria cooks for an army on Fridays so you don't poison the family over the weekend."

Kate grinned at her. "You're just pissy 'cause you missed all the fun."

An hour later they were pushing back from the table. Mac patted his stomach and belched.

"What did I just eat anyway?" Janice asked. When Rose started rattling off the names of dishes in Spanish, she held up

her hand. "That was a rhetorical question. It was all delicious."
She raised her wineglass to them, her eyes shiny. "Thank you all
so much."

"Aw, damn. She's gonna get mushy on us," Mac grumbled.

Blinking away the tears, Janice grabbed the wine bottle–the
second of the evening–and topped off her glass from the dregs.
"Seriously, I really appreciate your help. And I won't be under foot
long. I've got a hearing in the morning, but tomorrow afternoon
I'll start looking for a new place."

~~~~~~~

It wasn't as easy to fit apartment hunting into her busy schedule
as Janice had hoped it would be. By Wednesday, she'd managed
to see several places but wasn't thrilled with any of them. She'd
discovered, however, that the idea of having a place all to herself,
with no one to answer to but the cat, was downright exciting.

She was in her office bright and early Wednesday morning,
hoping to get caught up enough on some critical paperwork to be
able to look at a few more apartments that afternoon.

Her admin assistant buzzed to tell her that State Senator Tobias
Robinson was on line one. Janice picked up her phone. "Good
morning, Senator."

"Not so good, I'm afraid," the senator responded. "My son
was arrested last night for driving under the influence."

"No, not good." Janice listened while the senator barked in her
ear for a few minutes. Then she said, "Let me call the Baltimore
County State's Attorney. See what I can do."

She placed the call herself. "Hey, Phil," she said when the SA
came on the line. "How are the wife and kids?"

"Cut the crap, Janice. What do you want?"

"Ah, Phil, you're always a breath of fresh air. I believe one
of your boys in blue arrested Senator Robinson's son last night
for DUI?"

"How the hell would I know? They don't call me in for every
pissant thing."

"Of course not. Let me rephrase the question. Suppose one
of your good officers had arrested a senator's son on a DUI, and

suppose said senator had shredded the boy's driver's license and was in the process of getting him admitted into a thirty-day rehab facility. Could we make said DUI go away without the press ever getting wind of it?"

"Get me the shredded driver's license." The SA disconnected.

Janice called the senator back. Then she called Skip. "Hey, Tex. I hate to degrade you by using you as an errand boy but I have a matter that requires the utmost discretion."

"You sound pretty damn chipper for a filly who just got herself unhitched from her stallion."

Janice snorted. "Stallion, schmallion, he hasn't been getting it up for years."

"Way too much information," Skip said, but with a chuckle in his voice.

"Sorry. On a serious note, I need you to go to Senator Robinson's house out in Reisterstown and get an envelope for me."

"Am I allowed to know what's in the envelope?"

"His son's driver's license, shredded. The dumb kid's only been driving six months and he got a DUI last night."

"And the shredded license will accomplish what, other than keeping the rest of us safe on the roads?"

"SA's going to drop charges if I prove Daddy's holding Sonny Boy's feet to the fire."

"Got it. What's the senator's address?"

Skip was in Janice's office with the envelope by ten. He dropped it on her desk, then plopped down in her visitor's chair, stretching his long legs out in front of him.

"So how's it going, Streak?" he asked.

She lifted an eyebrow. "Streak?"

"Hey, if I'm Tex, then you're Streak."

"Don't worry, I'll be out of your guest room soon."

"I'm not the least bit worried. Although you oughta be. My kids are gonna fight you tooth and nail for possession of Peaches."

Janice smiled. "Is it okay for them to have a kitten? I want to take them to the Humane Society and let them pick one out. I might get a companion for Peaches while I'm at it. She may get lonely without my loser husband hanging around the house all the time."

"Janice, are you really as okay about this as you're pretending to be?"

She chuckled. "Hell, if I'd known getting divorced could be this much fun, I would've done it years ago. I had a blast yesterday looking at new apartments. I'm gonna rent for a year, then see where I want to live. I might buy a townhouse, do a little gardening."

Skip cocked an eyebrow at her without saying anything.

"Yes, I'm really okay," she said in a more serious tone. "I feel... *liberated* is probably the best word for it. I hadn't realized just how much Richard was sucking the life out of me. Even homeless, I'm happier than I've been in years."

Skip smiled at her. "Don't feel like you've got to rush into a deal on a new place. We're happy to have you. Edie thinks you're awesome. And Billy informed me over breakfast that I need to learn how to make cool sound effects like Aunt Janice when I tell stories."

Janice grinned. "Sorry to have raised the bar there for you, Tex. You never answered me about the kitten."

"I'll have to ask Kate, and Maria for that matter, since she'll end up being the one to supervise the kids taking care of it."

Skip pushed himself to a stand. "Well, I better get going. See you tonight at the house." He froze, his gaze fixed on the *Washington Post* lying on her desk.

She leaned closer to examine the picture he was staring at. A stocky, bearded Hispanic stood next to an elegant woman. His head was turned to one side, looking at the President who was shaking the woman's hand. The First Lady stood off to the side.

Janice read the caption. *Ambassador Juan Garcia of Colombia and his wife attended a recent White House function. The Colombian president will be paying a state visit to the U.S. later this month.* The story didn't sound all that interesting to her but Skip seemed transfixed.

"What's wrong?"

"This is the bastard," Skip muttered.

"What bastard?" Janice asked.

"Remember when I told you Kate was upset about a client but couldn't tell me why..." His voice trailed off.

"Come on, Tex, you can't stop there."

Skip just shook his head.

Janice grabbed the paper and turned it around on her desk so she could study it. "So one of these guys is the bastard who did what? Not the ladies and I would hope you're not referring to our President. So it must be this ambassador dude. What'd he do?"

Skip winced.

Janice made a gimme motion with her hand. She wanted the juicy details.

"Man, you're like a dog with a bone," he said. "Sorry, but it's confidential. All I can say is that the situation has created some risk for Kate. We think we have things under control, but it might not be a bad idea after all, for you to find your own place soon."

Janice arched an eyebrow at him. When he didn't elaborate, she said, "You're killing me here with curiosity, but I certainly get client confidentiality. I'm looking at a couple more apartments later. I can probably get something temporary lined up in a day or two."

"Sorry. We should have thought about this before we invited you to stay."

"That's okay. You were responding to a friend in need, and I can't tell you how much I appreciate all your help."

Skip held up the newspaper.

"Take it," Janice answered the implied question.

Thanks," Skip said. He was pulling out his cell phone as he left her office.

She picked up her phone to call the State's Attorney and tell him she had the shredded license in her possession. Then she called the senator.

Janice operated in a world of *quid pro quo*. She gave the senator the good news that his son's record was being expunged, then she asked for a favor in return. If this Ambassador Garcia from Colombia was up to something that was putting American citizens at risk, maybe a discrete investigation would lead to him being recalled. It was the least she could do for Kate and Skip after all they had done for her.

CHAPTER NINE

Rob and Kate were having their first normal Wednesday lunch in weeks. They met at their favorite restaurant at twelve. Mac Reilly had inherited his parents' corner bar a decade ago. He had changed its name to Mac's Place and turned it into a thriving combination of seafood restaurant and Irish pub. Then he'd decided his talents were being wasted as a restauranteur and he'd gotten his PI license.

Mac's Place was now run by a manager who came over to Rob's and Kate's booth to greet them. "What happened to you two? I thought you'd deserted me."

"How's business, Jack?" Rob asked, without answering the manager's question.

"Not too bad, considering the current economy. Being across the street from the courthouse helps. All you fat cat lawyers coming in for lunch keeps things going for us. What can I get you all?"

Kate and Rob gave him their order and the manager headed for the kitchen door. Even after a year, Kate still felt a small twinge of sadness that Mac wouldn't be coming out of that kitchen to make some teasing crack.

"How's Liz doing?" she asked. "I haven't seen her in ages."

"She's good," Rob said. "She wanted me to ask if you had time to go furniture shopping with her this weekend. She wants to redecorate the family room."

"You don't want to go along to help pick stuff out?"

Rob gave a mock shudder. "Being an enlightened man does

not extend to enjoying shopping. I don't care what that room looks like as long as there's someplace to sit and watch TV."

"Spoken like a true man. I think I can get free for a few hours on Saturday. I wonder if Liz would mind if I invited Janice Browning along. You remember her from our cookout in August?"

"Janice is hard to forget," Rob said.

"She'll have a new place to furnish soon. She's divorcing Richard."

"Why am I not surprised?"

Kate snorted. She told Rob the story of going to the Brownings' condo on Sunday to retrieve Janice's belongings. "She's not fighting him for the condo itself since there's very little equity in it. She's staying with us until she can arrange for a new place."

Rob opened his mouth to say something, then closed it again as their crab cake sandwiches were delivered by a young waitress they didn't know.

"No fries with yours?" Kate asked, as Rob stole her pickle slices to add to his own.

"I've been gaining too much weight lately," he said, referring to his ongoing battle with middle-aged spread.

Kate started slathering tartar sauce on the bun of her sandwich.

"Are you sure it's safe to have Janice at the house?" Rob asked.

Kate cocked her head in confusion. "Richard's an ass but I don't think he's dangerous."

"No, I mean safe for her, with all that's been going on lately."

"Oh, damn. I hadn't even thought about that. I guess I'm not..." She paused to look around, making sure no one was in earshot. "I'm not so good at this international intrigue stuff, am I?" she whispered.

"It's probably okay now," Rob said, also lowering his voice. "It's been almost a week and nothing else has happened, so I guess our insurance policy is working. I sent out supplemental envelopes before coming over, with the ambassador's name. Did Skip call you about that newspaper article?"

Kate nodded. "He left me a message. Sorry you have to hassle with making those calls every day. How long do you think we should keep that up?"

"I'd say give it another week. Then I'll tell my guys to put the envelopes in a safe place unless they hear otherwise from me. Hopefully, we've successfully extracted ourselves from the whole situation."

"Amen," Kate said with fervor.

~~~~~~~~

Rob soon discovered this was wishful thinking. When he got back to his office, a swarthy, bearded gentleman was waiting in the reception area.

The man stood up, smoothing the jacket of his custom-tailored suit. "Your assistant said you were busy this afternoon but I waited, hoping you might have a few minutes to discuss a very important matter." His voice was cultured, his Spanish accent mild. "My name is John Smith," he added, with a small apologetic smile, and offered a manicured hand.

Rob shook it. "Come on back to my office."

Once seated on either side of Rob's desk, they sized each other up in silence. The man was the first to speak. "We have a mutual friend."

"Perhaps," Rob said. "How did you find me, Mr. *Smith*?"

Once again the man gave Rob a small smile. "I have an excellent security staff, Mr. Franklin."

"Who are now aware of my friend's connection to the late Mr. Dawson."

"Unfortunately, yes. But there should be no further risk to her, as long as she and her husband stop making inquiries into my business. I had thought I had made it quite clear to her how unhealthy that would be."

"And we have made it quite clear just how important it is to *your* well-being that she remain healthy." Rob's tone was steely.

"Ah, yes. I assumed that you were her 'concerned friend.'"

"Mrs. Huntington and Mr. Canfield have many concerned friends. But I can assure you that they are not investigating you. They have no desire to have anything to do with you or your business."

"Nonetheless, it has come to my attention that someone has been making inquiries–"

"It isn't them."

"Very well. I will take your word for that. But unfortunately I am not the source of the threat."

"Who is?" Rob asked.

"I'm not exactly sure. I thought I had taken care of the source, but more recent events indicate that perhaps the threat is coming from elsewhere."

Rob softened his voice. He wanted to get more information out of this guy if possible. "Who do you think it might be? As a lawyer, I'm bound to keep this conversation confidential, by the way." That wasn't true, not unless the ambassador actually hired him. But Rob had few qualms about lying to the man at this point.

The ambassador sighed. "My instincts for self-preservation are telling me I should not answer that question. I liked Mrs. Huntington, however, when I met her. And I do not want any more innocent lives disrupted because of this. Are you familiar with my country's recent history, Mr. Franklin?"

Rob nodded.

"Did you know that the president of my country is coming here for a state visit soon?"

"That was in the paper."

"It has occurred to me that certain parties may attempt to do something to undermine our current government, and the fragile peace we have been able to maintain. And they may intend to use their former association with me to gain my cooperation."

"The rebels? They're still active?"

The ambassador shrugged. "Some of them are."

"So they wouldn't want your 'former association' brought to light then," Rob said. "Wait, our own president could be at risk here."

"I had already thought of that possibility. I have informed the security forces who will be accompanying *el Presidente* that there may be a heightened risk, without giving any details. They will be extraordinarily alert, and they will inform your Secret Service of the heightened threat as well."

Rob thought for a moment. He was beginning to understand why Kate felt some sympathy for this man. The ambassador was on a sinking ship, madly trying to patch the holes in the hull. "My concern is for the safety of my friends," he finally said. "And my own for that matter. You're coming here has now drawn attention to me."

"I am relatively certain that your friends are safe now, but it is imperative that they not make any inquiries into my business."

"*I* am relatively certain that they haven't done so, but I will pass along the message."

"As to drawing attention to you," the ambassador said, "I have let those on my staff–those who are privy to Annabelle Gaston's role in my life, that is–I have let them know that I felt it more discreet to consult with a Baltimore lawyer on a certain matter regarding her. I would like to set up a trust fund in her name. Should things go awry and I have to leave the country in haste, I wish to be sure that her needs are addressed."

Rob's mind was rapidly processing several things at once. The trust fund for the mistress was a plausible cover story, but only those closest to the ambassador would know about it. What did that mean? He shelved that to dissect later. He didn't really want to have anything to do with this guy. But then again, what was the saying? *Keep your friends close, and your enemies closer.*

"I'll take care of that for you, Mr. Ambassador. You can give Fran, my assistant, the details. Her full name, address, the amount you wish to put in the trust, et cetera." Rob stood up.

The ambassador took the hint and stood as well.

"I feel compelled to warn you, sir," Rob said. "Should this blow up in our faces, the two concerned friends who delivered our insurance policy last week will be highly motivated to track you down. And they have the training to succeed."

The ambassador grinned, white teeth flashing against swarthy skin. "Are you referring to the young woman who threatened to skewer me like a stuffed pig?"

Rob couldn't completely stifle a grin of his own as he shook the man's hand.

After the ambassador left his office, Rob sat at his desk for a few minutes, staring into space. He wasn't sure to whom he should report this latest development.

Having finally decided on Rose, he walked down the hall toward his partner's office. Picking up the receiver of Jim Stockton's admin's phone, he said, "May I borrow this for a moment, Shirley?"

Shirley nodded, giving him a strange look.

Rose answered with her brusque "Hernandez."

"Just had a visit from the gentleman we're concerned about. Apparently someone is making inquiries into his business."

"Not good."

"I assured him that said inquiries were not coming from our colleagues."

"If they are, said colleague won't need to worry about other threats. I'll kill him myself," Rose said.

"For what it's worth, I think this guy's on the up-and-up, that he's not the one causing problems. But he doesn't know who is the cause. He thinks it might be his former associates. Can you get the word out that renewed caution is called for? And maybe get me some of those prepaid phones?"

"Will do." Rose disconnected.

Rob hung up. His partner's assistant was watching him intently.

"Thanks, Shirley."

"If Fran ever leaves," she whispered, "could I get a transfer? You're a lot more interesting than Mr. Stockton, but don't tell him I said that."

Rob winked at her and headed back down the hall.

~~~~~~~~

Rose was on her way to the offices of Canfield and Hernandez, Private Investigations, but she decided this couldn't wait. She punched the speed dial number on her car phone for Skip's private line.

"Canfield."

"Partner, you haven't been making inquiries regarding the gentleman we're concerned about, have you?"

"Of course not. Why? What's happened?"

Rose started filling him in.

Suddenly Skip said, "Shh. I just heard something."

Rose stopped talking.

She was pulling into the public parking lot a block down from the agency's building. From the speaker in her dashboard, she heard the clatter of a phone being dropped on a hard surface. She rammed the car into park and reached for the key.

Several male voices yelled in Spanish at the same time. Then Skip's voice dominated. "Freeze or I shoot your *compañero* here." A gunshot reverberated.

Rose tore out of the car and ran toward the street. She pulled her cell phone from her pocket and punched in 911. "Break-in in progress. Shots fired!" She yelled the agency's address into the phone.

"Get out of the way!" Pedestrians scattered at the sight of the gun in her hand. As she neared the building, a dark-haired man in a black business suit ran out the front doors.

"Stop!" she yelled, but the man kept running, zigzagging in and out of the pedestrians.

Rose reached the building's entrance. She shoved through the doors and ran up the fire stairs to the agency's offices.

Blood was pooled on the floor in Skip's doorway.

Rose doubled over. It felt like someone had punched her in the gut.

CHAPTER TEN

"Watch where you step." Skip's head came around the doorframe. "Did you call the police?"

Rose's knees wobbled. "Yeah," she said, her voice gruff. "What the hell happened?"

"Two guys. From what I caught of their conversation before they burst into my office, they were specifically looking for me. Hang on. I'll be right back." He ducked back inside his office.

After a few seconds, his foot came through the doorway, stepping wide over the blood on the floor. Rose's knees wobbled again when she got a good look at him. His arms were splattered with blood.

"Are you sure you're okay?"

"Yeah, the blood's all the other guy's. I grabbed the first one who came through the door and held my gun to his head. Yelled for the other bozo to drop his weapon. He shot his buddy instead and took off."

"Damn good thing the bullet didn't go through him." Rose's hand shook as she returned her pistol to its ankle holster, then pulled the cuff of her khakis down over it.

"Yeah," Skip said absently. He was busy rubbing blood off of one of his arms and smearing it on the gun in his hand.

"What the hell are you doing?"

"I'm not giving the cops my granddaddy's pearl-handled pistol. I didn't fire it, but they're gonna want to take my gun and test it. This is the piece I keep in my desk."

"Actually I hear them coming so you might want to put the

gun down." The words were no sooner out of Rose's mouth than two officers came through the fire door at the top of the stairs. Their guns were drawn. "Don't move, mister," one of them yelled.

"I'm the victim, officers. I'm going to slowly stoop down now and put my gun on the floor." The older of the two uniforms nodded. Skip bent his knees to place the bloody revolver beside the doorframe.

"One of the two men who attacked me is in my office there. He's dead. The other one got away. His buddy is the one who shot him, not me."

"Move away from the gun, sir," the senior officer said.

Skip complied. Both he and Rose kept their hands where the officers could see them. The younger one moved toward the doorway to look into Skip's office.

"I'm Rose Hernandez," Rose said. "This is my partner, Skip Canfield. We own this agency. I saw the one who got away run out of the building as I was approaching."

The senior officer acknowledged the nod from his partner. "Secure the outer door of the building 'til the detectives get here."

He turned back to Rose as he holstered his gun. "Hernandez. You used to be with BCPD?"

"Yup. Went private a few years ago. More money, less bullshit."

The cop smiled. "Bill Lindsey and I partnered for a while. He mentioned you a few times."

"Oh yeah. He and I used to catch a beer after shift. Tell him Rose says hey."

"Will do." He took out a notepad and asked Skip to repeat what had happened.

"Guy who got away musta been shooting at you and got his buddy by mistake," he said when Skip had finished.

"I don't think so, officer," Skip said. "My sense was he wasn't leaving anybody behind who could ID him, or whoever he's working for."

The cop snorted. "Doubt he's working for anybody. Just a couple of thugs looking for somethin' to steal."

"Let's refrain from jumping to conclusions, officer," a female voice said from behind him.

~~~~~~~

An unbecoming shade of red crept up the uniform's face as a tall, thin woman with a cap of short dark hair stepped around him. "Yes, ma'am," he mumbled.

The woman was wearing a white tailored shirt and snug black slacks. A gold badge and holstered gun were clipped to her belt. Her only jewelry was a man-sized gold watch and small gold rings in her ears.

Avoiding the pool of blood, she leaned through the doorway to get a look at the victim. "Don't see too many thieves wearing business suits," she observed.

"No, ma'am," the uniform answered, standing at attention.

"You got here fast, Detective Anderson," Skip said.

The detective turned. The light shifted in her eyes as she recognized him. "Canfield, right?"

"Yes, ma'am. You've got a good memory."

She arched an eyebrow at him. "What'd you shoot this guy with?"

Skip shook his head. "I didn't shoot him. His buddy did. Guy's gun looked like a .45. Only got a brief glimpse of it though. The dead one's gun is on the floor somewhere. I knocked it out of his hand, then grabbed him as a shield. Told the other guy to drop his gun. He shot his buddy instead and took off."

"Guy was coming out as I was coming in," Rose said. "About five-seven or eight, Hispanic, black hair, medium build. Also wearing a suit. Didn't look all that scared. Ignored me when I yelled at him to stop, even though he'd seen my gun."

"Detective Anderson, this is my partner, Rose Hernandez," Skip said.

The detective shook Rose's hand, then pointed to the gun on the floor. "That yours?" she asked Skip.

"Yup. But I didn't fire it."

"Got any idea who these guys were?" Anderson asked.

Rose caught his eye and shook her head slightly.

Skip hesitated. Judith Anderson was Dolph Randolph's former partner and, according to Dolph, she was a top-notch detective. Plus she'd helped them out with a previous case. He hated to lie to her, but Rose was probably right. The police mucking around in this mess would no doubt make things worse, if that was possible.

"Nope. Best of my knowledge I haven't annoyed anybody lately, other than my wife."

"No pissed-off husband you caught shacking up with his honey and now his wife's divorcing him?"

"We don't do adultery cases," Rose said.

A middle-aged man in rumpled slacks and sports jacket came tearing through the stairway door. His rust-colored hair, liberally sprinkled with gray, was standing straight up in places. He raced toward them. "You guys okay? What happened? I had a helluva time convincing the uniform on the door to let me come up here."

When he saw his former partner, Dolph froze. "Aw, shit! Who's dead?"

"It's a pleasure to see you too, Dolph," the detective said.

"Sorry, Judith. How are you?" the older man asked in a distracted voice, as he looked around.

"The corpse isn't one of ours," Skip told him. He filled Dolph in on what had happened.

"You sure you're okay, son?" Dolph asked, eyeing his bloody arms.

"It's all the other guy's." Skip turned to Judith. "How soon can I get this gunk off of me?"

"Crime scene techs and M.E. should be here any minute."

~~~~~~~~

While Judith had Skip run through the whole event again, Rose called some of the agency's bodyguards and sent them to Kate's and Janice's offices and to the house. The guards were told to be discreet but to not let their charges out of their sight. She figured the kids, who only went to school for a half-day, would be home by now. She called Maria to check on them, and to tell her what was going on.

Two hours later, Skip was finally allowed to leave. He had

showered in the agency's locker room and donned the spare jeans and shirt he kept there. His bloody clothes had gone into an oversized evidence bag.

They had been told that it would be morning before they could get back into their offices. As they were leaving, they overheard the medical examiner telling Judith that there was no exit wound. He suspected the bullet had lodged in the victim's spine.

"You were damn lucky, partner," Rose muttered to Skip. She waited until they were outside, out of earshot of the young cop standing at parade rest by the front door of the building, to continue. "I made a couple calls while you were showering. Rob's waiting for us at his office. Mac's gonna meet us there."

"What's this all about?" Dolph asked.

"We need to tell him," Rose said.

Skip shook his head.

"This has gone way beyond what happened to Kate's client," Rose said. "They've invaded our offices. If anybody else had been there, they would've killed them to get to you. Our people need to know there's a risk."

Skip ran his fingers through his still damp hair. "Kate's gonna be pissed."

"She'll understand."

"So now you know my wife better than I do?" Skip snapped at her.

"Don't get pissy with me, partner."

Dolph had been standing, hands stuffed in his pants' pockets, swiveling his head back and forth. "You all gonna tell me what's goin' on? Or are you gonna stand here and squabble awhile longer?" He cocked one bushy, mostly-gray eyebrow.

Rose looked up into Skip's face. She didn't like what she saw. His jaw was clenched, his eyes muddy brown with emotion. Apparently the implications of the afternoon's events had sunk in. Skip could handle being shot at without batting an eye, but the one thing that could make him lose his cool was a threat against his wife or family.

In a gentle voice, Rose said, "If Kate's pissed, it'll be on me.

Meet us at Rob's office. Check your truck over good before you start it. And look for Hispanics hanging around Rob's building, just in case they're watching him now."

She turned on her heel. "Dolph, you're with me. I'll fill you in on the way."

~~~~~~~~~

Rob led Rose and Dolph down a hallway to a medium-sized conference room. Mac brought up the rear, carrying a cardboard box that he set at his feet as they settled around the table.

Fran followed them in, a carafe of coffee and a fist full of empty mugs in her hands. "Thought maybe a few of you could use a little pick-me-up." She tilted her head slightly toward Skip. He was sitting slumped in a chair at the opposite end of the table, his long legs stretched out to the side, staring at his feet.

"I'll be back with cream and sugar," Fran said.

"You got any more like her around here?" Rose asked. She was thinking the agency needed a Fran to run the office and, well, to take care of them.

"Nope, she's one of a kind," Rob said.

"Just have to steal her then," Rose said.

"You try it and I'll break both your legs," Rob replied good-naturedly.

Rose snorted. "You and what army?"

"For Fran, I'd fight to the death." They fell silent when the subject of their banter returned with the promised cream and sugar.

Fran poured a cup of coffee. "How's he take it?"

"Cream, no sugar," Rose said.

Fran added cream, then carried the mug down and placed it in front of Skip. He didn't seem to notice. He was still staring morosely at the toe of his sneaker.

"There's blood on my shoes. Guess I should've given them to the M.E.," he said, as Fran left the room, closing the door behind her.

"I don't think it matters, Skip. They've got your clothes," Rose said.

"What the hell are we gonna do?" Skip asked, his eyes still

on his shoe.

Rose and Dolph exchanged a worried glance. Rob caught the look and nodded at them.

"Drink your coffee, son," Dolph said.

Skip looked startled to find the cup in front of him. "Thanks," he said, not realizing the person who'd provided the coffee had left the room. He took a sip.

"I sent Manny Ortiz to Kate's office and a couple guys to the house," Rose said, partly to inform the others and partly to remind Skip that everyone was safe for now.

She'd decided on a strategy, for the meeting at least. She had no idea yet what they were going to do about the problem itself. "You're still lead on this, Mac, but if you don't mind, I'd like to summarize where we are."

Mac nodded.

Rose got up and walked to a large pad of paper propped on an easel at one end of the room. "Can I use this?"

"Of course," Rob said. "That's what it's for, to hash out strategies for cases."

Rose picked up the black marker from the tray and started writing. "What we know. One, Kate's client was murdered. Two, the ambassador's admitted he used to be a rebel. Three, he says he means us no harm but he doesn't know who's doing this. Four, Miller's house was torched."

"Five," Rob said. "The ambassador comes to my office, says somebody's making inquiries."

"Number six," Dolph said. "Two Hispanic hit men show up at Skip's office."

"Seven," Rose added. "When one of them's caught, the other guy shoots him. Anything else that we know for sure?"

After a moment, several heads shook.

Mac got up. "Anybody want any coffee?" Dolph raised his hand.

While Mac poured two mugs of coffee, Rose tore the top page off the pad and put it in the middle of the conference table. On the next page, she wrote *What We Think*.

"Number one," Rob said. "Ambassador Garcia may be telling

the truth that he's not behind all this."

Rose wrote, then added a number two. "The ambassador thinks the killer may be connected to the Colombian rebels."

"You didn't tell me that," Skip said.

"We hadn't gotten that far when we were interrupted. You want to fill everybody in, Rob?"

He gave them the details of his conversation with the ambassador. "And Garcia said something else interesting. He implied that I was protected because he had told those on his staff who knew about his mistress that he was seeing me to set up a trust fund for her. Makes me think he suspects someone in the upper echelon of his staff."

Rose wrote the number three, then *May be staff member close to ambassador.*

"If the ambassador's not the problem," Mac said, "whoever's behind this may not even know that we've taken out insurance."

"Were these guys today trying to kidnap Skip as their own insurance policy?" Rose asked as she wrote *4. Perp may not know about insurance.*

"Doubt it," Mac said. "If that was their agenda, they would've picked a different place. Most likely a parking lot. I think they were s'posed to take him out."

"Maybe they were going to use Skip's death as an example," Rose said. "Contact Kate and say the kids would be next if she didn't get Rob to get the envelopes back."

"Okay, so one of the things we think," Dolph said, "if these guys know about the insurance policy, is that they're not taking it lying down. They're trying to come up with a way to cancel out the threat that the ambassador's real identity will be revealed if anything happens to Skip or Kate."

Rose raised the marker to the paper, then hesitated. "How the hell do I summarize that?"

"Trying to cancel out insurance with counter threat," Rob said.

"Thanks." Rose wrote that down. Then her throat closed. She turned around to face the others. "The kids are really vulnerable here."

Everyone nodded, their expressions grim. Skip's jaw was

tight, his knuckles white where they gripped his coffee mug.

Rose turned back to the pad. The words blurred as she wrote. Those kids were her god-children, the closest thing to offspring she'd ever have. She and Mac knew damn well they weren't cut out to be parents. She blinked hard. With her back still to the room, she asked, "Anything else we think?"

After a moment, Mac said, "Can't think of nothin' else."

Swiping a forearm across her face, Rose tore off the page and tossed it on the table. On the next one, she wrote *What We Don't Know*.

"Who the hell's doin' this," Mac said.

"And why," Dolph said.

"Who's making inquiries," Rob added.

"How to stop the fuckers," Dolph said.

"Yeah, well, that's the next page," Rose said. "Anything else?"

"Who's doing this and how to stop them pretty much covers it," Rob said.

Rose tore the page off and wrote on the next one, *What We Could Do*.

"Send Kate and the kids away," Skip said.

Rose wrote it down but put a question mark after it. Turning around, she said, "I'm not sure they'd be safer somewhere else."

Dolph raised his hand. "Best problem-solving strategy is to write down all options first, without evaluating them."

Rose nodded and scratched out the question mark.

"Blow the whistle on the damned ambassador," Skip said. "Once the truth's out there's no reason to try to shut us up."

Rose wrote it down.

"Try to figure out who's behind all this ourselves," Dolph said.

Rose wrote *Investigate ourselves*.

"Kill the ambassador," Mac growled.

After a moment of stunned silence, Skip said, "Write it down, Rose."

"Try again to impress upon the ambassador and his staff that we won't tell if they leave us alone," Rob said.

Rose raised a skeptical eyebrow at that one, but she wrote it down. "Anything else?"

After several moments of silence, they all shook their heads.

Rose glanced at her watch as she tore the sheet off the pad. "Kate should be here soon."

Skip put his cup down so hard coffee sloshed over the edge. "You didn't tell her what happened, did you?"

"No, I told Manny to tell her everyone's safe but there'd been a development."

"I don't want her to know they came after me." His voice rose. "She blames herself for Ed's death. If she thought she'd brought killers down on me, it'd–"

"Take it easy, Skip," Rob said.

The big man jumped up and turned to him. "You of all people know what I'm talking about."

Rob stood and put a steadying hand on his friend's shoulder.

"You can't protect her from this," Rose said gently.

"Protect me from what?" Kate stood in the doorway, hands on her hips. "What the hell's going on?"

CHAPTER ELEVEN

Rob grabbed Skip's arm and nudged him past his wife. "We need to get something from my office. Be right back."

Skip looked over his shoulder but he allowed himself to be dragged down the hall.

Once in his office, Rob pointed Skip toward the sitting area off to one side of the room. Skip hesitated, then perched on the edge of a chair.

Taking a seat himself, Rob cleared his throat, searching for the right words. He'd wanted to diffuse the tension, keep Skip from blowing up, but now he was wondering if he was stepping over a line. Finally he said, "When you were Kate's bodyguard six years ago, when we were trying to track down Ed's killer, what was your impression of her then?"

Skip looked surprised by the question. He thought for a moment. "I was impressed by her strength. Especially after all she'd been through. And her courage."

"Did you love her then?"

Skip shook his head. "I didn't really give her another thought, not until you hired me to help your aunt." He paused for a moment. "If we hadn't connected up again that summer, she and I wouldn't be. Billy wouldn't even exist."

"Has she changed since then?"

"No, not really, other than worrying too much about something happening to me."

"Which is understandable, considering. But the thing is, she needs to deal with those fears herself. If somebody's stealing her purse or coming at her in a speeding car, by all means jump in and protect her. But if you try to protect her emotionally, it somehow..." Rob stopped, again reaching for the right words.

"Diminishes her," Skip finished for him.

~~~~~~~~

Kate was staring at *6. Kids vulnerable*. She tried to speak but her tongue stuck to the roof of her mouth. She coughed and tried again.

"So they attacked Skip, and now you think they'll go after the kids," she was saying when Rob and Skip returned to the conference room.

"You and the kids need to be someplace safe, as of tonight," Skip said.

"We *all* need to be safe as of tonight," Kate said. Her stomach clenched. She turned to Skip. "Janice!"

"Rose sent a guard to her office, but I'll call and make sure she's taking the situation seriously."

"Wait." Mac leaned over to the box at his feet and then tossed a cell phone to Skip. "Pre-paid cells. Harder to trace. If your regular phone's turned on, even though you're not usin' it, someone can track your location. These are good 'til you call someone who might be under surveillance. Once the phone number's captured, these can be traced too."

While Skip was calling Janice, Mac pulled out more phones and passed several to each person. Then he passed around sheets of paper with the phone numbers listed next to their names. "The numbers are taped to the backs of the phones. The ones with the numbers in red, those you only use when both people are in secure locations. The others, once you've called somebody whose phone might be tapped, or either person's somewhere the call can be intercepted, you destroy that phone." Mac rattled the box. "More where those came from."

Skip disconnected. "Janice is apartment hunting. Our guard's with her."

"How feasible would it be to send the kids away?" Kate asked. "Can we come up with someplace that would truly be safe?"

"Three challenges," Rose said. "Where to send them? How to get them away without them being followed? How to keep them safe once they're there?"

"You come up with a good place, I'll get 'em there an' keep 'em safe," Mac said. "Got some old Army buddies who'll likely help out."

"Do you think these guys would figure it out if we sent them to my mother's in Ohio?" Rob said.

"It'd probably take 'em awhile," Mac said.

"Are our siblings or parents at risk?" Kate asked.

Mac thought for a moment. "Maybe, if the kids aren't an option. But it's a lot harder to hold an adult hostage. 'Specially for a long time."

Most of the others' expressions looked as confused as Kate felt.

"You can hide the fact that kids have been kidnapped," Rose said, "by threatening to kill them if the parents tell anyone. And parents can readily cover for their kids' absence. Nobody's likely to question it if they say the kids are sick or visiting their grandparents. Holding an adult for any length of time is a lot harder. Somebody–a friend, co-worker–is likely to contact the authorities and report the person missing."

"These guys, they're tryin' to operate under the radar," Mac said. "Last thing they want is a police investigation."

"The attack today," Rose said. "They were probably planning to make it look like a robbery gone wrong."

"But they seriously underestimated you." Rob grinned at Skip.

Kate was surprised that she wasn't more upset by the attack on Skip. She found the fact that he had fended off his attackers reassuring. Her husband really was quite good at taking care of himself, as he and Rob had frequently pointed out to her.

"So sending the kids and Maria out to Rob's mom would buy us a few days at least," she said.

"You're going too," Skip said.

"No, I'm not. If I go with them, they won't be safe." Kate heard the sharpness in her own tone, but she wasn't sure she regretted it.

Skip opened his mouth but Rose cut him off. "She's right. The kids disappear, that's a lost opportunity to neutralize the threat. They may not even look for them. But Kate *is* the main threat. She disappears, they'll assume she's about to blow the whistle and they'll look for her long and hard."

Rob jumped in. "I'd like to try to talk Liz into going with the kids. She can help Maria take care of them, and that gets her out of harm's way."

"You should go too, Rob," Kate said. "I never should've involved you in this."

Rob and Rose were both shaking their heads before she'd finished her sentence. "Same applies to him as you," Rose said. "If these assholes know the ambassador came to see him today—"

"That's real likely," Mac said.

Rose nodded. "If any of the three of you disappear completely, they're gonna try to track you down. You don't want your trail leading them to the kids."

"But you don't think they'll be all that concerned about Liz?" Skip asked.

Mac pursed his lips. "She probably hasn't registered on their radar yet, but she will eventually. Now's the best time to get her out of the game."

"I'd sure feel a lot better knowing she was with the kids," Kate said. Then horror washed over her at another thought. "Rob's girls!"

Rob had gotten up to get a cup of coffee from the credenza. He turned back to the group. "I've thought about that. Hopefully they're far enough away to be safe. Shelley's out of the country." His voice was calm but his face was ghostly pale.

Kate's eyes stung as she watched him put his coffee mug down on the table with a shaky hand. *I brought this into our lives.* She shook her head, pushing the thought aside. She'd deal with her guilt later. Right now they needed to make sure everybody was safe.

"She's on an archeological dig in Egypt," Rob said.

"What about Samantha?" Kate said. "They could send someone out to her school in California. Rose, can you get a PI agency out there to put guards on her?"

"Be expensive," Rose said.

"Doesn't matter. I'm paying." Kate held up her hand as both Rob and Skip started to protest. "No arguments, guys. We're in this mess because of my client, and I can afford it."

"I'll call the girls and warn them," Rob said.

Mac tossed him another throwaway cell. "That one's international. Don't say too much over the phone."

"Let's get over to the house," Skip said. "I know there are guards there now, but still."

"What about looking normal?" Dolph said as they all stood and headed out of the room. "It's not gonna look all that normal if we all descend on your house."

"*You* go home, Dolph," Rose said. "If you're seen at the house, then you and your wife will be in danger. The rest of you go in the front. Mac and I'll slip in the back."

"I'll call Liz," Kate said. "Tell her to meet us there."

~~~~~~~~~

Janice had beat them to the house by just a few minutes. She was standing inside the front door when Kate and Skip arrived. Grinning, she held up a set of keys. "I found a great apartment, guys. And the best part is it's vacant. I can move in as soon as I get some furniture delivered."

Her face fell as their expressions registered. She looked at Skip. "The guard's not just a precaution, is he?"

"No. We've got a pretty bad situation here."

Rob had lingered on the porch to wait for Liz, who had just pulled up. They came inside. Skip closed the door behind them, throwing the deadbolt lock.

"Anybody going to tell me what's going on?" Liz asked.

Rose and Mac came around the corner from the back door. "You guys fill them in," Rose said. "I'll explain things to Maria and get her and the kids ready."

"Ladies, have a seat." Rob gestured toward the sofa and

armchairs in the living room.

"Got some more calls to make." Mac headed for the study and closed the door behind him.

Rob sat down on the sofa next to his wife and took her hand in his. "That dilemma Kate had that I couldn't tell you about, it's morphed into something that affects us all."

He looked at Kate. She took a deep breath. As succinctly as possible she summarized the events of the last couple weeks. By the time she got to those of that day, both women's eyes were wide. Janice's mouth was hanging open. Liz's was set in a grim line.

"I know this is a lot to digest all at once," Skip said. "But time is of the essence at this point."

"Mac's taking the kids tonight to my mother in Ohio, to get them out of harm's way." Rob glanced nervously at Kate.

She gave him what she hoped was an encouraging look.

"Hon, we'd like you to go with them. Help Maria keep them calm in a strange place."

Liz narrowed her eyes at her husband.

Kate jumped in. "I know it's a lot to ask, to just suddenly pick up and go. But whoever's doing this is ruthless. We've got to get the kids beyond their reach. I'd feel so much better knowing you were with them. That it's not just an elderly woman and an English-challenged nanny looking out for them."

"And if we don't have to guard you, that frees up more resources to keep the rest of us safe," Skip said.

"The girls are covered," Rob said. "Rose has a PI agency near Stanford sending two men to guard Sam. I called her and Shelley, and I talked to Dr. Sherman. He said they already have guards to keep poachers away from the dig. He'll have one assigned to Shel at all times."

Liz's eyes were still on her husband's face. "How much danger is he in?"

The question was aimed at Skip but Rob answered her. "Not nearly as much as Kate and Skip are."

"We're not going to let anything happen to Rob," Skip said softly.

Liz turned to him. Her green eyes held his in a steady gaze. "I know you'll do your damnedest to keep that promise."

Billy and Edie erupted from the kitchen and raced up the stairs. "Road trip!" Billy yelled. Maria trailed behind them.

Rose came into the living room. "I've convinced them this is a big adventure. I don't think it's quite sunk in, though, that Mommy and Daddy aren't going. Maria's helping them pack a few things."

Kate's throat closed for a moment. She looked at Skip. Her own worry and guilt were mirrored in his eyes.

Liz leaned over and took her hand. "I'll go with them."

Kate breathed a sigh of relief. She squeezed Liz's hand. "Thank you."

Then the doorbell rang and she just about jumped out of her skin. *Damn! I'm a nervous wreck.*

Trying to get her breathing and heart rate under control, Kate hurried over to the door where Rose was standing on her tiptoes, trying to see out the peephole that was set at Kate's eye level. Rose stepped aside and she looked out.

Her heart raced again when she saw the Hispanic man standing on her porch. Then her brain belatedly sent the message that it was the bodyguard who had escorted her to Rob's office earlier. "It's Manny."

Rose opened the door and stepped outside.

She was back in less than a minute. "Dark sedan, two men in it, watching the front of the house. They weren't there before." She turned to Liz. "No time for you to go to your house to pack. And you can't use any credit or debit cards while you're out there either."

Janice spoke up for the first time. "Liz, my things'll be a bit big for you but you can alter them."

Before Liz could thank her, Rose turned to Kate and Skip. "You all need to act as normal as possible during the day, at least 'til the kids are well away from here. But it isn't safe for you to sleep here tonight. You're not going back home either, Rob."

Janice dangled her keys in the air. "I've got the perfect safe house. No furniture, but the carpet's plush."

"These guys may have had somebody following you," Rose said.

"I looked at a bunch of places the last few days. How would they know which one I picked, or even that I picked any of them, since I came back here tonight."

Rose nodded.

"We leave first," Skip said. "Act like we're just going out to dinner. Draw these guys after us. Lead them around town for a while, then shake them. The cat will have to go with Liz and the kids."

"Okay," Rose said. "I'll follow you a few cars back. Keep an eye on your tail."

Mac came out of the study. "Four men on their way who're willin' to go to Ohio with us."

"That's quite a sacrifice they're willing to make for strangers," Skip said.

Mac shook his head. "Not for strangers, for my family. 'Sides they're itchin' for a bit of adventure."

"Don't know how adventurous it'll be, once you all are out there," Kate said. "Thanks so much, Mac."

Skip stood up and grabbed Mac's hand to shake it. "Yeah, thanks, man. Oh, and by the way, you've got a cat to deal with."

Mac grimaced.

Skip turned to Kate. "Pack light, darlin'. We can't look like we're moving out or they'll make a greater effort to follow us."

"I'll get the cat," Janice said. "I think I'll slip her a quarter pill of Xanax to keep her quiet."

"I'm going out back now," Rose said. "I'll circle around and be in my car to follow when you leave, Skip." She headed for the back door.

Within minutes, Liz had stuffed some of Janice's clothing into the duffle bag Kate provided. After depositing the cat carrier by the back door, Janice crammed a change of underwear in her pockets and a rolled-up blouse into her purse. Kate came out of the bedroom with a small tote bag that would pass as a purse.

"I'm so sorry we dragged you into this, Janice."

The other woman waved her hand in the air. "Not your fault, and I owe you guys. Glad to be able to provide *you* with a roof for a few days."

Maria came down the stairs carrying a bulging tote bag. The children trailed behind, each with a backpack.

Maria looked nervous but her mouth was set in a determined line. Kate gave her a hug.

"*¡Dios mio!* You watch out, Kate. *Los Colombianos*, dey bad *hombres*."

"We'll be careful."

Maria crossed herself.

Kate plastered a bright smile on her face and turned to Edie and Billy. "You guys are going to have so much fun. You're going to meet Uncle Rob's mother!" She reached down to give Edie a hug. "You both be good now and listen to Maria and Aunt Liz, okay?"

Skip scooped Edie up, as Kate hugged Billy.

"Aren't you and Mommy coming?" the little girl asked.

"No, Pumkin," Skip said gently, holding her tight. He planted a kiss on top of her head. "But we'll be together again real soon. Either we'll come get you, or Aunt Liz'll bring you home in a few days."

He set Edie down and then swooped Billy up in the air over his head. "Be good, little man!" The child giggled and grinned down at his dad.

Edie's little face was pinched with worry. Kate shot Skip an anxious look. He set Billy back on his feet. Stooping down in front of both children, he faked a cheerful voice. "We're going to play a game. You and Uncle Mac and Aunt Liz, you're all on a secret mission. When Uncle Mac says it's time to go out the back, you've got to be real quiet. Don't make any sound at all, okay? Or the enemy agents might hear you."

Billy's eyes lit up with excitement. Edie looked confused. Skip kissed her on the nose. "It'll be fun, Pumkin. Now you two do exactly what Uncle Mac tells you. He's the commando leader, okay?" They both nodded, Billy eagerly, Edie solemnly.

Kate glanced over to where Liz and Rob were hugging and

whispering their goodbyes. She quickly turned away, pretending she hadn't seen Rob's face as he'd reluctantly let his wife go.

She heard Liz whisper, "Be careful, hon." Then Liz started herding the children toward the laundry room and back door, helping them put on their little backpacks as they went.

A throwaway phone rang in Mac's pocket. He listened for a moment, spoke into it in a low voice, then disconnected. "My men are here. Let's get this show on the road." He picked up the cat carrier and peered in. Peaches was staggering around drunkenly. She let out a pathetic meow, then slumped over onto her side.

"She gonna be okay?" Mac asked.

"Yeah, I've given her Xanax before, to take her to the vet."

Mac nodded at Skip. He and Kate headed for the front door, Janice and Rob behind them.

Walking down the sidewalk, they loudly debated which restaurant they should go to, then climbed into Skip's Expedition. Once the doors were locked, Skip breathed a small sigh.

Kate looked over at him. On the surface, he was his usual calm and collected self, but she suspected he was almost as big a wreck inside as she was.

He glanced at her and smiled, but it didn't reach his eyes. "I'm going to drive around the commercial district a while," he said in a low voice. "Make it look like we're still trying to decide where to eat. Then I'll go to that Chinese place on York Road. We'll go through to the back parking lot, then I'll take off out the back exit and hopefully lose them."

Kate nodded. Matching his low volume, she said, "Why are we whispering?"

"They might've planted a listening device on the truck somewhere."

Kate's heart pounded. She felt a surge of rage at whoever was doing this to them. It was followed by a wave of frustration that she had no idea where to point that rage.

~~~~~~~~

While the others were leading the bad guys around town, Mac was turning on the radio in the kitchen and the TV in the living room. Then he joined Liz and the kids in the dark laundry room by the back door.

Liz heard the purr of a vibrating phone coming from his pocket. He answered it. After listening for a moment, he whispered, "Love you too, honey bun."

Liz pretended she hadn't heard him.

"Okay, troops, time to move out," Mac said to the kids, stooping down and peering into their faces. "I'm takin' Maria and the cat first. You need to be totally silent when I open the door, okay? I'll be back in a minute for you two." Two small heads nodded.

Standing, he punched a number into the phone in his hand. "We're coming," he whispered into it, then disconnected.

He slowly opened the door, then picked up the cat carrier in one hand and motioned for Maria to follow him.

Her bag was slung over her shoulder, the children's car seats in her hands. She mumbled something in Spanish under her breath and went out the door. Liz carefully closed it behind them.

Holding the children's hands in the dark laundry room, she looked out the window in the door. Squinting, she could just barely see Mac and Maria as they slipped around the perimeter of the dark backyard under the pine trees. Then they disappeared behind the garage.

In less than three minutes, Mac was tapping lightly on the door. Liz opened it.

Picking Billy up, Mac put an index finger to his lips. He nodded at Liz and stepped back out the door. She slid the duffle bag onto her elbow and took Edie's hand. With the other hand, she pulled the door closed quietly behind them. They started the circuit around the yard under the pines.

Edie was dragging her feet, either from fatigue or anxiety. Liz tapped Mac's shoulder, then motioned to the child. Mac handed Billy to her. "Shh," Liz breathed in the little boy's ear.

Mac picked up Edie and whispered, "Not a sound." He started moving forward again, Liz following as closely as she could.

The area beside the garage was inky black. "Watch your step, sir," a quiet voice came out of the darkness. Liz jumped and collided with Mac's back.

She sensed him stepping over something in his path. She put out her foot. It nudged up against a soft obstacle. She felt Billy being lifted from her arms as Mac whispered, "Quiet now, champ. Almost there."

A black man in Army battle fatigues materialized out of the darkness. Liz stifled a scream. He took her bag in one hand and her elbow with the other. "This way, ma'am," he said quietly.

He half lifted her over the unconscious body lying on the ground. At least she hoped the person was just unconscious. She shuddered as it sank in that this *was* life or death.

Then she was being helped into the back of a dark Hummer in the alley. It was idling with no lights on, outside or in. Even the dashboard was dark.

Liz could just barely see Edie in her booster seat. Maria was next to her, holding a finger to Billy's lips as he sat on her lap. Mac climbed into the front passenger seat.

Liz heard a quiet voice say, "We'll clean up, sir. Right behind you."

Then the Hummer moved silently down the alley, its headlights still off. Liz looked out the back window and made out the outline of another truck behind them, also with its lights off.

Maria was now kneeling on the floor of the Hummer, trying to get Billy to sit still in his car seat so she could strap him in. Liz turned to help her.

The two vehicles crept along several side streets until they came out on a country road. The headlights came on behind them. A radio squawked. The driver picked it up from its holder on the dashboard. He mumbled into it, listened, then mumbled again.

"All clear, sir," he said as he switched on his headlights.

"Uncle Mac?" Edie's voice wavered.

"It's okay, little one," Mac said. "We're safe now."

"Were we good secret agents?" Billy asked.

"The best, champ!"

Liz sat back in her seat and let out the breath she hadn't realized she'd been holding.

CHAPTER TWELVE

The five of them sat in a circle on the plush carpet of Janice's new living room. One of the throwaway cell phones was in the middle of the circle, set on speaker. Mac was on the other end. Kate heard faint road noises in the background as he reported on the only minor glitch, as he called it, in their departure from the house.

Kate's heart pounded at the thought of a man hiding in the dark behind her home, and the others in the car out front. What would those men have done if they hadn't decided to leave tonight, if they'd put the children to bed and gone to sleep in that house? She shuddered.

The kids are safe. We're all safe. She took a deep breath and let it out slowly.

Rose had spread the *What Could We Do* list out on the floor in front of her. "Anybody got a pen or marker?"

"I do." Janice rummaged through her purse and produced a red Sharpie.

"Thanks." Rose put a check mark next to *Get kids away*.

Kate skimmed the rest of the list. "Can we even think of a safe way to contact the ambassador again?" she asked.

"I've got the trust fund papers as a good excuse to contact him," Rob said.

"I'm not sure talking to him again is going to do much good," Skip said. "I vote for blowing the whistle on him."

"We're signing his death warrant if we do that," Kate said. "He'll be sent back to his own country and executed."

"Yeah but the man knew the risks goin' into the game," Mac's disembodied voice came from the phone. "You all have gotten caught up in this 'gainst your will."

"Who would we even tell?" Rob asked. "The CIA or the FBI?"

Kate looked at her watch. "It's not going to be that easy to get through to somebody tonight. And that still doesn't keep us safe while they investigate. They're not going to just march into some foreign embassy and arrest the ambassador on our say-so."

"I'm thinking we might as well try to figure out who's doing this ourselves," Skip said. "Promising not to poke around isn't stopping these guys from seeing us as a threat."

"How about we do both," Kate said. "Investigate ourselves and confront the ambassador again."

Rose bracketed those two options together and put a red number two next to them.

"Going to his mistress's house on Friday would be the most discrete way to confront him," Rob said.

"So we see what we can find out tomorrow," Rose summarized. "Confront him Friday. Reassess Friday evening to decide if it's time to move on to..." She put a red three next to *Blow the whistle on ambassador.*

Everyone looked at Kate. She nodded.

"Dolph and I'll take care of the investigating," Rose said. "Our computers at the agency have a thick firewall."

"Scratch killing him off the list," Rob said. "We wouldn't know how to do that anyway, without getting caught."

Skip shook his head, just as Mac's voice growled from the phone. "I do."

"Put a four next to it," Skip said after a beat of silence. "Last resort." He pushed himself to a stand and offered a hand to Kate.

She stared at it for a beat, then looked up into his face. This man had killed once in his lifetime. It had been ruled a justifiable homicide since he was defending Kate and Rob at the time, but it had still torn him up inside for months afterward. And now he was talking about cold-blooded murder.

What the hell have I gotten us into?

Skip's eyes softened. "I doubt it will come to that," he said quietly.

Kate took his hand and let him hoist her to her feet.

He put an arm around her waist and steered her toward one of the unfurnished bedrooms. "Goodnight, y'all."

Once settled on the floor, Skip's jacket bunched up under her head as a pathetic excuse for a pillow, Kate stared at the ceiling. Skip lay beside her, his pearl-handled .38 within easy reach. He put an arm around her waist and snuggled up against her. "'Night, darlin'."

"Goodnight."

A minute went by, then she felt him squirm next to her. "Plush carpet or not," he muttered. "The floor underneath it is damned hard."

Kate felt her lips curve into a small smile. "Love you, sweetheart," she whispered.

"Love you too, darlin'."

After a while, she felt his body relax into sleep.

She stared at the shadow of the window blinds, cast against the ceiling by the lights from the street below, until she eventually drifted off.

~~~~~~~~

After showering the next morning and changing into the somewhat rumpled spare clothes from the tote bag, they found Rose and Janice at the breakfast bar that divided the apartment's spacious kitchen from an even more spacious living room. The women were drinking from Starbucks coffee cups.

Grinning, Janice handed one to each of them. "One of the perks I love about this building. Starbucks on the ground floor delivers to the residents. There's also a wine shop. Same arrangement. So liquid refreshment is always available for both ends of the day."

"Thanks. Where's Rob?" Kate asked, then took a sip from the steaming cup.

"Up and gone already," Rose said. "Breakfast meeting with a client. He went home first to change." At the worried look in Kate's eyes, she added, "I had four of our men outside the building last night. One of them is now Rob's chauffeur, since we left his car at your house. A guard will go with each of you as well. They'll be replaced by fresh ones by mid-morning. You may not see them, but they'll be there."

"Why not have them visible, as a deterrent?" Kate asked.

Rose paused for a moment, trying to put words to her gut instinct. "These guys are highly trained professionals. Either mercenary hit men or members of a guerilla organization. If they see the guards, they can devise a plan to get past them. If they think you're unguarded, they'll focus on you. Then the guards can jump in and stop them."

Skip nodded his approval. "We don't want to let on that we're all that worried. During the day, we act as normal as possible. Let them assume that we think the guys at my office were thieves. You got anybody on our house, Rose?"

Rose shook her head. "We're spread too thin for that, but I'm going to drum up somebody to watch the apartment while we're all gone."

"Probably not necessary," Janice said. "Concierge doesn't let anybody come up to the apartments without permission from the tenants, and there are two security guards in the lobby to enforce that."

Rose gave her a skeptical look. "The building's security is no match for these guys. There's a dozen ways they can slip past those guards and the concierge."

"How about Lilly?" Skip said. "Do you think she'd be offended if we asked her to act as a bodyguard?"

It was Janice's turn to look skeptical.

Skip grinned at her. "Don't let her name fool you. Lilly is quite formidable."

Rose flashed a grin of her own. Lilly was a licensed investigator. She'd only been working for them for about six months, but she was proving to be as tough as they come. Rose paused for a second to consider the irony that they were both named after flowers.

"I don't think she'll mind. I'll call her."

"I'm going by the house on my way to the office," Skip said. "Be good to know if anyone's been inside."

"Unh, uh," Rose said. "If they haven't figured out that you've vacated, you going *in* instead of coming out, will make them suspicious."

"Easy enough to sneak in."

"Janice and I need to pick up our cars," Kate said. "If we're aiming for normal, we can't all be riding around in strange cars with big burly men."

"Okay, I'll take you, and go over your cars for bugs." Rose turned to Janice. "You okay with us coming back here tonight?"

"Sure. Can you get some more clothes out of the house while you're there?"

"Shouldn't be that hard to do," Skip said.

Rose's mind had turned to other things. Had they covered all the bases? They'd been at risk before, had to put guards on everyone. But those times, their enemies hadn't been well-trained international operatives. She couldn't think of anything they'd missed. She said a silent prayer, crossing herself.

She glanced up to catch Kate following suit. The two lapsed Catholics exchanged a small smile.

~~~~~~~~~

Skip's brain was multitasking. One part was watching for anyone following him, other than the car right behind him that contained one of his own employees. Another part was figuring out how he wanted to approach the house. And, in the background, were the emotions he was trying to sort out, or *process*, as Kate would say. He smiled to himself. Living with a psychologist was challenging at times.

The attack at his office hadn't scared him all that much. He'd been in tight spots before, and the calm detachment that kicked in at such times had not failed him. What worried him was the implication that these guys, whoever the hell they were, meant business. They weren't going to leave any loose ends, and his wife was a huge loose end.

His chest ached a little when he thought about his children being shipped off to Ohio, but he knew Mac would do everything in his power to keep them safe. He shoved aside his worries about them to focus on the bigger issue. *Kate.*

His mouth went dry at the thought of her walking around in the world with just one invisible guard trailing discreetly behind. Rose said she was putting Manny back on Kate as of this afternoon. That eased his anxiety some, but not much. Manny Ortiz was their best guard, smart and dedicated, but he was just one man. Skip wanted to surround his wife with an army of men.

He realized he was getting close to his house. He pulled over to the curb and got out as the car behind him cruised on by. It parked several houses up.

Skip stepped out of his truck and made a slight come-here gesture toward the car, then turned the movement into the act of running his hand through his hair.

A man of average height but with a thick muscular build got out of the car. He put a baseball cap on and headed Skip's way.

As he neared, he slowed slightly, as if he were just greeting a neighbor while taking his morning constitutional. "Hey, boss," he said softly.

"Good morning, Claude," Skip said in a cheerful voice, then quietly added, "We go in the back. It's quite possible someone's in there."

The man sketched a friendly wave in his direction and kept walking.

The two men made their way separately to the alley behind the house. They pulled out their guns, then silently spread out across the end of the yard. Moving slowly forward, they checked behind bushes and trees. The yard was empty of human beings.

They approached the back door. Skip slipped his key in the lock, then tilted his head toward the right before swinging the door open.

Claude went right, Skip left, guns extended in front of them. The laundry room, crammed with boots, snow shovels and a washer and dryer, didn't offer many hiding places.

Skip nudged open the door into the L-shaped living room. They swung to each side of the back section of the room. Skip checked behind the dark big-screen TV while Claude eased up to the corner.

He peered around it, then nodded without looking back and kept going. Skip moved quickly into the main part of the room, checked behind the sofa, then slipped into the entryway and cautiously opened the coat closet.

The doorbell rang. Skip looked through the peephole to verify it was Rose. He unlocked the door.

As he re-locked it behind her, Rose leaned down to pull her gun from her ankle holster. "Nobody watching out front," she whispered. "The cars were clean."

Skip silently pointed her toward his study. She moved past him, gun extended in front of her. He signaled to Claude and they cleared the kitchen.

Skip pointed to the bottom of the steps. Claude walked to that spot and kept his eyes and his gun trained up the stairs while Rose and Skip cleared the master bedroom and bath.

They moved up the stairs, Claude bringing up the rear. It took another fifteen minutes to check the upper floors, and then the basement. Next Rose swept the house for listening devices.

"Clean," she said, as she returned to the living room.

"Hard to believe nobody's been in here," Skip said.

Rose headed for the bedroom. "I'll get some more clothes for you guys."

"Backpack's on the floor of my closet," Skip called after her. "Bring the one from Kate's closet for Janice's stuff. I'm gonna get my other gun."

He went into the study and reached up to the top shelf of the bookcase for the fake book in which he kept the key to his gun safe. The book was there. The key was not.

"Shit!" Pulling out his key ring, Skip found the small key and unlocked the gun safe's door. The safe was empty. He banged his fist down on top of the metal box.

The noise brought Claude and Rose around the corner, pistols extended in front of them. They relaxed when they saw that Skip was the only one in the room.

"Shit!" He banged his fist again on the gun safe.

"What's the matter, boss?" Claude asked.

"My 380's gone."

CHAPTER THIRTEEN

"You need to report it stolen asap," Rose said. "They may use it in a crime and then frame you for it."

"Yeah, but I think I'll tell the police it was taken from the office. I don't want them crawling all over the house. That wouldn't exactly look normal."

"I'll dust the safe for prints. See if any show up besides yours," she said. Starting to hand him the empty backpack, she added, "Grab some stuff for Janice."

"Uh, let's reverse that, partner. You handle Janice's undies. I'll dust for prints."

Rose broke out one of her rare but gorgeous smiles, transforming her relatively plain face into a thing of beauty. Claude's mouth fell open.

Despite his concerns about the stolen gun, Skip had to stifle a grin of his own. Rose's smile usually had that effect on men the first time they saw it.

There were no prints on the safe but his own. The thief had apparently worn gloves. He used the house phone to report the gun stolen. No point in wasting a throwaway cell.

Skip handed Claude his keys. "You take the backpacks and get my truck, please. I'll ride with Rose so it looks like she stopped by to pick me up for work. You follow at a distance. See if we pick up a tail."

Rose did a discreet sweep of her car with the debugging device. Skip waited until they were well away from the house with no sign of a tail before he called Mac.

"Reilly."

"Mac, did you leave lights on in the house last night?"

"Yeah, and the radio and TV."

"Would your guys have gone back in to turn them off?"

"Nope. Wanted the house to look occupied 'til we were well away. Why?"

"They weren't on this morning. Hang on. Let me see if this cheapy phone has a speaker function. We're in Rose's car."

Once Skip had found the correct button, they filled Mac in on the missing gun.

"They turned the TV and radio off so they could hear if anybody came home while they searched the place," Mac said. "I agree with Rose. Stolen gun's gonna end up at some crime scene."

"But why aren't they watching the house?"

"They may have limited personnel," Rose said.

"'Specially now that two of their men are outta the game," Mac said.

"What happened to the guy your men knocked out?" Skip asked.

"We swung south a bit and dumped him outside an emergency room in Virginia. Doubt he'll remember what happened. My man snuck up behind him and whacked him good. He was still out cold when we dumped him."

"Bad news is these guys have probably figured out that the kids are gone," Rose said.

"We've got 'em tucked away here," Mac said. "I'll keep 'em safe."

"Thanks, Mac." Skip swallowed the lump in his throat. "Thanks for everything."

~~~~~~~~

Rob was staring at the document in front of him, trying to register the words in his mind instead of just reading them with his eyes. Hard to get excited about a civil suit regarding an alleged patent violation when practically everyone near and dear to him was in jeopardy. Not to mention, he hadn't slept much the night before. He was getting too old to sleep on the floor, even if it was covered with plush carpeting. And he had missed Liz horribly.

The intercom on his phone buzzed. Fran's disembodied voice announced, "Two gentlemen to see you, Mr. Franklin."

Rob was instantly alerted. Fran never called him Mr. Franklin. He was Boss at the office or Rob at social events. He started to press the intercom button, then thought better of it. He picked up his phone instead and called Fran's extension.

"Mr. Franklin's office," she answered.

"Who are they?" Rob asked.

"Oh, hi, Mr. Ceeiya," Fran said.

"Ceeiya? They're CIA?" Rob suspected Fran's attempt at subterfuge wasn't fooling whoever was standing in front of her desk.

"Yes, that's right," Fran said. "Your appointment's at four."

"Do they look Hispanic?"

"No, no, of course not. Mr. Franklin will understand if you're a little bit late. He'll have your paperwork ready."

"They have credentials."

"Yes, that's right. Okay, see you then."

"Thanks, Fran."

Through the intercom, Rob said, "Send the gentlemen in."

Rob stood up as his admin ushered in two men. Rob guessed they were around his age, early to mid-fifties, but the taller one seemed to be fighting tooth and nail to defy the aging process. He was lean and fashionably dressed in a well-tailored suit. His dark brown hair screamed *hair dye*. His partner's off-the-rack suit was a bit rumpled already at ten-forty in the morning. He sported a middle-aged paunch and his salt-and-pepper hair was combed over to hide the beginnings of a bald spot on the top of his head.

His ice-blue eyes bored into Rob's as he extended his hand. "Nicholson. He's Phelps. CIA."

Rob shook their hands. "What can I do for you, gentlemen?"

Nicholson held out a picture of the Colombian ambassador. "What do you know about this man?"

Rob hesitated for an instant. He had no idea why but his gut was telling him something was off about these two. "He's a new client. Came in yesterday."

"Yes, we know that," Phelps said, impatience in his voice. "What did he want?"

Rob waved his hand toward the two chairs in front of his desk. "I'm afraid I can't tell you that," he said, as he walked over to his desk chair. "Client confidentiality."

"National security trumps client confidentiality," Nicholson said, settling into one of the visitors' chairs. Phelps remained standing at parade rest.

"May I see some credentials, gentlemen?"

The two men exchanged a quick glance.

Nicholson pulled a flat leather wallet out of his inside jacket pocket. Rob held out his hand. The agent flipped the wallet open and leaned forward across the desk, flashing it in Rob's general direction.

Rob withdrew his hand, resisting the implied expectation that he would lean forward and attempt to read what was in the wallet from a distance. He sat back in his chair instead. "Gentlemen, please put your credentials on my desk so I can examine them."

After a slight hesitation, they both complied.

There now, that wasn't so hard. Rob picked up one and then the other of the small wallets to examine their contents.

He nudged them back across the desk and the agents retrieved them.

"My client identified himself as John Smith. He asked me to write up papers to take care of a routine financial matter." Despite the legitimate-looking credentials, Rob's instincts were running up red flags.

"I repeat, Mr. Franklin, national security trumps client confidentiality," Nicholson said.

"Not without a court order, it doesn't," Rob replied. "Perhaps if you told me why you're interested in my client, I might be able to be more helpful, without violating lawyer-client privilege."

Phelps snorted.

"Or perhaps not," Rob said amicably. He stood up. "We seem to have reached an impasse, gentlemen. If you would leave your card, I'll contact you if I become privy to any information that would not be covered by client confidentiality."

The two agents exchanged another look. Nicholson pushed up out of his chair and picked up one of Rob's cards from a holder on his desk. He wrote a number on the back of it, then handed it to Rob. "You can reach us there."

Rob waited five minutes after the two men had left his office before taking out one of the throwaway phones and the list of phone numbers for the others. He started to punch in a number, then thought better of it. Leaving his office, he walked to his partner's office again.

Knowing Stockton was in court, he asked Shirley, "Is Bill in?" She responded in the negative.

"I'll just leave him a note then." Rob entered his partner's office. He nudged the door closed, then took out the cell phone and punched in a number.

"Hernandez."

"Rose, I just had a couple of interesting visitors. Not sure what to make of it."

"Hispanic?"

"Nope," Rob said. "Claimed to be on the payroll of the taxpayers, but there was something off about them. I didn't tell them much."

"Wonder what that means." There was silence on the line for a moment. "We've been doing some research here. I'm thinking we should meet for lunch, pool our info. Say in an hour. We'll come to you."

"Sounds good. Oh, and bring your little gizmo. Just in case these guys left me a present."

~~~~~~~~

Rose had swept Rob's office for listening devices and pronounced it clean by the time Skip and Dolph joined them. She called Mac with a throwaway phone, put it on speaker and set it in the middle of Rob's desk. On his end, Mac also hit the speaker button so Liz could join the conversation.

Rob's heart swelled at the sound of Liz's voice booming from the small clump of plastic. "Kate's gonna be royally annoyed that she's not in on this."

"She's doing her best to get through the day with her clients," Skip said. "I'm not about to call and upset her. She said she had two people scheduled today who are in a rough place."

"We'll fill her in this evening," Rose said. "We're going back to Janice's tonight. After that we're going to need another safe house."

"'Specially after you all confront the ambassador tomorrow," Mac's gruff voice came from the phone. "I'll make some calls. See what I can come up with."

Rob described his visitors, and their resistance to showing him their credentials or leaving a business card.

"Could've been macho posturin'," Mac said, "or they could be rogue."

Dolph opened his laptop. "You got wireless here? Any kind of a decent firewall?"

Rob shrugged. All he knew about firewalls was that they were supposed to keep viruses from eating his computer files.

Rose got up and went out to Fran's desk. A minute later, she returned. "Firewall's decent. And if they're hacking into the system, they'd expect Rob to check on them."

Dolph began tapping on his keyboard.

"We've confirmed that Ambassador Garcia did not exist before the age of twenty," Rose said. "Which is when he bought his way onto the Colombian police force with the appropriate bribes. His driver, Raul Pérez, also did not exist, with that name at least, before he started working for Garcia six years ago. Had a bit more luck with him. We think he was Raul Dias, a lieutenant in a right-wing paramilitary group under the *Autodefensas Unidas de Colombia,* or AUC. The AUC came into being in the late 90's to supposedly suppress the left-wing insurgency groups, like the one Garcia was in. Their methods were quite extreme. They were accused of killing hundreds of civilians and the Colombian government saw them as a greater threat to peace than the insurgents. The previous *presidente,* Álvaro Uribe, negotiated a demobilization treaty with them, but some of their members just went underground instead.

"Raul Dias vanished from the scene about two months

before Raul Pérez was hired on to Garcia's security staff by his then security chief, José Álvarez. This was when Garcia was Assistant Minister of Defense for Colombia. Garcia's wife's a bit interesting. She was christened Consuela Maria Fernandez Delgado Rodriguez."

"Good Lord," Liz's voice broke in from the phone on the desk. "How many last names does one person need?"

Rob chuckled.

One corner of Rose's mouth quirked up in a half smile. "Families that claim a relatively pure Spanish lineage just keep adding the prestigious family names to the list. In person she would probably introduce herself as Consuela Rodriguez de Garcia. Her Spanish lineage plus the fact that her family's quite wealthy spells hard-core law-and-order politics in Colombia."

"So she may not know her hubby's an ex-rebel," Skip said.

Rose shook her head. "Kate said Garcia had talked to his wife about Dawson."

"So she knows," Rob said. "Any indication how involved she is in politics herself?"

"Not at all that I can tell," Dolph said. "Her daddy was though, before he died. A behind-the-scenes kind of guy. Tended to back politicians who advocated destroying the rebels over negotiating with them. The Garcias have been married eleven years. She's nineteen years younger than him, currently thirty-three to his fifty-two. According to her Facebook page, which is under the name Maria Delgado, with a very limited circle of friends and the strongest privacy settings Facebook provides, she's three months pregnant."

"I want to thank the judges for my second place ribbon in the world's best hacker competition," Liz's voice boomed from the table. "It's an honor to have lost to Mr. Randolph who is an inspiration to all of us who aspire to hacking excellence."

"I humbly decline the honor of first place," Dolph said with a chuckle. "Hacking into a Facebook page is hardly difficult." His fingers were still dancing around on his laptop.

Rose nodded to Skip. "I went to D.C. to check out the

ambassador's *hacienda*," he said. "Fort Knox has less security. I lingered across the street, pretending to consult my street map. *Hombre* immediately materialized at my elbow, suggesting I move along."

"Not too surprising," Rose said. "Considering that Colombia's still a bit unstable, despite claims to the contrary in their travel brochures."

Skip shook his head. "You really think *anybody* would mistake me for Hispanic, Rose? They're not worried about their own countrymen taking out the ambassador. This felt like something else."

"It's understandable that the ambassador would be paranoid," Liz said.

"Yeah," Skip said. "But he's trying to keep a low profile–everybody's best friend, please don't question from whence he came. Blatantly extreme security would be more likely to draw attention, which is the last thing he wants."

"What the hell's going on in the Colombian government," Mac's growl came from the phone, "that they hire people with suspicious backgrounds?"

Rose shrugged, even though Mac couldn't see her. "Bribery's rampant, I'm sure. And there may be a certain amount of mutual looking the other way going on, now that the country's supposedly at peace."

Dolph jumped in. "Not getting anywhere with trying to get into the CIA's personnel records."

"Not surprising," Skip said.

"I did find something interesting on their mission statement page, however. There's a link to another page of fine print that defines the perimeters of CIA activities. If an American is suspected of espionage or other acts of treason, they aren't the ones who'd investigate. It would be the FBI. They're not allowed to even *question* U.S. citizens."

"That would explain the weird vibes I was getting," Rob said.

Dolph nodded. "I'm leaning toward these clowns are rogue."

"They could be Dawson's connections, the ones who tracked

down the mistress," Rose said. "When he turned up dead, they decided something was fishy."

"And that's who's been investigating," Skip said.

"Passing that information along may reassure the ambassador and his cohorts that we're not the ones they should be worrying about," Rob said.

"We need a game plan for tomorrow," Rose said, "when we show up at the mistress's house."

"I go in with the trust papers and deliver our message to leave us the hell alone," Rob said. "You guys stand guard outside."

"Mac's vigorously shaking his head on this end," Liz reported.

"Driver's way more than a chauffeur. He needs to be neutralized," Mac said.

"Manny and I'll do that," Rose said.

"I'm going in this time," Skip said. "No point in my keeping a low profile now. At some point we bring Raul into the house and question him. One of them might let something slip in front of me, not realizing I speak Spanish."

~~~~~~~~

Janice didn't normally mind working ten hours or more a day. She'd always figured it was part of being a successful lawyer. But she too hadn't slept well on the floor the night before. At four o'clock, she decided to call it a day. She would take her laptop home so she could do some work later in the evening.

But first she needed to get herself and her guests some better bedding. She headed for the nearest Sears store, watching in her rearview mirror for a glimpse of the bodyguard who was supposed to be following her. She saw no sign of him but decided that probably meant he was good at his job.

Getting off the escalator in the furniture department, she located the bedding area, and quickly encountered an obstacle. Yes, they had plenty of mattresses in stock, but the earliest delivery time available was between noon and four the next afternoon.

Janice picked out a basic bed frame, box spring and mattress for her bedroom but decided to wait on the other rooms until she knew how she wanted to decorate them. This was the first home she'd ever had that she could decorate however she wanted, without trying to please anyone else. She wanted to savor the experience.

As she returned her credit card to her purse and signed the paperwork for her bed, she asked the salesman, "Any thoughts on how I can get something temporary for tonight? It's not just me. I have some guests as well."

"You might try sporting goods, ma'am. They should have air mattresses and the pumps for them. Wife and I have a couple for guests. They're pretty comfortable."

"Great idea." Janice headed for that department. Thirty minutes later she was lugging two huge bags out to her car.

~~~~~~~~

Rose had swung by Kate's office at the end of the day to escort her safely back to Janice's place. When they arrived there, Lilly was standing in the hallway outside the apartment.

On first blush, Rose's name seemed appropriate for a short woman with a gorgeous smile, until one got to know her and realized she was no delicate flower. In Lilly's case, the mismatch between name and owner was instantly apparent to Kate. The blue-eyed, blonde was over six feet tall and probably weighed close to two hundred pounds, most of it muscle.

"She's been shopping," Lilly told her boss.

"Uh, oh," Rose said.

"What's the problem?" Kate asked.

"Hopefully there isn't one. But she's been staying with you. Now nobody's at your house. They might have been watching for her to show up at work today to tail her back to you."

Rose called the guard assigned to Janice that day. After disconnecting, she said. "Says he spotted what he thought was a tail as she was leaving the shopping mall. He got between them and slowed down so Janice got through the next light and they got stopped. He kept the guy blocked in until she was out of sight. Still, I'll tell the guards to be extra vigilant tonight. Can you stay, Lilly?"

"No problem," the big woman said.

When they opened the door, they were greeted by an

horrendous noise. It sounded like someone was demolishing the master bedroom with a jackhammer. Rose and Lilly pulled their guns and raced toward the room, just as the noise stopped. Janice was shoving the plug into the last of the air mattresses.

"Hey, Rose, I got us some better accommodations for tonight. Could you drag the bigger one into Kate and Skip's room for me?"

Rose stifled an eye roll and holstered her gun. She nodded to Lilly, who returned to her post outside the door. Rose grabbed the designated mattress and wrestled it out of the room.

Janice caught sight of Kate. "I've got sheets and pillows, too. Come get the ones for your bed. How 'bout Chinese for dinner? We can have it delivered."

Rose dropped her burden and returned to the doorway. "No. That would be a bit obvious if you order a bunch of food on your credit card, and have it delivered here."

"Well, what the hell are we going to eat then?" Janice asked.

"She's got a point," Kate said.

"Hang on. Let me call Skip. He and Claude can get the food. I'll call it in, but not to the place you usually use, Janice."

Janice threw her hands up in the air. "How did life get so complicated?" she asked no one in particular, but there was no rancor in her voice. "Is it okay if I get the wine shop to send up a couple bottles? And some glasses and a corkscrew."

"Do you have to use your credit card?" Rose asked.

"Nope, they keep a running tally. Don't have to pay up until the end of the month."

"Don't see a problem then."

~~~~~~~~

The next morning, Janice resisted the idea of going to the new safe house with them that evening. "If you're willing to leave a guard with me to make sure nobody follows me home, I should be okay. I've already forwarded my mail to the office. I'll leave it that way for now."

Neither Rose nor Skip responded as they drank their Starbucks coffee and ate the muffins the coffee shop had delivered.

Janice brushed crumbs off the front of yesterday's rumpled

blouse. "Thanks for bringing some more of my clothes, guys. I'm gonna go get dressed for work."

Once she'd left the room, Rose said, "She's kind of a loose cannon. Might be better to not have her with us."

"And better for her if we distance ourselves from her," Skip said. "Is it time for her guard to become more visible?"

Rose paused for a moment. "Yeah, 'cause then they'll be able to stop her from doing something dangerous. Like running around Sears buying sheets and pillows."

When Janice returned to retrieve her coffee cup from the breakfast bar, Rose said, "You need to realize that until this is all completely resolved you're in danger. They know you're a friend of Kate and Skip, that you were staying at their house. They may assume you know what's going on. Or they may try to kidnap you, to use you as leverage. So you just come and go from here to work. I'm putting two people on you. You're going to ride with one of them in their car. The other will stay here to rest up for the night shift, but also to guard the place so you don't have any surprises when you get home."

~~~~~~~~

At nine a.m., the delivery department at Sears received a phone call. "Hello, you have a delivery going out today for Janice Browning. I am her assistant. She wanted me to verify that she gave you the correct address. Since she has just moved, she was not positive that she remembered the street number correctly."

The clerk in the delivery department pulled up the relevant order on her computer. "Yes, that delivery's going out this afternoon to 3943 York Road, Towson, apartment 901."

"Yes, that is correct. Thank you."

CHAPTER FOURTEEN

At precisely three o'clock, Juan Garcia stepped out of his limousine in front of the luxury townhouse owned by Ms. Annabelle Gaston.

Garcia had not realized that Annabelle was a high-priced call girl when he had first met her at a private party in Washington. She, on the other hand, had assumed he was privy to this knowledge, since the party was the kind to which gentlemen did not bring their wives.

They had talked for hours, ignoring for the most part the festivities around them. At three in the morning, the host, who had imbibed far too much alcohol, rather clumsily announced it was time for *the girls* to leave. Garcia was shocked when the graceful and elegant young brunette said goodnight to him and got up to join the women who had been entertaining various guests in the upstairs rooms all evening. Halfway to the door, Annabelle had glanced back over her shoulder. Seeing the look of dismay on his face, she had come back to plant a gentle kiss on his lips. It was the first time they had touched.

She had taken his hand. "I had a delightful evening conversing with you, monsieur," she said in her soft French accent. When their hands parted company his held an embossed card with nothing but a phone number on it.

He had called the following day and asked her to consider an exclusive arrangement. That was three years ago.

Garcia came to Annabelle not just for sex, indeed not even primarily for sex, although their physical relationship was certainly more satisfying than the one he had with his wife, who knew dozens of subtle ways to remind him of the discrepancies in their backgrounds. No, Garcia came to Annabelle's house three times a week primarily to *talk*. It was the only time he was able to relax, to let down his guard.

But today was not destined to be a normal relaxing visit. Five minutes after he entered the townhouse, while Annabelle was still making him a drink, the doorbell rang.

Garcia and Annabelle exchanged a look, hers concerned, his annoyed–not with her but with Raul for once again allowing someone to disturb them.

The doorbell rang a second time. Annabelle started for the door but Garcia stopped her. "No, *querida*, I will see who it is."

He went over and nudged aside the thin curtain over the window nearest the door. The man on the doorstep was the lawyer he had visited outside Baltimore two days ago. Garcia looked over to his limousine parked on the street. The young woman who had threatened to skewer him like a pig was leaning against its side. She appeared to be conversing nonchalantly with his driver but Garcia suspected she was holding him at gunpoint.

Furious, Garcia opened the door.

"Mr. Ambassador," the lawyer said. "I have those papers you asked me to prepare. And I have another urgent matter I need to discuss with you."

"How dare you come here–"

Garcia's angry tirade was cut short when a tall muscular man suddenly appeared next to the lawyer and shoved the door wide open.

He stepped into the doorway, forcing Garcia to take a step backward. Nodding to Annabelle, he said, "Please excuse the intrusion, ma'am. Mr. Ambassador, allow me to introduce myself. I'm Skip Canfield, Kate Huntington's husband."

~~~~~~~~~

Skip was impressed with how quickly the ambassador composed himself.

"Come in and close the door, please."

Skip and Rob complied.

"Do you realize how dangerous it is for you to come here, especially you, Mr. Canfield. I am not certain that I have eradicated those zealots who are over anxious to protect me."

"Sir, you most definitely have not eradicated them. Two men came to my office on Wednesday and tried to kill me."

"Annabelle, please excuse us," the ambassador said without taking his eyes off Skip. She gracefully slipped from the room.

"Have a seat, gentlemen." Garcia headed for the loveseat. "Tell me what happened."

Rob sat down in an armchair. Skip remained standing.

The ambassador listened without comment as Skip summarized the attempt on his life, including the fact that the dead man remained unidentified and that his companion seemed to have shot him on purpose.

"We have a pretty good idea who's been making inquiries," Rob said. "Two CIA agents came to my office yesterday asking about you. I invoked client confidentiality. Mr. Dawson had asked someone he still knew within the intelligence community to check you out. Apparently that request set something in motion."

"Who are these individuals?" Garcia asked.

Skip snorted.

"We have no desire to add names to someone's hit list," Rob said.

Garcia sat back, covering his face with a meaty hand. "You are quite right, Mr. Franklin." Then he lowered his hand and looked at Skip. "My deepest apologies, Mr. Canfield, for all of this."

"I'm afraid apologies are an inadequate response at this point," Skip said.

"What then do you want from me, sir?" the ambassador asked, straightening his back.

"Let's start with a description of your staff."

"I am hardly personally acquainted with all of the people who work at the embassy."

"With all due respect, sir, that's bull hockey. You're a man with a secret and a lot to lose if that secret comes out. You're not going to let just anybody wander around your home. You may not know them all personally but someone senior on your staff has carefully vetted them, and probably has reported to you in a fair amount of detail regarding their backgrounds. Who's in charge of security?"

"There are two people in that role. Captain Juan Martinez of the Colombian Army is in charge of the military guards. Raul Pérez, my personal bodyguard, supervises a small staff."

"How small?" Rob asked. He was taking notes on a legal pad he'd removed from his briefcase.

"Normally six men, but that number has been increased to twelve in anticipation of the upcoming visit by *el Presidente*. The military guard has also been doubled."

"Housekeeping staff?" Rob asked.

"Five Colombian women, carefully vetted as you put it, Mr. Canfield. Three cleaners, a cook and her assistant. They all report to the housekeeper, Ingrid. I do not recall her last name. She is Scandinavian. She answers to my wife. I also have an aide, who has two assistants, and my wife has her own secretary. They have all been with us for some time."

"We'll need their names," Skip said. "Housekeeping staff hasn't been increased due to the impending visit?"

"No. *El Presidente* and his wife will bring their own personal staff. They will be housed in a separate wing of the embassy specifically dedicated to their use."

"So what do you know about the new people on your security staff?" Skip asked. He noticed the ambassador hesitate, his eyes shifting for a moment.

"Nothing. They are Raul's responsibility. But they have all been sent from Colombia. They are not just hoodlums he hires off the street."

"Did you know any of them before, in Colombia?"

Again the slight hesitation. "No."

"Ambassador Garcia, the only thing keeping us from telling the world who the hell you really are is my wife's conscience. I personally voted for just shooting you and being done with it.

So I'd suggest you stop lying to us. What do you know about the new members of your security staff?"

Garcia sighed, then stood up and paced across the room away from them. Skip's hand went to his gun at the small of his back under his windbreaker.

Garcia turned and paced partway back to them. "I am not at all sure, but one man looks familiar, although I did not recognize his name when Raul gave me his report on the man."

"Who does he look like?"

This time the ambassador's hesitation was more straight-forward. He looked at Skip for a long moment, then took a deep breath. "He reminds me of someone I encountered in my rebel days."

"You fought with him?" Rob asked.

"No, against him. He was an officer in the military at that time. Later he joined one of the paramilitary groups organized by certain wealthy citizens to combat the rebel forces."

"What's his name?" Skip demanded.

"We called him *El Diablo*. He was quite ruthless. His actual name was Ricardo Delgado."

"Any relation to your in-laws?"

"A cousin. My father-in-law was one of the main backers of his organization."

Silence reigned for a moment as Skip digested that information. Then he said, "We need to talk to Raul Pérez."

Garcia bristled. He opened his mouth.

"That was not a request."

The ambassador started to reach into his pocket.

Skip's hand was back on his gun. "Bring it out slow."

Garcia carefully pulled his cell phone out of his pocket. He hit a speed-dial number, spoke a few words of Spanish, then listened. He held the phone out to Skip. "Please tell your associate to let him come in."

Skip took the cell. "Bring him in," he said, then disconnected and handed the phone back to Garcia. "Sit down, Mr. Ambassador, and keep your hands where I can see them at all times."

Skip strode to the door and opened it halfway. A moment later, Raul, his hands out to his sides, palms up, nudged it the rest of the way open and entered the room. Rose was behind him, her gun in her hand.

"*Señorita*, since you have disabled my bodyguard, would you be so kind as to stand guard outside the door?" Garcia asked.

Skip pulled out his pistol, then nodded at Rose.

Once she had stepped back outside, Garcia said, "Raul does not speak much English. I will question him. I am as anxious as you are, Mr. Canfield, to get to the bottom of this."

Skip just nodded.

Garcia and Raul exchanged several spates of Spanish. Finally Garcia said, "*Gracias,* Raul, you may go."

"Not so fast," Skip said, waving the .38 in his hand. Raul didn't move. "What'd he say?"

"The gentleman in question checked out when Raul looked into his background. He is who he says he is, one José Gonzales. He was sent ahead as a liaison between my staff and that of *el Presidente*. His resemblance to the man I once knew is coincidental, it seems."

Rob stood up and handed his pad to the ambassador. "Have him write down the names of all the embassy staff."

The ambassador passed on the pad and the instructions. Raul wrote for several minutes, then held the pad out.

As Rob took it, he said, "We want to be certain that Raul understands the consequences if anyone near and dear to us should come to harm. Please inform him, in our presence, of the insurance policy we've taken out regarding that."

After only a slight hesitation, Garcia nodded. He spoke to Raul in Spanish for several moments.

Skip stepped over to the much shorter bodyguard. Looming over him, he said, "Additional attacks against my friends or family will have the opposite effect of the desired result. And I'll come back and dismember you very, very slowly. I'll start with eyelashes and fingernails, then move on to larger appendages. You understand, *hombre*?"

Garcia started to translate. Skip held up his hand. "I think Raul gets the picture, don't you, Raul?"

The man had remained expressionless throughout Skip's speech. He now nodded.

Skip stepped away from him and looked at Rob. "You have something for the gentleman?"

Rob pulled a clump of papers from his briefcase. "The trust. It requires your signature, and that of two witnesses. I believe Mr. Canfield and Mr. Pérez will serve for that. Then you merely transfer the assets into the trust."

Rob handed the papers to the ambassador who looked them over quickly.

"Please sign all three copies. One is yours, one is for Ms. Gaston, and one I will take and file with the court for you."

As Garcia and then Raul signed on the lines Rob indicated, Skip walked over to the front door and opened it. Rose entered the room.

"Raul's done here. Escort him back to the car please."

Once they were out the door, Skip picked up the pen with his left hand and made an indecipherable scribble on the witness line of each copy as Rob flipped through them. Rob handed two of the copies to Garcia, then headed for the door.

Skip followed him out.

Once they were back in their vehicles and several blocks away, Rob called Rose and put the throwaway phone on speaker.

"Rose, there's a new guy on the security team at the embassy," Skip said. "Names supposedly José Gonzales, liaison with the Colombian president's staff for the upcoming visit. The ambassador thought he looked a bit like a guy by the name of..." Skip looked at Rob, who was leafing through his notes.

"Ricardo Delgado," Rob said.

"This Delgado chap was in one of those paramilitary groups, this one supported by Garcia's father-in-law."

"So he could be just another Colombian," Rose said, "trying to remake himself in the new regime–"

"Or he could be in the U.S. for another reason," Skip finished for her.

"I'll check him out."

"Garcia never mentioned his secret to Raul *per se*," Skip said. "He referred to our having some 'detrimental information' so Raul may or may not know the ambassador's true identity. Also, Garcia lied to us, twice. One, Raul speaks English just fine."

"Ah, thus the elaborate threat," Rob said.

"Yup–"

"He understood Mac the other day," Rose said.

"Yeah. Garcia also claimed Raul had already checked this Gonzales guy out," Skip said. "Raul actually said he'd examined the man's papers and had contacted someone to verify his identity. He rattled off a name too fast for me to catch it, but I assume it's someone back in Colombia. Then Raul said he would dig deeper. Garcia wasn't happy with him."

"So Garcia wants to clean his own house," Rob said.

"Can't blame him there," Rose said. "We already know too many of his secrets. Manny and I'll swing by Kate's office and relieve her guard." She gave them the address of the new safe house Mac had arranged for them. "See you there tonight."

~~~~~~~~~

Janice got out of court much earlier than expected that afternoon. She figured the judge was just looking for an excuse to take off early on a Friday. Standing outside the courthouse, she glanced at her watch. Three-fifteen. Debating whether to go back to the office or go home, she was leaning toward the latter. It had been a long and gruesome week.

Her bodyguard approached and pointed out that she shouldn't be standing around in the open.

"Very well. Home, James," she said in a fake British accent.

The twenty-something Hulk Hogan wannabe gave her a confused look. "Ma'am?"

"It's an expression." When his face remained confused, she added, "An *old* expression apparently." Suddenly she felt every one of her fifty years.

As they headed for her new home, Janice was having mixed emotions. The sense of relief that she no longer had to concern herself with Richard's moods had not diminished. But the thought of returning to a bare apartment, without even the cat for company, did not have much appeal. She would have no furniture but the bed, no food in the house, no television or other form of entertainment except her laptop.

When she entered her building, she was greeted by the concierge who assured her that her bed had arrived. "Also, Ms. Browning, a lad from the wine shop brought this in." The young man held up a bottle of a relatively expensive Merlot, not her favorite vineyard but a decent one. "He said the sender gave him a message to deliver as well. I wrote it down. 'Let us part amicably and with fond memories, Richard.'"

Janice narrowed her eyes. She pulled out her cell phone and found the message, the earlier call from Richard that she'd ignored. She played it.

"Janice, darling. There's no need for us to fight, not after all we've meant to each other. We can come to an agreement ourselves, without outside interference. Please call me."

Janice frowned while Phillip, the concierge, waited, a neutral expression on his face.

What did Richard mean by *outside interference*? Was he referring to Kate and Skip, or to lawyers? Probably the latter. The man was too cheap to spring for a divorce attorney, so he'd try to sweet talk her into a settlement. Except she wasn't susceptible to his sweet talk anymore. Why hadn't she noticed before just how smarmy his voice sounded when he was trying to sweet talk her?

Janice smiled. The evening might not be a total wash after all. She'd enjoy Richard's wine, and then she'd trounce him in court. Taking the bottle from the patient concierge, she thanked him, then headed for the elevators.

Lilly was leaning against the outside of her apartment door. Janice raised the wine bottle. "Wanna join me?"

"Can't, ma'am. On duty," the young woman replied. "But thanks for asking."

~~~~~~~~

Sitting in the waiting room while Kate finished up with clients, Rose put the time to good use composing a draft of an anonymous letter on her laptop.

Finally, Kate and her last client came out of her office. Kate escorted the client across the waiting room, then locked the outer door behind her. Turning to Rose, she said, "Sorry about that. An earlier client was feeling suicidal. I ran overtime with her and it threw my whole schedule off. I had to give her the number of one of my throwaway cells, in case she starts feeling worse over the weekend."

Rose winced inside while keeping her face neutral, a skill she'd learned in the Army and fine-tuned as a police officer. She didn't like the idea of a phone number being out there that could be traced back to Kate, since the phone would have to stay on in order for her to receive emergency calls. "Okay, but if she calls you, then you have to destroy that phone right away."

Kate shot her an odd look.

"Just because you're paranoid, and all that jazz," Rose said.

Kate smiled. "Let me get my briefcase and we can get out of here."

In the parking lot, Rose went over Kate's Prius with the debugger. When Kate started to get in the driver's side, Rose put out a hand to stop her. "Better let me drive, just in case."

"In case of what?" Kate asked.

Rose handed her own car keys to Manny. "Follow us in my car. Watch for tails." She turned back to Kate. "In case fancy driving is needed."

She soon discovered these were wise precautions.

A block from Kate's office, Rose glanced in the rearview mirror. A dark sedan had cut between her and Manny. "Hang on." She sped up, then turned right at the next corner, then right again. The dark sedan also sped up and made the same turns. It was following so closely now that it hit the rear of Kate's car when Rose slowed to avoid a truck at the next intersection.

Rose ignored the screech of metal and the stop sign. She

jabbed the button to lower her window as she whipped around the corner. "Get down!" Swinging the car to the curb, she jammed on the brakes and reached down to her ankle holster.

The dark sedan rounded the corner only seconds after them. Rose shot out its far front tire. The sedan veered into the path of an oncoming taxi. The driver's efforts to avoid the cab threw the car into a spin. It slammed into a postal service mailbox across the street.

The driver's door of the sedan flew open. A black-sleeved arm slashed at the air bag that had deployed. Rose jammed her gun into her pocket, but kept her hand on it. She ran across the street, dodging between the cars that had stopped at odd angles.

The man attached to the arm had fought his way out of the car. He glanced back, then took off between two buildings.

A siren could be heard several blocks away. Rose weighed her options. The sedan might not have been traveling alone. She returned her gun to her ankle holster and loped back to Kate.

Rose stuck her head in the open window. Kate had managed to fold herself into the foot well on the passenger's side.

"Are you okay?"

"Yeah. Can I get up now?"

Rose looked around before answering. Manny had pulled to the curb behind them. He jumped out. His gun disappeared as a police cruiser–lights flashing and siren fading with a sickly squeal–stopped beside the dark sedan across the street.

"Yeah." Rose's brain was churning through ramifications and options. She motioned Manny over. "Kate, give me your driver's license. Then go with Manny to the new safe house. I gotta do some damage control here." Once again she crossed the street.

A uniformed officer had stepped out of the police car and was examining the wreckage. He didn't notice when Kate slipped out of the passenger door of her banged-up Prius. She and Manny edged their way through a gathering crowd of onlookers to Rose's car.

"Guy was going too fast," Rose told the officer, while memorizing the license number of the sedan. "Hit me when I stopped at the corner and shoved me into the intersection. Then he tried to swerve around me and lost control of his car." She was hoping that none of the gawking crowd had seen her gun, or had made the connection between the loud bang and the sedan spinning out of control.

The top of the license plate was muddy, while the rest of the car was polished to a high shine. Stepping closer, she brushed away the dried mud.

"Diplomats' kids." The cop was unable to keep the disgust out of his voice. "Come over here from D.C. Think they can joyride around town and nobody can touch 'em 'cause of diplomatic immunity."

"Yeah, well, I think Daddy may do more than touch him when he comes home on foot, without his shiny new car," Rose said, a fake smirk in her voice. "Love to be a fly on the wall at that embassy tonight."

The cop nodded.

Rose handed over Kate's license. He barely glanced at the picture, as he wrote the license number, name and address on his pad. She gave him Kate's home phone number.

"Is your car driveable?" the officer asked.

"Yeah," Rose said. She'd take a cab if it wasn't. She didn't want to deal with a tow truck.

The cop handed back the license along with a slip of paper with the police report number on it. "You'll need that for the insurance company."

"Thanks, officer."

Jogging back across the street, Rose slid behind the wheel of Kate's car, hit the lock button, raised the window and then let out her breath.

As she started to pull away from the curb, a throwaway phone rang in her pocket.

"My charge is on her way to the hospital," Lilly said when Rose answered.

CHAPTER FIFTEEN

"What the hell happened?"

"Looks like a suicide attempt," Lilly said. "Cops are on the way."

"You still at the apartment?" Rose asked.

"Yeah. The other guard's following the ambulance. She's being taken to St. Joseph's."

"Catch the cops at the elevator. Stall 'em. Act hysterical, whatever it takes. I need to see that set-up before they move anything."

On a busy Friday night, investigating a possible suicide when the person was already on their way to the hospital was low on the Baltimore County police department's priority list. Rose got to Janice's building well before the cops, sparing Lilly the indignity of pretending to be an hysterical woman, a role for which she was ill-suited.

As they loped down the hall to the apartment, Lilly told Rose that she'd knocked on Janice's door to ask to use the bathroom. When there was no answer to her repeated pounding, she'd kicked in the door and found Janice lying in the living room, a wine glass next to her.

Rose zeroed in on the note. It was on the living room floor, one edge under the air mattress she had slept on the previous night.

"It was almost completely under there," Lilly said, "until an EMT kicked the mattress out of the way to get the gurney past."

Rose stooped to examine the note without touching it.

Typed, no signature. "'Please forgive me, friends and family," she read aloud, "but without Richard, life is not worth living.'"

She spun around and headed for the wine on the counter.

Lilly informed her that Janice had the bottle with her when she came home. Rose sniffed the top without touching it, then pulled out her handkerchief and used it to pick up the circle of foil that had been removed from the top. She held it up by its edge. The light from the kitchen shone through a small hole in the middle of it.

Syringe through the cork.

She carefully replaced the foil on the counter. "I need something to put some of this wine in."

"I have evidence bags," Lilly said. "Well, they're just baggies I carry just in case."

They heard the elevator ding down the hall.

"Have to do." Using the handkerchief, Rose grasped the bottle toward the bottom, where she was less likely to smear fingerprints. She tilted a small amount of liquid into the baggie Lilly held open.

She'd just barely got the bottle back on the counter when two uniforms came through the open doorway of the apartment. Lilly held the baggie behind her back as she sealed it.

Lilly succinctly told the officers how she'd found the apartment's tenant on the floor, leaving out that she was guarding the woman. One of the cops wrote down what she said in his notepad.

"It's not a suicide attempt," Rose said.

"Your name, ma'am?" the older of the two officers asked.

"Rose Hernandez. We're both friends of Ms. Browning. I used to be with BCPD. Now I'm private. You need to treat this scene as a possible homicide attempt."

The officer looked skeptical.

"Note's totally out of character. It implies he left her. Other way around. I was there the night she got her stuff out of their condo. She was relieved to be rid of him."

"Where's her stuff?" the officer asked.

"Still in storage. She just got this place."

"And what did she use to try to kill herself? No weapons," Lilly said. "Had to be something in the wine. Something pretty potent since she hadn't even finished the bottle."

"If she put something in the wine, where is it?" Rose asked.

The other officer had zeroed in on Janice's purse at the far end of the breakfast bar. Using a pen, he maneuvered it so that the contents spilled out on the counter. "Got a prescription for Xanax here," he called over to his partner.

Lilly used the distraction to slip the baggie of wine into her jacket pocket. Rose caught the movement out of the corner of her eye and prayed the bag wouldn't leak.

"Is the pill bottle empty?" she asked, craning to get a look at it without being too obvious.

"No, 'bout half full," the cop said.

"Probably not enough to make her pass out after just a few glasses of wine. And why did she bother to put the pill bottle back in her purse?" Rose said.

The senior partner shrugged. "Logic don't always apply when it comes to why folks do things." Left unsaid was *especially when they're depressed*.

Rose decided it was time to take advantage of the cops' resistance. "Look, we've got to get to the hospital and make sure our friend's okay." She scribbled a throwaway cell number on one of her business cards and handed it to the senior partner. "That's where you can reach us. If you don't want to believe us, fine, but to be on the safe side, you should send the note and wine to the lab." She gestured for Lilly to follow her as she headed for the door.

When the elevator doors had closed, Rose said, "So two mysteries. Where did she get the wine, and how did the suicide note get in there?"

Suddenly Lilly stiffened beside her. Staring straight ahead at the elevator door, she said, "I'd like to tender my resignation, Ms. Hernandez."

"Say what?"

"I screwed up. A bed was delivered this afternoon. I went into the bedroom to watch while they set it up, in case they were bogus deliverymen there to plant a bug or something. The door was locked, but I didn't flip the deadbolt. Someone could have popped the lock with a credit card and slipped in with the note."

She bought a bed?!? Rose suppressed the urge to curse a blue streak. Her employee would assume it was aimed at her rather than Janice.

"Honest mistake. And the guys we're dealing with are extremely well-trained."

Rose caught Lilly's sideways glance of confusion. She hadn't told the young woman any details, had just instructed her to guard Janice and to be highly suspicious of Hispanics. Lilly had no doubt found that politically-incorrect instruction especially strange coming from her Hispanic boss.

Lilly shook her head. "I should've–"

Rose cut her off. "I got no problem with the way you handled yourself here. Let's get over to the hospital. Mind if we take your truck?"

~~~~~~~~

Kate and Manny arrived at the new safe house a few minutes after Skip and Rob. It was the fishing shack of one of Mac's buddies, nestled amongst some trees on the edge of the Chesapeake Bay on the Eastern Shore.

It was not quite as bad inside as its ramshackle outward appearance implied. The main room was quite dusty and contained only a card table, four folding chairs and an old-fashioned porcelain sink. A bare lightbulb hung from a cord over the table.

Kate wrinkled her nose at the musty smell. "I guess it's not safe to open the window or leave the door open?"

Rob was in the process of wiping the worst of the crud off the table and chairs. He looked skeptically at the only window in the room, that was almost completely obscured by cobwebs. "I seriously doubt you could get that open."

Kate held up the bags in her hands. "We went through the drive-thru at the KFC in Chestertown." She unloaded the feast of grease and chicken, with mashed potatoes, biscuits, and cole slaw on the side.

Manny took some of the food outside to the other guards.

They had no plates so they passed the side dish containers around, eating out of them with the plastic sporks provided by the restaurant.

Skip's jaw tightened as Kate told them about the dark sedan that had followed them and hit her car. Then he and Rob filled her in on their encounter with the ambassador that afternoon.

They were just finishing their meal when they heard a ringing phone. It took a moment to figure out which of the throwaways in their various pockets it was.

Skip answered it. "It's Rose." He put the phone on speaker and placed it in the middle of the table.

"Kate tell you about the car?"

"Yeah. Did you get a look at the driver?" Skip asked.

"A quick one. I did some research this afternoon on Delgado. Sounds like a nasty dude. I found one picture of him. He was a lot younger in the picture, but there is a definite resemblance to the guy who rear-ended us."

Kate didn't like hearing that they were being chased by a 'nasty dude.' But at least now their enemy had a face and a name.

"Also talked to Mac," Rose said. "He thinks this guy may be here to assassinate the Colombian president, then blame it on Garcia, i.e., the rebels."

"Or blame it on the crazy violent Americans to undermine our relationship with Colombia," Rob speculated. "We need to report this to the authorities."

"That's what I thought, too," Rose said from the phone on the table. "I composed an anonymous letter to send to the Secret Service. Let me read it to you. See what you think. 'It has come to our attention that there may be a plot to assassinate the president of Colombia during his state visit the end of this month. It is possible that Ambassador Garcia is unaware of this plot, but a man by the name of Ricardo Delgado has infiltrated the embassy's security staff, under an alias, José Gonzales. If you check into Delgado's background you will find he is not a fan of the current regime in Colombia. We are forced to bring this to your attention anonymously. Our lives are in danger because we have this information. Sincerely, several concerned citizens.'"

"Sounds good," Skip said. "Enough info to get them on the

right track, but nothing that leads back to us."

"Why can't we just go to the Secret Service or the FBI and tell them all this?" Kate asked. "They'd take the threat more seriously if we told them in person, gave them all the background."

"Mac assured me that they'll take the threat seriously," Rose said.

"Anything that hints of danger to our president is going to be fully investigated," Rob agreed. "No matter how far-fetched it sounds."

Kate's jaw dropped. "You think this sounds *far-fetched*?"

"Not to us it doesn't, darlin', 'cause we've been living it the last few days. But the authorities will probably think we're a bunch of conspiracy nuts."

"They'd still protect us, though, wouldn't they?" Kate asked.

"Maybe, maybe not," Rob said. "They might just thank us for the information and cut us loose."

"And if they did put us in protective custody, we'd have no means of communicating with anybody," Skip said. "No way to make sure the kids are okay. I'd rather take our chances with our own security."

"I agree," Rose said from the phone.

"So how and where do we send this letter?" Kate asked.

"Tomorrow I need to get to the agency office so I can print it out. I'll send it from Towson."

"Snail mail may be too slow, and what if the letter doesn't get through to the correct person?" Skip said. "Check with Dolph. He'll know how to e-mail it so it can't be traced back to us."

"Maybe we should send it both ways to be sure," Rob said. "Since we can't exactly ask for a return receipt on either one."

"Okay, I'll call Dolph," Rose said from the phone. "Get him to research who we should be sending it to. Uh, I'll be over there in a little while."

~~~~~~~~

Rose called Dolph and filled him in on all that had happened, including the fact that she hadn't yet told the others about Janice. Then she dropped the phone she'd been using on the sidewalk and stomped on it.

Was she doing the right thing, keeping Kate and Skip in the dark? She knew what their reaction would be. They'd feel guilty, big-time guilty. And Skip would tear back across the bay wanting to investigate. Nope, better for all of them to stay safely tucked away on the Eastern Shore, until Janice woke up and could tell them what happened.

She walked back inside the hospital to join Lilly in the ER waiting area.

They had handed over the baggie of wine, that had miraculously stayed intact in Lilly's pocket. Rose had told the ER nurse there might be Xanax and possibly other substances dissolved it. The nurse said she'd get it to the hospital lab right away.

Rose was hoping that they'd gotten to Janice in time. She hated to think what would have happened if the woman had laid there all night.

It was well over two hours before a doctor came looking for them. "Are either of you Mrs. Browning's next of kin?"

"I'm her sister," Lilly lied.

Rose hid her surprise.

"Are you her health care surrogate?" the doctor asked.

"What's that?"

The doctor frowned. Her question had effectively answered his. "Is there any other family member who has written permission to receive medical information about Mrs. Browning?"

"Doc, will ya please just tell me if my sister's okay?" Lilly asked, with a plausible amount of anxiety in her voice.

The doctor frowned again.

"Is she dead?" Lilly belatedly brought her hand to her face in a gesture of horror.

When the doctor still hesitated, Rose growled, "Seems like a pretty simple yes-or-no question to me?"

The doctor sighed. "I wish I had a simple answer for you. She's alive but still unconscious."

When the doctor didn't elaborate, Rose said, "Look, Doctor, the only other relative is an estranged husband who may have tried to kill her tonight."

The doctor's eyebrows shot up. "The police said it was a suicide attempt."

"No, the killer set it up to look like a suicide attempt, but the note was totally bogus and there are several other things that don't add up."

"And you are?"

"Rose Hernandez, private investigator, and a friend of Ms. Browning." She pulled out her PI license to show him. "Her husband's not the only suspect here. I've been investigating a situation for her, for a few days now."

The doctor blew out air. He glanced over at the busy nurses' station. "I'm due for a break. Let's go down to the cafeteria."

Once settled at a table far from the few other occupants of the cafeteria, the doctor took a careful sip from the cup of hot coffee in his hand.

"Was it Xanax?" Rose asked.

"Yes, quite a bit of it. Pumping her stomach didn't do much good. The wine had already been absorbed. We gave her a drug to counter the effects, but those effects are exacerbated by alcohol." He shook his head.

"Nothing else in the wine?" Rose asked.

"No, and we did additional blood work as well. Nothing else in her system."

"She'd had two thirds of a bottle of wine, and her pill bottle was half empty. Bottle about this big." Rose held up her hand, fingers two inches apart. "Would that be enough to account for the amount found in the wine?"

"Does she have a serious anxiety disorder?" the doctor asked Lilly.

"She's a trial lawyer," Rose quickly answered. "I think she has the Xanax just to calm pre-trial jitters." *And to subdue her cat.* She opted not to share that.

"So probably a mild dose." The doctor looked thoughtful as he drank more coffee. Then he shook his head. "Half a bottle wouldn't be nearly enough to account for the concentration we found in her bloodstream or the wine."

"That's what I figured," Rose said. "The wine was doctored before she got it. And the suicide note implied her husband left her and she couldn't go on without him. She was the one who left him, and seemed pretty happy about it just this morning."

"So somebody's done their research," Lilly said. "Knows she's separated from her husband, but doesn't know who left who. Knows she likes wine and has a prescription for Xanax."

"A good enough set-up to fool the cops, but not those of us who know her."

"Maybe, whoever did this only wanted to fool the cops," Lilly said.

Rose gave Lilly an approving look. "Excellent observation."

The doctor drained his cup, then cleared his throat. "I'm only supposed to tell next of kin this..." He looked at Lilly.

"I'm just gonna tell Rose as soon as you walk away."

The doctor sighed. "I haven't given up hope completely, but it doesn't look good."

Neither Lilly nor Rose had to fake a look of horror. "*¡Ay, dios mio!*" Rose crossed herself.

"In the absence of a health care surrogate, the husband would legally be the one with the authority to make decisions."

"We need to leave him out of the loop," Rose said, her tone sharper than she'd intended.

"I won't go out of my way to find him, but if he shows up..." The doctor shrugged. "Where can I reach you all?"

"We're staying right here tonight, Doc," Lilly said. "I'm gonna sit outside her door and make sure nobody gets to her."

The doctor stood up and patted Lilly's shoulder. "You should go home and try to get some rest. She's in the ICU. The nurses won't let just anybody in."

"They'd let her husband in," Rose said.

"True. Until the police say it's an attempted homicide investigation, we can't stop him from seeing her."

Rose clenched her teeth. *You can't but we can.*

CHAPTER SIXTEEN

At the fishing shack, the others were exploring their new home away from home. In the only other room there was another lightbulb dangling from the ceiling. It revealed two Army cots. There were four sleeping bags rolled up on one of them, with a half-inch layer of dust on top of everything.

Off of that room–Kate was unwilling to call it a bedroom–was a tiny lavatory, with a toilet and small sink.

She sent the men outside to shake out the sleeping bags. There was a broom in the corner of the lavatory. Half its bristles were missing but she managed to sweep the dust off the cots. Then she swept the debris on the floor into a corner, on the alert for anything that moved.

Back in the main room, she rummaged through the metal cabinet under a porcelain sink that might have been new in 1950. On one of the sideboards of the sink rested a two-burner hot plate and a toaster. That constituted the entire "kitchen."

"Eureka," she said to Rob and Skip as they came back inside, sleeping bags dangling from their arms. She held up a rusty can, the label so faded the word *Comet* was just barely visible. Armed with the vintage cleanser and the leftover KFC napkins, she tackled the grungy bathroom fixtures

Once they had brought in the bags with their meager supply of spare clothing, Kate said, "I guess we should draw straws to see who gets the cots." Her tone implied they would be only a slight improvement over sleeping on the floor.

Rob's expression said he agreed with her.

"What's the matter? Can't handle roughing it for one night?" Skip said, a chuckle in his voice. "Guess this is when the men are separated from the girls."

Rob raised his hand in the air. In a falsetto voice, he said, "Hi, my name is Bobbi and I'd like a cot, please."

They all cracked up. Skip, still chuckling, said, "You guys take the cots. I'll sleep out here on the floor, between you and the door."

Shortly all were settled in their sleeping bags and the lights had been turned out. Kate lay on her cot, trying not to think about what might be cohabiting with them despite her efforts. She was fairly sure she would not get much sleep tonight.

Was that a scuttling noise she'd heard, coming from the corner? She had almost convinced herself it was her imagination when Rob whispered, "I vote we leave the light on."

"That motion carries unanimously," Kate said, getting up to feel around for the dangling pull cord.

"Wimps!" Skip called from the next room when the light came on. Rob and Kate ignored him.

Miraculously Kate did sleep and relatively soundly, until a ray of sunlight found its way through the grime on the small window high on the wall. It danced across her eyelids, refusing to be ignored.

She slipped out of her sleeping bag, made use of the facilities and then tiptoed into the front room. Skip was sitting at the table. Kate walked over to him. He snagged her around the waist and drew her down onto his lap.

Putting his lips right next to her ear, he whispered, "Do you realize that's the first night we haven't slept together in over a year?"

The last time had been when Kate was in the hospital, recovering from an attack by a killer. *How do we get ourselves into these messes?*

"Let's take a walk," she whispered back. "So we don't disturb Rob."

~~~~~~~~

They stepped out onto the rickety porch. Skip closed the door quietly, then took Kate's hand. They walked past the row of vehicles parked on the packed dirt and weeds passing for a lawn.

They were about twenty feet down the road–that was barely more than two dirt tracks through the scraggly grass–when Skip saw a flicker of movement. He stepped in front of Kate as he drew his gun. "I hope that's you behind that tree, Claude," he called out softly.

Claude stepped out from the tree, gave Skip a small salute, then disappeared again.

Skip smoothly slipped his gun back into the holster at the small of his back. They walked down the road a bit further, stopping at the edge of the woods.

"How many men are out here?" Kate asked in a quiet voice.

"Hopefully only our three." He drew Kate against him, wrapping his arms around her. He dared not kiss her. He needed to stay alert just in case there were more than just their men in the woods.

He doubted there were though. Claude and the other guards would have been in frequent communication via two-way radio during the night. Anyone hanging around would have been spotted by them.

He rested his chin on the top of Kate's head and took in the scenery as he held her. Before them spread a fallow cornfield. The dry, brown stalks were cut off a foot from the ground. Skip smiled when he felt what he'd been waiting for–his wife's body relaxing against him.

They both jumped when an elderly voice said, "You two lovebirds buy that old shack from Fred?"

Skip quickly positioned himself between Kate and the old man standing ten feet away. Blue eyes squinted at them from a wrinkled face turned leathery tan by hours in the sun. His cheeks and head were covered with gray stubble. He wore faded jeans and a plaid flannel shirt that looked almost as old as he was.

In his peripheral vision, Skip saw two shadows emerging from the trees. He made a slight gesture with his hand. His men retreated.

"You all ain't exactly dressed for roughing it," the old man observed. They were still wearing the clothes they'd worn to work the day before.

Skip opted not to try to explain their attire. "Are you one of our neighbors?"

"Yup, live right over that little rise, near the main road. Where are my manners?" He stepped forward, rubbing his right palm against his jeans, then reached out to shake Skip's hand. "Name's Sid Pierce."

"Uh, Steve. Steve Williams, and this is my wife, uh, Sally Mae." Skip grinned down at Kate. "To answer your question, Fred lent us the place for a few days."

"Please ta meet ya, ma'am," Pierce said, still eyeing their inappropriate clothing. Then he shrugged.

"Have you lived here long, Mr. Pierce?" Kate asked.

"All my life. Born just a few miles from here. I'm a waterman, mostly retired now."

Kate smiled at him. "So I have you to thank for all those delicious crab cakes I've eaten through the years."

"Yes, ma'am, some of 'em, at least. Well, I better be gettin' back 'fore the missus thinks I fell in the bay. You all need anything, just holler." The man started walking down the dirt road away from them.

"Pleasure meetin' you, sir," Skip called after him.

Pierce turned back toward them. "Where ya from, son? Can't place that ax-cent."

"Texas."

Pierce chuckled. "So it's true. They really do grow everythin' bigger down there."

"Yes, sir." Skip smiled at the old man.

But his expression quickly sobered once the man had turned away again. "Rosie's gonna be hoppin' mad."

"Why?"

"Our guys didn't know Pierce was taking a stroll through the woods."

"They are a bit out of their element, out here in the boonies," Kate said.

They started back toward the shack. Skip's left arm was draped over Kate's shoulders, but his right hand was now resting on the butt of his gun behind his back. He nervously eyed the woods around them.

"I think you need to leave town until we get this mess resolved," he said.

Kate stopped walking. Skip nudged her forward. "We need to get back to the cabin. If the guys missed Pierce, they might've missed somebody else."

That got her moving again. "I can't leave town, for a variety of reasons. First, where would I go that would be truly safe? Second, I have clients depending on me, one of whom is suicidal at the moment."

They neared the porch. "We've tightened the perimeter, sir," a tree said quietly.

"Good," Skip said.

"It should be safe to sit out here on the steps then," Kate said. "Rob's probably still asleep."

They settled gingerly on the wobbly steps. Kate took Skip's hand between both of hers. "Sweetheart, if I go away," she said quietly, "I'm not sure I'd be any safer. I definitely wouldn't *feel* safer. I'd be scared to death in some hotel room, not knowing what was going on."

He drew her against his chest. "I know it'd make you crazy, but you would be safer, if we could spirit you away to someplace these guys would never think to look. When I almost lost you last year..." The words caught in his throat. "I don't know what I'd do without you," he whispered.

Kate leaned back in the circle of his arms. "They seem to be just as determined to get you. Besides you're always the one telling me that we can't protect each other from life."

Skip snorted. "This is hardly normal life."

"True." Kate stared off into the woods for a moment. "I wonder if God's testing us, trying to get us to realize that one of us is bound to die before the other."

"Not necessarily. I was thinking maybe we'd do a Thelma and Louise off a big cliff when we're in our eighties."

Kate smiled as she shook her head. "Nope, even in their

forties, that would traumatize the kids."

"Now that's hard to wrap one's mind around. Edie and Billy in their forties."

"Do you miss them, Skip?"

"Every minute." He looked down at her. "Claude, eyes front and center while I kiss my wife," he called out.

"Yes, sir," the tree replied.

~~~~~~~~

Inside the back room of the cabin, a cell phone rang in Rob's pocket. He sat up on the edge of the cot and answered it, his voice rough from sleep. Rose's words brought him fully awake.

Covering his eyes with one hand, he said into the phone, "This is going to tear them up."

CHAPTER SEVENTEEN

Kate was still smiling at Skip's Thelma and Louise fantasy when they walked back inside the cabin. She stopped. Skip froze beside her. Rob was sitting at the table, his expression grim. In a voice gruff with emotion, he said, "Sit down, guys."

Kate's heart thudded in her chest. "My God, what's wrong?"

"Janice..." Rob stopped and cleared his throat. "She's dead."

They stared at him in stunned silence. Then Skip stumbled over and sat down hard in one of the chairs. His Adam's apple bobbed in his throat.

Tears pooled in Kate's eyes, threatening to blind her. This couldn't be real. Shaking her head, she stepped over behind Skip's chair and put her hands on his shoulders.

"What happened? Where the hell were her guards?" Skip said.

"Best to call Rose and let her explain." Rob picked up the phone lying on the table. He hit redial, then put it on speaker.

"Hernandez."

"Skip wants to know what happened," Rob said.

Rose told them about Lilly finding Janice, the note, the doctored wine, and that Janice had stopped breathing an hour ago.

At the words *stopped breathing*, Kate's tears broke loose. She dug her fingers into Skip's shoulders, struggling against the urge to sob.

Skip banged his fist down, making the phone jump. Then he crossed his arms on the table and dropped his head onto them.

The pressure was building in Kate's chest. Her ears started ringing. She thought she might faint. She moved to one side and sat down in a chair, leaving one hand on Skip's upper arm. Without lifting his head, he covered her hand with his own.

"So we've got a bogus note and a doctored bottle of wine to check out." Rose's voice shifted from sympathetic to matter-of-fact.

Kate looked across the table at Rob. His eyes were worried but he took the hint from Rose's tone. "If we're still aiming for acting normal during the day, I'd like to go to my office today. I've got a case coming to court next week I need to prep for."

Skip lifted his head. His jaw was clenched. "That building's concierge might know something. I'm coming over there to interview him."

"I'm not staying here by my..." Kate's voice broke. She blinked hard and swallowed the lump in her throat. "I need to get us some money for supplies for the weekend. It doesn't really matter if the bad guys trace my debit card to an ATM in Towson."

After a beat, Rose said, "Skip, bring Kate to the agency first. I could use her help with some stuff."

~~~~~~~~

As she and Lilly walked to the hospital parking lot, Rose called Manny. After filling him in on Janice Browning's death, she said, "You drive Skip's truck. Wrestle the keys away from him if you have to." She disconnected, then called the agency office.

Dolph answered, "Canfield and Hernandez."

"Janice Browning's dead."

There was a long silence, then Dolph said, "Damn it to hell! Is there anything I can do?"

"Yeah. Skip's on his way to her place. Head over there. 3943 York Road. Try to keep him from killing anybody who doesn't deserve it."

"I got the address for the Secret Service and the name of the person we should direct that letter to."

"Good. Leave it on my desk."

~~~~~~~~

There was only one suspicious-looking car, containing a dark-haired driver wearing sunglasses, parked near the front of the agency's building. No one was watching the back. After escorting Kate in the back entrance and up the fire stairs, Manny drove Skip to Janice's apartment building.

Skip was hoping the concierge today would be the same one who had been on duty the previous day. It would be a lot more complicated if they had to track the guy down.

It was the same young man, and Dolph was standing next to his desk.

Skip frowned, then nodded at the older man. He pulled out his private investigator's license and introduced himself to the concierge, whose small green badge, pinned to his shirt pocket, read *Phillip*.

The young man recognized him. "Yes, sir. You're one of Ms. Browning's guests. How is she doing?" His expression was worried.

"She didn't make it, son," Dolph said.

The concierge's face paled. He shook his head. "I can't believe she killed herself. She was so happy yesterday."

"Yeah, well we need to talk to you about that." Skip's tone was harsher than he'd intended as he struggled to control his emotions. "We need to see her apartment too."

Phillip's eyes went from Skip's face to Dolph's, then back again, as if he were assessing their motives. Finally he said, "I'll have to accompany you, sir." He motioned to a nearby security guard to take over the desk.

"Stay down here," Skip told Manny. "Watch the door."

On the ride up in the elevator, he said to the concierge, "Mrs. Browning had a bottle of wine with her when she came home yesterday. Do you know where it came from?"

"Yes, sir, a delivery boy brought it in right before she got here."

"From the wine shop in this building?"

"I assumed so," Phillip said. "Although it wasn't the regular delivery person. He said it was a gift for Ms. Browning and he gave me a verbal message for her. Lemme think. Something about parting amicably and having good memories."

"From Richard?"

"Yes, sir. That's the name the kid said."

"You said he wasn't the wine shop's regular delivery person,"

Dolph said. "Can you describe him?"

Phillip nodded. "Normally it's one of the women who works in the shop. But this was a black kid I'd never seen before."

"A kid? Don't you have to be over twenty-one to handle alcohol?" Skip asked.

The elevator doors opened on Janice's floor and the concierge led the way toward her door. "Now that you mention it, the guy couldn't have been twenty-one. He was more like sixteen or seventeen."

There was a hasp and padlock on the apartment door, above where Lilly's kick had splintered the doorframe. Phillip pulled a small key out of his pocket and unlocked the lock.

Dolph put out a hand to hold the young man back as Skip entered the apartment, on guard in case it had gained any unwanted occupants since the night before. After clearing the rooms, the two men returned to the living room. The only evidence of the wine bottle was a red ring on the breakfast bar. No sign of the note.

"At least the cops took Rose seriously enough to preserve the evidence," Dolph said.

"Seriously about what? What's going on?" Phillip asked.

"She didn't kill herself. The wine was doctored with Xanax, to make it look like a suicide," Skip said.

The young man turned green and clapped a hand over his mouth. "Oh, my God," he whispered.

"It's not your fault. But we need to find that kid."

"He was tall, real thin. Skin tone halfway between milk chocolate and dark. His hair was in corn rows tight against his head. He was wearing a white shirt and dark dress slacks. Kind of fidgety in his clothes. Like they were new, maybe scratchy. And they didn't fit him real well. Pants were too short, shirt kind of baggy."

Skip was impressed. "That's a very detailed description of a kid you saw for maybe five minutes."

"Less than that. He didn't stick around. But that's part of the job. You gotta notice every little thing. The concierge services and security are an important part of the package for our tenants."

Phillip stopped abruptly and dropped his gaze to the floor, swallowing hard.

Skip put a hand on his shoulder. The guy was barely more than a kid himself. "Phillip, you did your job. There was no way of knowing the wine was doctored. We had a trained PI guarding the apartment, and she didn't see any reason to be suspicious of the wine. Whoever did this figured out a very clever way to get past our defenses."

The young man nodded. They headed back to the elevator.

In the lobby, Skip signaled to Manny and the three of them walked outside. "Let me guess," Skip said to Dolph. "My wife bugged Rose into sending you as back-up."

"Don't think Kate had anything to do with it. Rose told me to keep you from killing anybody who didn't deserve it."

Skip snorted.

Dolph pulled a small electronic device out of his pocket, switched it on and started walking around the vehicle. "My new toy. Picks up GPS devices as well as listening bugs. And guess what? You've got one of each."

He walked over to his own car. "And so do I."

Skip looked at the Expedition for a moment, a vague plan forming in his mind. "Manny, stay here, please. Keep an eye on the vehicles." He started down the sidewalk. Dolph fell into step with him.

Once they were well away from the truck, Skip said, "We need to find that kid."

"You sure he's from around here?"

"Nope. Whoever gave him the doctored wine might have picked him up anywhere. But let's poke around here for a while. See what we can find."

~~~~~~~~

They didn't find Jamal Johnson. He found them. They had been walking up and down the streets around Janice's building, looking down the alleys behind buildings, trying to figure out where a black kid would hang out in a rather lily-white section of town.

Dolph had decided it was a lost cause. He voiced this thought and Skip agreed.

They were headed back toward the truck when a voice hailed them from behind. "Hey, mister, you got any errands or odd jobs I can do for you?"

Turning around they saw their quarry coming toward them. Tall, skinny black kid with neat corn rows, baggy jeans hanging low on his hips, black T-shirt with some rapper's picture on it.

Dolph pulled out a twenty-dollar bill. "Actually we're looking for some information."

Skip had moved behind the kid to block him should he try to take off.

"For your own safety, son, we can't be seen talking on the street," Dolph said. "Let's go down that alley a little bit."

The boy's eyes went from friendly to wary. He turned to bolt but Skip grabbed his arm. "We're not going to hurt you, but it's really important we talk to you." He pushed the kid into the entrance of the alley. Dolph followed.

"Hey, man, I ain't that kinda hustler, ya know whad I mean?" The boy was trying to sound tough but his voice wavered.

"We do, son," Dolph said. "You're just trying to pick up a little spending money doing odd jobs."

"Yeah, but it's for my college fund. Let me go, man. I'm not gonna do nothin' for ya. I'm not queer."

"We didn't think you were," Skip said. "What's your name?"

The boy was starting to tremble, his eyes wide. "Jamal."

"Honest, Jamal, we're not going to hurt you," Dolph said. "We just need to ask about a job you did yesterday afternoon. You delivered a bottle of wine to a lady's apartment building."

"Man, I can't be tellin' ya nothin' 'bout dat. My rep, man, it's built on dis-cre-tion." The boy dragged the word out.

"It's important to maintain a good reputation," Skip said. "But the problem is that bottle of wine was poisoned."

"Yer shittin' me!"

"No shit, Jamal. The lady died. We need to know who gave you that bottle."

"I don't know nothin' 'bout no poison." The boy was pulling hard against Skip's grip. "I'm just tryin' to get money for college. My grandma, she's a retired school teacher. I lives with her. She wants me to go to college so bad she said she's gonna mortgage her house when the time comes. I can't let her do that, man."

"Where do you live, son?" Dolph asked.

"Few blocks from here. Please let me go, mister, I didn't know nothin' 'bout poison."

"Jamal," Dolph said. "Something tells me if your grandma lives in this section of town and she's a retired schoolteacher, she raised you to speak standard English. Not that there's anything wrong with the street jive when you're hangin' with your friends."

"Street jive? Don't nobody call it that no more, old man."

Skip shook the kid's arm. "Show a little respect for your elders."

Suddenly Jamal straightened out of the rebellious adolescent slouch and hitched up his sagging jeans. "You're right, sir. I'm sorry. The jive talk's an act I put on. For some reason white folks are more suspicious of me when I talk like them and politely tell them I'm trying to raise money for college. If I act like a hustler, they're more likely to hire me to do little stuff, like delivering wine bottles."

Skip cocked an eyebrow at him. "But you still tell them you're raising money for college?"

"Yeah, but they don't believe me. They just pretend they do so they can convince themselves they're not contributing to my drug habit." This was said in a matter-of-fact tone.

Skip gave the teen a small grin. "Jamal, you should major in psychology. You've got human beings pretty well pegged there. Now about the guy who gave you the wine bottle. Did you know him?"

"Nope. He was white, had a tan. Dark hair. About two inches shorter than you, sir." He pointed to Dolph, who was six foot even.

"Anything else you can remember about him? Scars, facial hair?" Skip asked.

Jamal shook his head. "He was kind of old, wore a suit."

Skip nodded. "Now what do we do with him?" he asked Dolph. "It's not safe to leave you roaming the streets, Jamal."

The kid misunderstood. His eyes grew wide with fear again. He struggled to get free. Skip opened his mouth to reassure him.

"Hey, down there. Leave that kid alone!" They all turned toward the voice coming from the street.

Jamal pulled loose from Skip's grip and raced down the alley. Skip took off after him. Dolph pulled out his PI license and started toward the man who had yelled at them. But the guy disappeared around the corner.

Dolph stopped, his cop instincts kicking in. He pivoted and tore after Skip.

He rounded the corner at the end of the alley and caught a glimpse of pants leg and sneaker as Skip disappeared down another alley, a block away. Dolph ran as fast as he could. Racing around that corner, he almost collided with Skip, who had stopped in the middle of the alley.

"Kid ducked in here, then disappeared. He's got to be hiding somewhere," Skip said, gesturing toward the dumpsters, trash cans, and boxes that were scattered along the alley.

Dolph grabbed his arm and dragged him toward the nearest back door of a shop. He tugged on the doorknob. It was locked. He ran for the next door, dragging Skip along with him.

"What the hell are you doing, Dolph? We've got to find that kid."

"It's a trap. I'd bet money on it." The third doorknob Dolph grabbed turned in his hand. He threw open the door, pushed Skip inside, then dove through the doorway himself, shoving the door closed behind him.

They were in a dimly lit back room of a shop, surrounded by boxes of gourmet delicacies. Dolph felt around on the door, found a deadbolt knob and turned it. Then he put an ear to the door.

"Have you lost your mind?" Skip whispered from behind him.

"Shh," Dolph said. There it was again. The faint sound of male voices, getting louder as they came closer. They were speaking rapid-fire Spanish.

The doorknob turned. Dolph backed up quickly and collided with Skip. The door rattled but the deadbolt held.

They both drew their guns and eased further away from the door.

CHAPTER EIGHTEEN

"Now how the hell do we get out of here without getting shot by the storekeeper?" Skip whispered after several uneventful minutes had passed.

"We sure ain't going back through that alley," Dolph whispered back. He slipped his pistol into his pocket. "Wait, I've got an idea. Follow my lead." He sidled up to the edge of the doorway leading into the shop. "Police safety inspectors coming through here," he called out and moved into the store holding up his PI license as if it were a badge. Skip holstered his gun and followed suit, holding his own license up.

"Sir, we're going around this section of town checking on the shops. Looking for ways that thieves can get in." Dolph was talking fast, walking toward the man behind the counter, license held high in one hand. "Did you know your back door was unlocked? You need to be careful about that, sir. Anybody could have walked in here from the alley."

"I... I thought it was locked," the man stammered. Dolph kept moving toward the front of the shop, Skip in his wake.

"Gee, thanks, officers," the shop owner said to their backs. He came around the counter and headed for the back room to check the door himself.

Dolph race-walked to the front door, then slowed when he reached it. He and Skip sauntered out onto the sidewalk, looking around for Hispanic men.

"When we get to the vehicles, get rid of the bugs but leave the tracking devices for now," Skip said quietly. "I'll keep an eye out for the bad guys."

While Dolph located the button-sized listening devices stuck to the back windows on the driver's side of each vehicle, Skip told Manny to follow them in Dolph's car. Dolph dropped the bugs into the gutter.

Once they were in his truck and pulling away from the curb, Skip said, "That was a rather obvious spot."

"Only if one's looking for a bug," Dolph said. "They had to put it on the glass in order to pick up what we said inside. Anywhere else outside and they'd just get road noise. So what are you thinking here?"

"You got a throwaway cell on you?" Skip asked.

"Yeah."

"Call Rose. Every vehicle that's going to the safe house needs to be checked."

Dolph made the call. "Rose, we got several little presents recently from our friends," he said into the phone. "A couple of bugs which I removed and a GPS device planted on each of our vehicles. They're still active. I think your partner's got a plan hatching. Let me put you on speaker."

"You finished your errands, Rose?" Skip asked.

"Almost. We're headed out to send off the letter."

"Good. Dolph's got a new toy that detects GPS devices."

"Sweet. Hope your mama taught you to share your toys, Dolph."

Dolph chuckled. "I was planning on turning in the invoice for reimbursement once I was sure it worked, so technically it's your toy."

"Excellent. What are you thinking, partner?"

"Did you check for a listening device in your car?" Skip asked.

"We're in Lilly's truck and yes, I checked. No bug."

"We had bugs and tracking devices planted on both our vehicles while we were inside Janice's building," Skip said. "But there wasn't anybody watching the house yesterday and only one guy out front of our office building this morning. What's that say to you?"

"Limited personnel but money and access to technology," Dolph answered.

"Yeah," Rose agreed. "My guess is they all were in that group brought in from Colombia for the president's visit. So at most a dozen men."

"I suspect it's more like five or six," Skip said. "I want to spread them really thin. Minimize the risk of them tailing us to the safe house. I'm going to send Manny, in Dolph's car, to Bel Air. I'll head north toward Westminster. Where's a good place for Dolph to meet you all to check your vehicles for GPS devices?"

"Hmm, Manny's going east. You're going north," Rose said. "How about southeast. Sparrows Point, the old Bethlehem Steel plant."

Dolph grinned. "Good choice." Bethlehem Steel had once been the largest steel mill in the world. After changing hands multiple times, it was now in bankruptcy. It wasn't completely shut down, but there wouldn't be much happening there on a Saturday. "If we find any tracking devices, we throw them over the fence. They'll spend hours chasing their tails, looking for us in all those buildings."

Skip glanced at his watch. "Okay, call Rob's guard and you all meet Dolph at the main entrance of Beth Steel in an hour, at one-thirty sharp. We all dump the GPS devices at the same time. We'll meet you in Centreville, that first town off of Route 301 headed out toward the shack."

"Sounds good," Rose said and disconnected.

"You and your wife need to join us at the safe house," Skip said.

"That had already occurred to me."

"I'm going to drop you in front of a hotel to catch a cab and go get her."

"I think I can sell Sue on a little weekend get-away without scaring her too much."

"I think you need to scare her a little, Dolph. She needs to know how serious this is. And don't oversell the accommodations.

They suck, and they're going to be very crowded tonight."

~~~~~~~~

Kate felt downright giddy with relief when she spotted Skip's truck pulling into the parking lot of the only shopping center in Centreville. She jumped out of Lilly's pick-up and ran toward the Expedition. Skip got out and caught her up in a quick hug.

Dolph stepped out of his wife's car. Rose came over to join them. "Any problems?" Skip asked.

"Nope. Lilly's truck was clean but Rob's bodyguard had a couple attachments on his car." Dolph tilted his head toward the white sedan parked nearby, a burly guard behind the wheel. Rob sat in the passenger's seat. "They're now in the tall grass next to Beth Steel's parking lot."

"We need internet to send the e-mail to the Secret Service," Rose said.

"We also need supplies," Kate said. She had been weighing the merits of the few decent-sized towns between Route 301 and the shack. "I think our shopping options will be better in Chestertown."

"Next stop, Chestertown then," Rose said. "Lilly and I'll bring up the rear and watch for tails."

Skip and Kate climbed into his truck. "Did the snail-mail version get dispatched okay?" he asked as they headed out of the parking lot.

She pulled a latex glove from her pocket and waved it at him. "Yes, and never touched by human hands. Dropped it in the drive-by mailbox at the Towson post office."

Skip nodded.

After a few minutes of silence, Kate snuck a peek at her husband. His eyes were on the road, his mouth set in a grim line. "How're you doing?"

"I'm okay." His tight jaw said otherwise.

Her own chest ached at the thought of Janice. She knew he had to be hurting too. But she let it go. He was focused on keeping them safe. Grief would have to wait.

In the shopping center parking lot in Chestertown, they climbed out of their respective vehicles and gathered in a huddle.

The bodyguards surrounded them, facing outward and scanning the parking lot for anyone who looked like they could be trouble. But the people coming and going from their cars to the stores were ignoring the strangers.

"We need an internet connection," Dolph said.

"I'll go find out where there's wireless around here," his wife volunteered.

Both Skip and Rose nodded their approval. Sue Randolph was as nondescript as they come. Short brown hair, pleasant but not particularly pretty face, average height, slightly plump with middle-aged spread. No one was likely to remember talking to her five minutes after the conversation ended.

"This place looks like it'll have a lot of what we need," Kate said, tilting her head toward the sign on the brick storefront that read, ironically, *Rose's Discount Department Store*. She dug some cash out of her wallet. "There's an Acme down there. Can somebody get us some groceries?"

Rose gestured toward Lilly, who took the money from Kate.

Sue walked briskly back in their direction. "Both the public library and a coffee shop downtown have wireless. I think people are ignoring us because they get a lot of tourists here on the weekends."

"The coffee shop. Tourists would be more likely to go there than the library," Dolph said. "Did you get directions?"

"Of course."

"I'll ride over to the coffee shop with Manny," Rose said. "Rob, shopping or coffee shop?"

"Coffee shop."

They scattered, some returning to their vehicles, others heading for the stores.

Inside the department store, Kate made a beeline for the cleaning supplies and paper products. This wasn't a time for leisurely shopping. She figured the sooner they got done and got out to the shack, the safer they'd be.

"Grab one of those big coolers from over there," she said to Skip. "And get a couple shirts for Rob. He doesn't have any spare clothes with him."

By the time Skip returned with a second cart, she had loaded towels, sheets and blankets into hers and was staring at a shelf piled high with boxes of air mattresses. The sign said $10. "How can they sell these so cheap?"

Skip shrugged. "The sign did say *discount* department store."

They filled the rest of Skip's cart with mattresses and an air pump. Kate gingerly turned her own top-heavy load toward the front of the store.

"This is gonna stick out in the clerk's mind," Skip whispered as they neared the cash registers.

That had already occurred to her. "Got it covered. If I ask you a question, just grunt." She headed for the youngest cashier, who was snapping her gum and looking bored.

Kate started dumping stuff onto the counter. "Just moved into a new place. Boy, what a mess. The previous tenants were total slobs."

"Where's your new place?" the clerk asked the obligatory question in a flat voice, without looking at them.

"Oh, I keep forgetting the address. Where is it, honey?"

Skip grunted.

"That's right. It's kinda small but it'll be real cute by the time I get it fixed up. You all have such good prices here. I'm gonna bring the kids in to get some school clothes."

The clerk's eyes were glazing over. "One hundred, sixty-nine, twelve," she said in a bored voice.

Kate handed over a fistful of twenties. "Once we get the place cleaned up, I'll be back for some curtains and rugs."

"Ten, eighty-eight's your change." The clerk dumped the money into her hand.

"Have a nice day," Kate trilled as she pushed her cart full of bags toward the door. Skip followed with the second cart.

"You too," the clerk mumbled, already turning toward the next customer in line.

As they neared the Expedition, Skip started to snicker. Then he burst out laughing.

Kate grinned at him as relief washed through her. His sense of humor was returning. "Come on, you're blowing it, sweetheart. People are going to remember the giant laughing his ass off in the parking lot."

"That was some performance, darlin'." Skip was still chuckling as he unlocked the back of the truck. They started stuffing their purchases inside.

Lilly arrived with a cart full of grocery bags. Kate helped her load them into the back of her pick-up while Skip called Rose.

"She said to go on out," he told Kate after disconnecting. "The wireless keeps crapping out on them, but they should be done soon."

~~~~~~~~~

It was almost an hour before Rose and Rob arrived at the shack. By then Kate had scrubbed all the floors, wiped down the cots and had found several hooks on the walls that had been buried in cobwebs. The groceries were stacked in the kitchen area, the perishables iced down in the cooler. The cots had been dragged out into the front room and Skip was blowing up the air beds.

He came out of the backroom. "It's wall-to-wall bed in there now."

"We finally got the damn e-mail sent," Rose said. "Dolph went through several steps I didn't quite understand but he swears it can't be tracked back to his laptop by the Secret Service or hackers."

"Great," Kate said. "Now grab some blankets and start making up beds."

"Never knew she could be this bossy," Rose said to her partner, her tone teasing.

"She's on a roll. You should've seen her in the store. She was a speed-shoppin' demon. Filled two carts to overflowing in less than fifteen minutes."

Rose frowned. "Clerk's gonna remember that big an order."

"Nope." Skip told the story of Kate's Sally Mae Homemaker routine, with only a few small embellishments. They were all chuckling when the door opened.

The smiles faded as each person saw Dolph's face, gray and

drawn. Sue stood beside him, biting her lower lip, tear tracks on her cheeks.

Kate's heart was in her throat, terrified that something had happened to the kids.

"I brought my police band radio along. Turned it on while we were coming out here," Dolph said. "There's a BOLO out on you, son."

"Say what?" Skip said.

"Wanted for questioning regarding a homicide. I didn't put it together at first, with the call a few minutes before about a homicide in Towson. I called a buddy on the force. Your stolen gun. It was found next to the body."

Dolph swallowed hard. " The boy's dead, Skip. Jamal's the homicide victim."

CHAPTER NINETEEN

The room was silent. No one moved. Kate looked from Skip's pale face to the distress on Dolph's. She had no idea who Jamal was but this couldn't be good.

"No," Skip whispered. Then he roared, "No!"

He turned and slammed his hand against the partition between the rooms. The flimsy wallboard cracked. Before anyone could react, he had gone into the backroom. The whole building started shaking as he pounded on the walls.

"What's a BOLO?" Kate asked in a choked voice.

"Be on the look out," Rose answered. "Who's Jamal?"

"Kid who delivered the wine bottle to Janice," Dolph said. "We talked to him this morning. Good kid. Hustling for odd jobs to make money for coll..." His voice broke.

Sue wrapped her arms around her husband. Rob swore under his breath.

"Everybody stay out here, please," Kate said unnecessarily, heading for the backroom.

Skip was curled up on the air mattress in the furthest corner facing the wall. The hand she could see was clenched in a fist, the knuckles raw and bleeding. Her heart ached for him.

She gave up on walking the narrow paths between the mattresses and crawled over them instead. Wrapping herself around her husband's back, she laid her cheek on his.

She couldn't think of a thing to say. She wasn't sure she'd be able to push words past the tightness in her throat anyway. So she just held him.

Eventually Skip sat up, cross-legged on the wobbly air mattress.

"Come on out. Let your friends help," she said softly.

"I'll be out in a minute." His voice was gruff, just barely above a whisper.

She kissed his cheek, then edged off the mattress and walked the narrow path to the open doorway.

The others were scattered around the front room. Rose sat on one of the cots. Rob was at the table. The Randolphs were sitting on the other cot, Sue's arm around Dolph's shoulders. He was staring into space.

Kate sank down on one of the chairs at the table. "You guys didn't cause this," she said to Dolph.

He nodded. "I know. That kid was doomed the minute he wrapped his hand around that bottle."

"I'm having trouble believing Janice's husband would do this," Kate said. "I can see him trying to poison her, but kill an innocent kid? And he definitely wouldn't have the nerve to break into our house and steal Skip's gun."

Dolph rubbed his hand over his face. "Boy said the guy was white, with a tan. A little shorter than me, dark hair. Kinda old, which probably covers anyone over thirty-five."

"That describes Richard," Kate said.

Skip appeared in the doorway, clothing disheveled, hair sticking up. No one spoke as he moved across the room and sat in the remaining chair at the table.

"Kid's description would fit Delgado too," Rose said. "He doesn't match the Hispanic stereotype. Taller and not all that dark-skinned."

"Did we draw them to him, Dolph?" Skip's voice was raw.

"No, son. They were already hanging around Janice's building, watching for the kid. We just gave them a bonus attraction when we showed up."

Skip didn't say anything. He stared at the older man.

"Skip, if the kid hadn't run, we could've saved him. We didn't kill him. Delgado's boys did. They're ruthless."

"They would view Jamal as a worthless peasant kid," Rose spat out.

"The BOLO?" Skip said, shaking his head. "The cops want to talk to me?"

"Your stolen gun was found beside the kid. They're assuming it's the murder weapon."

"I'm a suspect? But I reported the gun stolen days ago."

"They got a witness says he saw you chasing Jamal down the alley," Dolph said.

"I should go in. Get it sorted out."

Rose was vigorously shaking her head as Dolph said, "You can't be in a cell, son, even for a little while. Delgado will send somebody in to kill you."

Kate felt the blood drain from her face. She must have looked as close to fainting as she felt because the next thing she knew Rob was kneeling beside her chair.

He gently pushed her head down into her lap. "Deep breaths, sweetheart."

"Great, just great." Skip said. "Innocent people are getting killed all around me, and now I'm a fugitive from the law."

Kate raised her head. "You didn't cause this. This all started with *my* client, remember?" She got up and moved around the table to his chair. He pulled her down onto his lap and buried his face in her hair.

"None of us caused this," Rose said quietly. "We're just trying to deal with it." She stood up abruptly, grabbed the bag of blankets and headed for the backroom.

Kate laid her cheek against Skip's chest. She could hear his heart beating erratically. Again she tried to think of something comforting to say, and failed.

She caught movement in her peripheral vision and glanced up.

Rose was dragging an air mattress on its side through the doorway into the front room. Dolph and Rob got up to help her.

Kate felt tears pooling in her eyes. She knew what they were doing even before Rose tapped her on the shoulder and softly said, "Backroom's all yours."

"Thank you," Kate whispered, then stood to pull her husband to his feet and lead him to bed.

Rose had tucked a blanket around the two remaining air mattresses in an attempt to create a full-sized bed. Skip stretched out on it and stared at the ceiling. Kate carefully lay down beside him, aware that a wrong move might cause the air mattresses to part company and dump them on the floor.

She stroked her hand down his shirt front, then rested it on his stubbled cheek. He didn't move.

Gentle tugging on his shirt finally got a response. He turned on his side to face her and wrapped his arms around her. She slipped an arm under his to stroke his back, the way she would Edie's or Billy's at bedtime.

Again he buried his face in her curls. She felt him take in a long shuddering breath. After a very long time, his body relaxed into sleep.

~~~~~~~~

Kate's growling stomach woke her the next morning. She was alone on the air mattress. The fragrance of cooking eggs made her stomach grumble again. They never had gotten around to eating dinner last night.

In the front room, Rose stood by the hot plate, scrambling eggs in a large skillet. When she spotted Kate, she said, "Took me half an hour to scrape the crud off this thing. The toaster's beyond redemption. We'll have to settle for plain old bread. Won't be fancy but it'll fill us up. Water in that pan is hot," she tilted her head toward the other sideboard of the sink, "if you want to make yourself some tea or instant coffee."

"Where is everybody?" Kate asked.

"Skip and Dolph are checking on the guards. Rob and Sue are getting some fresh air. Told them to stick close to the cabin."

"Want me to set the table?" Kate asked.

"Yeah. I called Mac last night. The kids are doing fine. A little homesick, but Liz and Rob's mom are keeping them occupied."

Kate nodded. She set out paper plates and plastic forks, a loaf of bread and the tub of margarine. Pulling the cots over to the table to serve as benches, she sat down on one of them.

A wave of longing for her children threatened to overwhelm her. She closed her eyes for a moment and imagined she was hugging them. She felt her lips curl into a smile when her imaginary Billy squirmed off of her lap.

Rob and Sue came in. They took seats at the table as Rose scooped eggs onto several of the plates. She went back to the hot plate and broke more eggs into the pan. "Don't know if this food's gonna last more than a day. After we've eaten, I've gotta feed the guards."

"Hopefully we'll only be here another day or two," Kate said.

Dolph and Skip came through the door. Kate patted the empty end of her cot and Skip joined her. She kissed his cheek, then dug into her food.

He poked at his.

Rose brought the skillet to the table again, dishing out eggs for Dolph and herself. She dumped the rest from the pan on top of the yellow heap already on Skip's plate.

"What are you doing?"

"That's your second serving. Eat it while it's hot," Rose said.

Skip took a bite, then poked some more. Kate shot him a look out of the corner of her eye. Rose put the skillet in the sink. She sat down at her place and glared across the table at him.

"Eggs are excellent brain food," Kate said. "They promote the production of the neurotransmitter that helps us concentrate." She knew full well her pretense that she was just making conversation was fooling no one.

"I think you'd better eat up, son," Dolph said. "Your womenfolk are ganging up on you."

Skip started shoveling eggs into his mouth. His attitude was that of someone digging a hole to bury his dead dog.

Rob complimented Rose's cooking. She thanked him. After that, they gave up on table conversation.

When they'd finished eating, Kate gathered the empty plates into a pile. "Rose needs to feed the guards, but first we should figure out how much to tell them?"

Rose was about to respond when the door swung partway open. Three guns came out. Manny's head appeared around the edge of the door.

"Don't do that, Manny," Rose said. "You almost–"

"We got company," Manny interrupted, his voice cheerful. "Our neighbor from down the road."

He paused until the guns had disappeared, then nudged the door all the way open. Sid Pierce was standing behind him.

"Come on in, Mr. Pierce," Kate said, faking a smile.

"Call me Sid, ma'am," the old man said. "I just wanted to stop in and say howdy."

"Then I'm Sally Mae, Sid."

Rob snickered softly. Kate located what she thought was his shin under the table and kicked it gently.

"Ouch," Dolph said.

"Sorry," Kate whispered. "I was aiming for somebody else."

Sid Pierce was looking around the room. He let out a low whistle. "You sure do have a bunch of folks crammed in here."

Kate spread her hands in a what-can-you-do gesture. "This is what happens when you tell your friends you've found the perfect place to get away from the craziness of the city." She turned to Manny. "Did you and Claude catch any fish?"

She was counting on his quick thinking. This was, after all, a fishing shack.

Manny did not disappoint her. He blinked twice, then said, "No, but the others are still trying."

Rose got up. "You'll have to settle for eggs then." She reached into the cooler for the second carton.

"Lordy, how many people ya got stayin' here?"

Kate gave Sid a rueful smile. "I didn't realize the place was quite this small when I said, 'sure come on and join us.'"

~~~~~~~~

Skip was beginning to think more clearly. Maybe there was something to Kate's eggs as brain food concept. An idea was hatching. He stood up and stretched. "I think I need to work off that second helping. Come on, Sid, I'll walk up to your house with you."

Halfway to the main road, Skip stopped walking. "Sid, I gotta tell you something but you can't tell a soul. Lives depend on it."

Sid turned to face him, eyebrow cocked, waiting.

As Skip had suspected, the old man was no dummy. He knew there had to be more to the story when that many people were sharing a two-room shack.

"All of those folks back there," Skip said. "They're involved, one way or another, in a big trial coming up. A drug trafficking ring. Two of them are witnesses, two are lawyers. The rest of us are guarding them. Fred's letting us use his place as a safe house until right before the trial starts. These drug lords are ruthless. They've already killed three people who could've identified them."

Sid was nodding. "Best place in the world to hide in plain sight is around here. Way off the beaten track, but we get 'nough tourists an' summer folks that we don't pay much attention to strangers."

'Well, if these guys figure out where we are–which is unlikely, we covered our trail pretty good–but if they do come around, they'll stand out. They're Hispanic."

"Well, now, not nec'sarily. We see Mexicans 'round here. Work for the rich folks in Chestertown doin' yard work and such. They don't live out this way though. But folks wouldn't pay all that much mind to a car load of 'em drivin' round."

"These guys aren't Mexican. They're Colombian."

Sid looked at him as if to say, *What's the difference?*

"I doubt they'll be wearing work clothes, and they may be a bit taller and lighter skinned than the Mexicans you've seen." Skip opted not to get into the whole Central/South American class system that was based not just on money but on how much Spanish versus Indian blood the person possessed. "They may look more like a white person with a tan."

"Gotcha. I'll keep an eye out."

"That'd be great. Let me give you my cell number. If you see anybody coming around that looks like that, don't try to talk to them. Don't even let on that you've noticed them. Like I said, they've already killed three people." Skip had pulled out one of his disposable cells to get the number off the back.

Sid surprised him by producing a state-of-the-art iPhone. He plugged in the number that Skip read off.

"Tell your wife to avoid them if she sees them, and to let you know right away. But you can't tell her all that background. It's highly confidential. My boss would skin me alive if she knew I was telling you all this. But I could tell we didn't fool you for a minute with our 'we're just here to get away from the city' routine."

Sid nodded. "I'll tell the missus I heard some Hispanics escaped from prison and might be headin' this way. That way if she sees 'em, she'll skidaddle inside and call the police."

Skip tried to think of a way to discourage calling the police. Then again, if the bad guys were driving down the lane, the cops showing up might be a good thing.

"Thanks, Sid, and I'm sorry we brought this possible danger to you."

"Shucks, boy, don't 'pologize. I haven't had this much excitement in a helluva long time. By the way, which one of them gals is your boss? Sally Mae?"

"No, she really is my wife. I was afraid to leave her at home for fear these guys would kidnap her, use the threat of hurting her to make me lead them to the witnesses. The one cooking breakfast is my boss."

"You're pulling my leg. That little gal!"

Skip grinned. "I've seen that *little gal* take down men twice her size. I tried arm-wrestling her once. She won."

Sid gave him a skeptical look.

"Okay, that time I *was* pulling your leg, but I'm serious about her taking down the big guys. It helps that they tend to underestimate her."

As Skip started back toward the cabin, the image of Jamal's bright-eyed young face popped into his mind. He felt his jaw clench. He silently said a short but fervent prayer that God would protect Sid Pierce and his wife.

CHAPTER TWENTY

Two of the guards sat at the table, wolfing down their breakfast. Rose was beating yet more eggs into submission in the skillet.

She waved Skip over to the makeshift kitchen. "To answer Kate's earlier question," she said quietly. "I'm thinking the guards need to know what's going on so they can do their jobs."

"Even that I'm suspected of murder?" he whispered back, not sure how he felt about sharing that little tidbit.

Rose paused, her expression thoughtful. "Manny, yeah, and I think Lilly's okay. These other two." She shook her head. "They haven't been with us all that long. But it's up to you. It's your hide on the line."

"We'll give these two the short version and send them back outside," Skip said. "Probably worth having Manny and Lilly brainstorm with us about where to go from here."

Skip sat down at the table. He gave the two guards a sanitized synopsis of how he, Kate and their friends had gotten into this mess. "These guys are totally ruthless. They stop at nothing. They've already killed three people and tried to kill me.

"I told the old man who lives down by the road a version of this," he informed the others as well as the guards. "He thinks the bad guys are drug lords and we're protecting witnesses for a trial that's coming up. So if he's running toward you yelling 'they're coming,' take him seriously. And do everything in your power to keep him and his wife safe."

Claude's expression hadn't changed much as he'd listened. "Got it, boss."

The other guard's mouth was hanging open. He closed it abruptly, then nodded.

"Oh, and don't call me boss if Mr. Pierce is around. My name is Steve and he thinks Rose is my boss."

Rose flashed one of her brief but gorgeous grins.

The guard's mouth dropped open again. Skip stifled a grin of his own. He stood up and gave the man a friendly pat on the shoulder. "You guys go back out and tell the others to come in, please."

Their eggs were a bit dried out but Manny and Lilly didn't seem to care. As they tackled the food, Skip gave them a somewhat more detailed synopsis, including what he had told Sid Pierce.

"And there's one thing we're not telling the other guys. The kid they killed, they set me up for it. One of my handguns was stolen a few days ago. They used it on the boy, then left it at the scene. There's a BOLO out on me even though I reported the gun stolen."

"You can't go in to talk to the cops," Manny said. "If they hold you even overnight, that'll give these guys time to get somebody on the inside to attack you."

"That's our take on it," Rose said.

Skip turned to Lilly. "You got a problem with harboring a fugitive for a while, until it's safe for me to be back in circulation?"

"Hell, no. This definitely smells like a set-up to stage a jailhouse hit," she said. "And I'd bet my next paycheck those guys used gloves so the gun's still covered with your prints."

Gonna have to give these two raises, Skip thought, *when this is over.*

~~~~~~~~

Once they'd cleared the breakfast debris off the table, Rose punched Mac's number into her phone, then hit the button for speaker mode.

"Reilly," Mac's voice growled from the phone as she put it down on the table.

"It's us," Rose said.

"Liz around?" Rob asked.

"She's tellin' the kids a story. They're gettin' restless, cooped up in the house."

The others didn't notice Rob's crestfallen look, but Kate did. She went over and sat on the cot next to him. "Use one of your phones to call her later," she whispered, patting his hand.

Rose was filling Mac in on the latest developments, including the BOLO on her partner.

Mac muttered a curse. "You're all safe? You there, sweet pea?"

Kate was startled by the anxiety in his voice. It hit her how hard this must be for him, to be babysitting several states away while the people he cared about most were in danger. "Yes, I'm here. We're all safe." She wanted to say more but she knew she'd just embarrass him.

There was silence on the line. Rose jumped in. "We need to figure out what to do next."

"Today's Sunday," Manny said. "You sent the letter and the e-mail yesterday. I'm thinking we need to wait a couple days. Give the Secret Service some time to investigate."

"I agree," Mac said. "And ta hell with actin' normal. I don't think you all should go to work tomorrow."

"So we just hang out *here*?" Sue said, looking around the bare room.

Kate grimaced. "I've got two clients in the morning I really need to see. One was feeling suicidal on Friday. Anybody else feel compelled to go in tomorrow?"

"I still have some prep to do for my court case on Wednesday," Rob said.

Kate turned to him on the cot. "Couldn't you get a continuance?"

"I can ask for one. The judge may or may not grant it."

"So we need to get Kate safely to her office tomorrow," Rose said. "And Rob to court on Wednesday, if this hasn't been resolved by then. Anybody else?"

Sue shot her husband a sharp look. "No job's worth getting killed for."

Kate felt a stab of guilt. Sue had been so relieved when Dolph retired from the police force and got his PI license. She'd confided to Kate that she could finally breathe easy because private investigators were rarely in physical danger. Things didn't seem to be working out that way.

"How will we know when the situation's resolved?" Lilly asked.

"Good question," Dolph said. "Either Rose or I need to take our laptops into town periodically and check the news online. See if there's any indication that our message has been received and acted on. I'll also try to find out what detective has been assigned to Jamal's case. That may make a difference in how we handle that whole issue."

"You got another safe house for us, Mac, in case we have to vacate this one in a hurry?" Skip asked.

"Yeah, place in Catonsville. Another friend of a friend. They're leavin' on vacation tonight. Said they'd leave a key with the neighbor across the street, tell her somebody's gonna come to house-sit."

Mac gave them the address, then signed off.

"Uh, is there any way we can get something to keep ourselves entertained?" Sue asked. "Some board games, or maybe a small TV?"

"We can't use credit cards," Dolph said. "In case they're tracking them."

Sue's face registered disbelief. "They can't break into bank records, can they?"

"If they've got a savvy hacker like your husband, they can," Skip said. "Google 'how to hack into credit card accounts' sometime. You'll be shocked at what comes up."

Sue turned to her husband. "Is it really that easy?"

"No," Dolph said. "A lot of those posts on how to do it are bogus. It's not easy, but a really good hacker can do it."

"We need more groceries," Rose said. "That's going to use up most of our cash."

"I've got a credit card in my maiden name, Susan Barrett. I use it for business travel expenses."

"That may be enough degrees of separation," Rose said. "Especially if we go far enough away from here to use it."

"I overheard some of the locals at the coffee shop talking about going to Middletown, Delaware to shop," Rob said. "It's about an hour's drive from here. Another state should throw them off pretty good."

Rose nodded. "Sue, Kate and I'll go to Middletown. Dolph, you go to town to check the news."

"I'm actually kind of tired," Kate said, faking a yawn. "I think I'll stay here." She nudged Rob's knee with her own. "Why don't you go, Rob? You can help them pick out the TV... And call Liz," she added in a whisper.

Rob flashed her a grin. "Good idea."

~~~~~~~~

Kate had decided to finish cleaning up from breakfast while the others were getting themselves organized to run their errands. She was scrubbing the cast iron skillet when Dolph, the last to leave, called out a goodbye from the doorway.

She waved a soapy hand without turning around from the sink. "Ugh, this water stinks. I hope there's nothing lethal in it."

Skip leaned over her shoulder to sniff. "I think it's just sulphur. Won't hurt us." He wrapped his arms around her waist from behind and rested his chin on top of her head. "You did a damn fine job of clearing the place out, darlin'."

She chuckled, grabbing for a paper towel to dry the skillet. She froze when she felt his body tense against her back. His forehead dropped to her shoulder. When he started shaking, she put the skillet down and lifted her arms behind her to wrap them around his neck. Awkwardly, she rocked them back and forth, tears now streaming down her own cheeks.

When the shaking stopped, she turned in his arms and put her still-damp hands on either side of his face. Looking up into pain-filled eyes, she said, "It's not your fault."

"I know."

Kate snorted softly. "Yeah, so do I, but I still feel guilty." She took his hand and led him to the table. They sat down across from each other.

"When I was a newbie therapist, Sally Ford taught me... You remember Sally?"

Skip nodded.

"She taught me a way to help clients deal with guilt. I'd

always thought that guilt was a pointless emotion, but Sally set me straight. She said that its job is to stop us when we're about to break a rule about how we're supposed to act in a civilized world. But a lot of those rules get internalized when we're kids. They're often too simplistic or absolute.

"So first you ask yourself what behavior you feel guilty about, then what rule is involved. Once you bring both out into the light of day, you decide if the rule is still valid or does it need modification. If the rule's still valid, you have to change your behavior. When you've got your behavior and the rule in sync with each other, then the guilt has done its job. You can thank it and let it go."

Skip sat for a minute, thinking. "We're both feeling guilty for involving innocent people in this mess."

"Yeah, that's the behavior. Now what's the rule?"

Skip didn't have to think very long this time. "You gotta protect the people you're responsible for."

Kate reminded herself to walk softly. That rule had come from Skip's father whom he idolized. "Was that how the rule was originally phrased?"

Skip thought for a moment. "No. My daddy taught me to protect my family. But as a cop, I was told to 'protect and serve' everyone, especially the innocent victims of crime."

"Kind of a heavy load to carry," Kate said.

"Yeah, and before you say it, I will. I'm not a cop anymore."

"So it all comes down to responsibility. Who are we responsible for?"

After a pregnant pause, Skip said, "And the answer is...?"

"I don't know. I'm not totally playing therapist here. I'm trying to sort this out for myself as well. Who do we take responsibility for? Our kids certainly, but even there we may not always be able to protect them from everything. Not without smothering them and not letting them live."

"My daddy also used to quote the Serenity Prayer at me on a regular basis."

"As in we shouldn't take responsibility for that which we cannot control, only what we can control."

"And that's the crux of the 'yeah-but' that keeps echoing in my head," Skip said. "If I'd insisted Janice come with us, she'd still be alive. If I'd kept looking for Jamal, he'd probably still be alive."

Kate resisted pointing out that more likely *both* he and Jamal would be dead.

"Now we've come to hindsight bias. Once we know the outcome, we assume we should have known it all along. We don't have crystal balls to predict the future, sweetheart. We can only make the best decision possible with the information we have at the time."

"And you're not doing any second guessing?" Skip said, his voice a bit defensive.

"Of course I am, all over the place. If I'd refused to meet Miller for lunch, none of this would have happened. But I had no reason to suspect that lunch would bring all this to pass."

"So what's your rule?" Skip asked.

It was Kate's turn to think for a minute. "It's similar to yours. Like doctors, we therapists get it drummed into us to 'do no harm.' Now it feels like anyone who even says hello to me on the street is at risk."

"Bottom line," Skip said, "We didn't create this mess, as Rose pointed out. We're just trying to deal with it."

"The people responsible are Delgado and his henchmen," Kate said.

Skip nodded. "You're darn good at this, darlin'. You should consider doin' it for a living."

Kate smiled, then sobered as her mind flashed to Miller's intense face across that lunch table from her. Her chest felt hollow. "In a way, it's a good thing Miller's not around to know what has happened. It would have destroyed him. Like you, protecting those he loved and felt responsible for, it was a big part of how he defined himself."

Skip took her hand. "You really admired him," he said softly.

"Yes. I wish you could have met him. You would have liked each other."

He lifted her hand to his lips and kissed her fingertips.

"I love you," she whispered.

Skip stood and drew her up with him. He held her hand against his chest. She could feel his heartbeat, strong and steady, under her palm.

"Did this help?" she asked, brushing his hair out of his eyes with her other hand.

"Yeah, I'm not totally okay yet, but I'll get there. And just being with you helps, even when you're not playing therapist." He smiled down at her. "You're healing balm for my heart."

"Oh, how romantic." She gave him a teasing grin. "I'm Neosporin."

He chuckled, then bent and swooped her up in his arms. "I figure we got about half an hour before Dolph gets back."

She just smiled up at him.

Unfortunately, the doorway between the rooms was too narrow. He couldn't figure out how to get both his bulk and her through it at the same time. Even sideways didn't work.

He set her back down on her feet. "I'm batting a zero here in the romantic department."

She preceded him through the door, then turned and started unbuttoning his shirt. "I think your batting average is about to improve."

CHAPTER TWENTY-ONE

Dolph had called his wife's office first and left a message on her boss's voicemail. Then he punched in the number for the Towson precinct where he had once worked. The evening before he'd been too stunned by the news to think to ask who'd caught Jamal's case. Now he was praying it was somebody he knew and liked, or more importantly someone who liked him.

His prayer was answered. "Detective Anderson isn't on duty at the moment, sir. Would you like me to relay a message?"

"No, that's okay. I'll call her tomorrow." He punched his former partner's home number into the throw-away cell. After three rings, an answering machine picked up.

"Hey, Judith, hope you'll forgive me for calling you at home but I wanted to touch base about–"

"That you, Dolph? I'm screening calls. Trying to get a little down time."

"Then I guess you don't want to discuss some information on the case you just caught. The black kid."

"What info?"

"The guy you've got the BOLO out on, the owner of the gun, Reginald William Canfield, the third. Do you realize who he is?"

It took Judith a second to connect the dots. "Skip *Canfield*, of course. I didn't make the connection, and I should've after the witness described him. Where is he?"

"Don't know exactly at the moment," Dolph said. It wasn't a lie. He didn't know *exactly* where Skip was at that moment–which room he was in, or he and Kate might be taking a walk.

"He and I were together yesterday. We interviewed the boy regarding a case. Woman was poisoned by a doctored bottle of wine. The kid was hired to deliver the wine. He was describing the guy who gave it to him when somebody yelled at the other end of the alley. Kid got spooked and took off."

"So why was Canfield chasing him?"

"Because we were worried that what did happen would happen, that the kid was in danger because he knew too much. I was right behind Skip, but the kid was too fast for us. We lost him."

"You got any suspects for the poisoning?"

"Maybe." Dolph hesitated, then decided he had to give her somebody else to chase besides Skip. "Might be the woman's estranged husband. He matches the kid's description, although it was pretty generic. White with a tan, five-ten, brown eyes, dark hair."

"Look, I know you got all that client confidentiality crap to deal with, Dolph, but I need names. A kid's dead. Grandma claims he was one of the good ones, no drugs, good grades, trying to raise money for college."

"You're preaching to the choir," Dolph said. "He struck us as a good kid. I'm happy to give you names. Janice Browning was set up as a bogus suicide on Friday night, died early yesterday morning. Husband is Richard Browning. Probably still living at the condo they own together in Towson. Don't know the address."

"Who's the detective working that case? I don't remember hearing anything about a poisoning."

"Well, that's why we were investigating. The uniforms who responded reported it as a suicide. But the note found in her apartment didn't ring true to those who knew her. We found out from her building's concierge that the wine was delivered as a gift, with a verbal message from her husband."

"Okay, I'll track down Browning, but I still need to talk to Skip. His prints are all over that gun, and nobody else's. Somebody steals a gun, you'd think they'd handle it some, then maybe wipe it clean after they use it in a crime."

"Or they use gloves so they can frame Skip for the crime. Skip and his wife were friends with Janice Browning. They helped her get her stuff out of the condo when she left her husband. From what I heard, it got nasty. Browning called the police, tried to get them arrested for breaking and entering. There should be a report on that call–"

"When was that?"

"I'm not sure. Early last week. Anyway, there's no love lost between Browning and Skip at this point."

"How would Browning get his hands on Skip's gun?"

"Don't have an answer for that one."

"Dolph, I'm getting real tired of repeating myself. I need to talk to Skip. Get his involvement, if any, cleared up so I can focus on finding the killer."

"What's the TOD?"

Judith sighed loudly into the phone. "Don't have one yet. Autopsy hasn't been done."

"Okay, but I'll bet you've got a general sense of when it went down. When was the kid found?"

"Around four Saturday afternoon. Shop owner took out some trash. Kid was behind his dumpster. Grandma hadn't seen him since breakfast, so we've got a real big window there."

"We talked to the kid about eleven. That narrows your window some."

"Also puts your boss at the scene."

"I can alibi him for the rest of the day."

"Every minute?"

"Almost, and into the evening."

Big sigh again. "I *still* need to talk to him. Find him and tell him to come in."

"I will, but could you cancel the BOLO? I don't want some overzealous rookie thinking he's a murder suspect and maybe shooting him. He's working another case today. I'll see if I can track him down, have him call you. Then he can come in tomorrow if you need him to."

"Okay, I'll cancel the BOLO but if I haven't heard from him

by morning, it goes back on."

~~~~~~~~~

At the department store in Middletown, Rose was working hard to keep from tapping her foot while Rob picked out a small TV and then Sue mulled over the selection of board games. When they got to the toasters, she'd had enough. She grabbed the cheapest one off the shelf. "Let's go."

In the grocery store parking lot, Rob stayed in the car to call Liz. Lilly got out and leaned against the front fender, scanning the lot.

Rose and Sue quickly filled a cart with the essentials they would need for the next couple days, keeping in mind their limited capacity for keeping perishables cold. At the checkout counter, Sue slid her credit card through the machine.

"It didn't work," the clerk said. "Try again."

She did.

"Sorry, ma'am. It's saying the card's not good."

Sue frowned. "Damn it, they did it to me again. What part of 'I use this card for travel' don't they understand?"

Rose dug in her pocket. Kate had given her the rest of the cash, just in case. "Here, this should cover it." She didn't want the clerk to remember them.

Once they were out of the store, Sue said, "That damn card company. They did that to me before. I used the card outside of Maryland and their dumb computer immediately flagged it as a possible fraudulent charge and blocked the card. I thought I had it straightened out, though. Now what do we do for cash?"

Rob had gotten out of the car to help load the groceries. "I've got my debit card with me."

Rose shook her head. "No, you're too involved. They may be watching for activity on your account."

"Does it really matter whose card we use," Rob said, "this far away from the shack."

Rose weighed the pros and cons for a moment. "Maybe not, but we'll use my card." She headed for the ATM machine outside the grocery store.

~~~~~~~

Dolph had intentionally lingered in town to give Kate and Skip some privacy. He'd done some window shopping at a travel agency. It was closed on Sunday, but he wrote down the website from the cruise line poster in the window. He figured when this whole mess was finally over, it wouldn't hurt to take his Susie on a real vacation, to mend the marital fences.

When he got back to the shack, he told Skip and Kate about his conversation with Judith. "You need to call her, son. Try to appease her so she doesn't insist you come in."

"I'd like to check on my client," Kate said. "We could drive back over the bridge to Annapolis, call from there."

Rose walked in the door with a load of groceries. The others straggled in behind her, laden with packages. "Who's calling who from where?"

Dolph filled her in on the police investigation.

"You'd better not take your truck," Rose said to Skip. "Just in case some local cop heard the BOLO earlier and recognizes it."

~~~~~~~

Lilly volunteered to take them in her pick-up. After they'd crossed the Bay Bridge, she took the first exit for Annapolis and pulled into the parking lot of a restaurant.

Skip called Judith Anderson's cell number that Dolph had given him.

"Hi, Judith. Skip Canfield. Dolph said you wanted to talk to me."

"Yeah, did he tell you why?"

"I can't believe those bastards killed that kid!"

"And which bastards would those be, Mr. Canfield?"

"Uh, does this mean I have to call you Detective Anderson? I thought we'd moved beyond that."

"*Which* bastards, Canfield?"

"Sorry, I wasn't trying to be cute. The ones that killed Janice Browning."

"I thought you suspected the husband. That's only one bastard."

"Yeah, well, we're not sure it's him. Janice is... uh, was a criminal lawyer. She had enemies. It just seemed like a rather huge coincidence that she was killed right after she left Richard. And to steal Dolph's favorite line, I'm allergic to coincidences. It's also occurred to us that Richard could've hired somebody. Personally I don't think he's got the, uh, guts to do it himself."

That elicited a slight chuckle. "You can say *balls* to me."

"Yeah, but I'm in the car with... one of my female investigators." He'd almost slipped and said he was with his wife, which wouldn't jive with what he was about to tell Judith. "I try not to cuss in front of ladies."

Lilly looked at Skip over Kate's head. She arched an eyebrow at him.

He managed to fake a touch of laughter in his voice. "From the expression on my investigator's face, she dislikes being called a lady."

He breathed a bit easier when Judith chuckled again. "Skip, I really need to talk to you, in person. There are a couple other details I need to clear up."

"Uh, that could be difficult. I'm out of town at the moment working another case, and I'm undercover. Even as far away as Baltimore County, I can't afford to be seen going into a police station. It would blow my credibility with the low-lifes I'm trying to cultivate."

"We could meet away from the station," Judith said. She named a diner frequented by police officers.

Skip stifled a sigh. He'd hoped to avoid a face-to-face meeting. But maybe he could at least control the location. "Too much of a cop hangout. How about Mac's Place, across from the courthouse? And it's my treat. My thanks for your help on that case last year."

"Okay. What time?"

"Uh, let me coordinate with the, uh, non-lady." He put his thumb over the cell's tiny mouthpiece. "What time is your depressed client coming in tomorrow?" he asked Kate.

"Eleven."

Into the phone, he said, "One o'clock?"

"Yeah, I can make that work."

"Okay, I'll see you there. If I'm late, it means I've picked up a tail that I had to shake first."

"See ya tomorrow."

After Skip disconnected, Kate asked, "Are you sure it's safe to meet with her?"

"Yeah, because I'm going to have several of our people nearby, just in case Delgado's gang shows up. And if they do, it'll be handy to have a police detective right there to arrest them."

"What if she tries to arrest *you*?"

"Highly unlikely at this point," Skip said. "We'll get out and give you some privacy so you can call your client."

He and Lilly climbed out of the truck and walked down several cars. They stood facing each other so it would look like they were having a conversation, but they could see anyone approaching the truck from any direction.

"We should pretend to be talking," Skip said.

Lilly took a deep breath. "Did Rose tell you I screwed up?"

"What do you mean?" Skip responded absently, scanning the parking lot.

"I left my post, when Mrs. Browning's bed arrived. I went inside to make sure the deliverymen were on the up-and-up. And I should've questioned her about the wine."

"Did she say anything about it being a gift?"

"No, she just waved the bottle at me and asked if I wanted to join her in a glass."

"Lilly, you didn't do anything wrong–"

"I didn't do much right either. She died on my watch."

Skip glanced at her. There was anger in her eyes, anger at herself. He went back to scanning the parking lot, while trying to think of something reassuring to say. "You had no reason to suspect anything about the wine."

"I should've–"

Skip cut her off. "How do you think I feel? Kate and I dragged Janice into this mess to begin with." He glanced her way again, then softened his tone. "But as Rose keeps pointing out, none of us created the mess, we're just trying to deal with it."

Lilly didn't look convinced. She turned away from him,

toward her truck. "I think Kate's finished her call."

~~~~~~~~

On the way back to the Eastern Shore, Kate's mind was working on the logistics for the next day. "I don't remember exactly who I've got scheduled tomorrow afternoon," she told Skip. "I need my appointment book which is in my briefcase, which is in my car. And I just realized I have no idea where my car is."

"Rose left it in a visitor's space at Mrs. Browning's building," Lilly said.

"I also need a shower before I see clients, and the two office outfits I have with me are not only dirty, they've been slept in."

"There's a laundromat near the Acme in Chestertown," Lilly said.

"That solves the clothing part of the problem. But how can I get a shower? You could use one too, Skip." Kate waved her hand in front of her nose. "Washing up in that tiny basin in the bathroom can only go so far."

"What, you don't like my new aftershave, *eau de* two-day-old sweat?" He grinned down at her.

She grinned back in relief. He seemed to be getting his emotional equilibrium back, again.

"We actually have a shower," he said. "Sort of. I didn't bother to mention it 'cause I didn't think you'd want to use it."

Kate cocked an eyebrow at him. "What does 'sort of' mean?"

"Very, very basic. As in garden hose duct-taped to a tree branch."

Lilly snorted. "That's pretty basic."

"I'm just desperate enough to use it. Lilly, could you stop at the Acme so I can get some shampoo?"

"Sure thing."

At the cabin, all were delighted to hear that a shower was an option. Enthusiasm dimmed somewhat when they learned they would be standing naked outside under a garden hose.

In less than an hour everyone had showered. No one lingered under the cold spray. Once the dirty clothes and towels were gathered up, Rose and Kate headed for town with two of the guards.

At the laundromat, Manny wandered down a couple stores, then leaned nonchalantly against a pole. He was watching for overdressed Hispanics. The other guard stayed in his car, also scanning the parking lot.

Kate and Rose loaded the laundry into several machines, then sat down to wait.

Rose shifted awkwardly in her seat, then cleared her throat. "Uh, how's Skip doing?"

Kate hid a smile. Discussing emotions was not Rose's favorite thing to do. "I think he's okay now. Or at least on his way to being okay."

They sat in silence for a few minutes while Kate debated with herself. Finally, she said, "Please don't tell him I talked to you about this, but I'm starting to think he's in the wrong profession. It hits him so hard when someone he perceives as an innocent is hurt or killed."

Rose pondered that. Kate waited patiently, used to her thoughtful silences.

"I can't imagine what else he'd do. It's all he knows. And the fact that he cares so much, it makes him a better investigator. I've never seen him just go through the motions, not even when a case is fairly routine."

"I just worry," Kate said, "that one of these times, he's not going to spring back."

"He will. As long as he has you."

"Rose, I don't think I've ever told you how much I appreciate our friendship."

"Aw crap, Kate! Don't go gettin' mushy on me."

"For Pete's sake, just accept the sentiment and say thank you." Kate smiled to take the sting out of her stern tone.

"Thank you. Aren't those washers done yet?" Rose jumped up to go stand over them as the machines started vibrating their way through the spin cycle.

They were taking the clothes out of the dryers and folding them when Manny entered the laundromat.

"What's wrong?" Rose said.

"That new guard, he's disappeared. One minute, he was sitting in his car. I did a scan of the parking lot, looked back and his car was gone."

Rose frowned. "Pull my car up front."

"What does that mean? Where'd the guard go?" Kate asked.

"Don't know, but we're getting out of here."

"I got a funny feeling he's gone AWOL," Manny said as they loaded the laundry into the car. "He's been acting strange all day."

CHAPTER TWENTY-TWO

It was starting to rain when the laundry brigade arrived at the shack. Dolph ran out to help them get the clean clothes inside before the sky opened up.

Rose told them about the missing guard.

Sue turned from where she was cooking dinner in the makeshift kitchen. "Is he likely to tell anybody where we are?"

Dolph winced a little at the anxiety in her voice. He quickly reassured her. "Not if he ever wants to work as a bodyguard again. He's not gonna admit that he deserted his post."

Over dinner at the crowded table, they ironed out the plan for the next day.

"Kate, I'm thinking you could wear your sweats and take your good clothes with you," Rose said. "We take the bucket and mop. Make it look like we're janitors coming in to clean up before folks arrive for the day."

"Good idea," Skip said. "Kate needs her briefcase from her car in the morning."

"I'd like to go by our house," Dolph said. "There's some stuff there I think we might find useful."

Sue shot him a concerned look. He carefully avoided eye contact with her.

"If I could get some papers from my office," Rob said, "I can work on the prep for my court case here. The judge may not grant the continuance. And it wouldn't hurt for me to be there when Skip meets with Judith, just in case my services are needed."

Rose's expression was thoughtful. "Lilly and I'll go with

Skip and Kate to her office. Rob, you ride with Dolph. Manny'll follow to watch–"

"We need to leave two guards here with Sue," Dolph interrupted. "It's too easy to sneak up on this place through the woods."

Rose frowned at him. "It's not all that safe for you and Rob to be running around Towson without back-up."

"Damn it!" Skip said. "Lilly could follow you guys. Rose goes to get Kate's briefcase."

Unh, uh," Rose said. "They will definitely be watching Kate's office. You two are the main targets. I'm not leaving you there by yourselves."

"We'll be okay, son. We'll take Sue's car. The bad guys don't know it." Dolph was looking everywhere but at his wife. Mentally he upgraded the four-day cruise he'd been considering to a seven-day one. "We all converge on Mac's Place at one. Some of us inside, some out. That's where you're most vulnerable, sitting still in a public place for at least a half hour."

"I'll call the manager in the morning," Rose said. "Tell him not to be surprised if some of us suddenly run out the back exit. Let's hit the sack. We need to be up by four-thirty, on the road by five-thirty."

That was met with a chorus of groans.

~~~~~~~~~

Rose's plan to sneak Kate and Skip into the building as janitorial staff worked beautifully. By eight o'clock, Kate had changed her clothes and Lilly had retrieved her briefcase.

Kate started making calls. Her fib that she was coming down with the flu met with sympathy. By nine, she was feeling vaguely guilty but she'd cleared her schedule for that afternoon and the next two days.

Lilly was sitting in her truck half a block from the building, with a two-way radio. She was watching the front entrance and the silhouette of a man in a dark sedan across the street from it. Skip was in the locked waiting room, Rose in the hallway by the elevators. They both had radios as well. Kate had given them a physical description of each of her morning clients. Skip would keep the waiting room door locked until he received the signal that the next client was on the way up.

~~~~~~~~

About the time Kate's first client was arriving, Dolph was rummaging through a set of shelves on one side of his garage. He pulled out two bullet-proof vests. "Got these cheap in the equivalent of a cop shop yard sale when BCPD upgraded. I figured they'd come in handy some day."

Rob frowned. "A standard-sized vest isn't going to fit Skip."

Dolph deposited the vests in the trunk of his wife's car. "One's an extra, extra large."

A corner of Rob's mouth quirked up. "You bought it for him."

Dolph could feel his face turning red. He considered repeating that they'd been cheap, which wasn't totally true. He'd paid two hundred apiece for them–half their original cost but still not a minor expenditure. He opted for honesty and voiced a sentiment he'd never shared with anyone but Sue. "I tend to think of him as the son I never had."

Rob smiled. "Those two grow on you, don't they?"

Dolph chuckled. "Next stop, your office."

At Kate's suggestion, Rob had worn one of the plaid flannel shirts she and Skip had bought for him in Chestertown. It did indeed make a good disguise for slipping into the building undetected.

But in the law offices of Stockton, Bennett and Franklin, Rob's entrance in his Joe Farmer costume caused a bit of a stir. By the time he and Dolph reached his office, he had been the recipient of several surprised comments and teasing barbs.

Rob gestured for Fran to follow them in and close the door. "I need to get the papers on the Harrison case but I'm not staying. Please clear my calendar for today and tomorrow. I'm going to work on the prep for court from home."

"Are you okay?" Fran asked.

"Yeah. I'm just involved in something right now that's kind of complicated. If anyone comes looking for me, I'm not here. I'll buzz you when I've got what I need gathered up, to see if the coast is clear."

Fran gave him a concerned look but asked no questions. She nodded and returned to her desk.

Dolph stepped over and locked the door. Rob began rummaging through the papers on his desk. He stuffed folders and a thick law book into a briefcase, then buzzed Fran. They were headed out again in less than five minutes.

As they neared the glass doors at the front of the building, Dolph grabbed Rob's arm to stop him. He tilted his head toward a black sedan parked across the street. It hadn't been there when they'd come in. Two dark-haired men were sitting in it.

Dolph and Rob pivoted toward the back of the building. "How we going to get to your car?" Rob was huffing a little as they race-walked to the back exit.

Dolph had been trying to figure that out. He wasn't thrilled with any of the options that came to mind. "Stay here for a minute." He went out into the back parking lot to look around. Seeing nothing suspicious, he returned to Rob.

"Give me the briefcase. You stay back here, hidden behind the dumpster over there. I'm going to get the car, check it for bugs and then see if they follow me. I'll double back for you once I'm sure I've ditched them."

Dolph moved around the side of the building. The two guys were still out front, acting like it was perfectly normal to sit in a car with your morning coffee, reading a newspaper. The hairs on Dolph's neck were standing at attention.

He walked to his car and shoved Rob's case over the seat into the back, then climbed in. Pulling away from the curb, he fumbled with his seatbelt with one hand while watching in the rearview mirror to see if the sedan followed.

It didn't do so immediately but when Dolph stopped at the red light at the corner, it pulled out and started in his direction. He was reaching under his seat for his new toy when he caught movement in the mirror.

He swivelled his head around. The sedan was not following him. It had just turned right onto a side street that led to the street behind Rob's building.

Ignoring the red light, Dolph swung his car into a right turn, narrowly missing a Honda that had started into the intersection. A horn blared as he raced down the block, then took the next right as fast as he dared. Approaching the back parking lot entrance, he saw the sedan parked in the lot. The two men climbed out and started walking toward the building's back door.

Dolph's neck hairs were vibrating. He pulled over to the curb as he dug out his own cell phone and turned it on. Finding the number under contacts for Rob's office, he punched send.

"Mr. Franklin's off–"

"Get out of there, Fran. Now."

The men started running.

"Now!" Dolph yelled. He frantically looked around the car. There was a small round object stuck to the lower back corner of the passenger's window. He jabbed at the button to lower the window, hoping the listening device wouldn't be able to pick up anything if it was down inside the door.

The men had disappeared through the building's back door. Dolph hit the accelerator and roared into the parking lot.

Rob ran out from behind the dumpster and jumped into the passenger seat. Dolph had the car moving again before he could get his door closed. The forward motion slammed it shut.

Dolph tore out of the parking lot. "Roll your window up. Let's see if the listening device is still there."

Rob gave him a confused look but did as he was told.

"Look for a little white button in the lower corner," Dolph told him.

"Don't see it."

"Shit! It's fallen off inside the door."

Dolph was making random turns as he moved away from Rob's building. When no one seemed to be following, he slowed on a side street, feeling under his seat with one hand for the device. He turned it on and swung it slowly around in an arc, still creeping down the street. "Listening device isn't showing so hopefully it's busted. We do have another tracking device, on the front bumper it looks like."

Dolph glanced in his rearview mirror. No sign of a tail. Handing the detector to Rob, he said, "Watch for bad guys."

He pulled to the curb, then jumped out and raced to the front of the car. Feeling along under the bumper, he found the bump that shouldn't be there. He yanked it off.

A Fed Ex truck was double parked two cars up. Dolph ran to it and jammed the device inside its back bumper. He was in the car and pulling away from the curb in seconds.

"Does Fran carry a personal cell phone on her?"

"Yeah."

"Call it. Make sure she's okay."

Rob punched the number into a throwaway phone, then hit the button for speaker. "Where are you? Are you okay?" he asked when Fran answered.

"I'm back by Shirley's desk. What's going on?"

"Can't explain right now. Call reception on Shirley's phone. Ask if two dark-haired guys in suits came in looking for me. I'll hold."

In less than a minute, she was back. "Yes, they pushed past the desk when she said she had to buzz me. They hurried back out again a minute ago."

"Call security. Have them search the building to make sure they're gone."

"Uh, hold on. Mr. Stockton wants to talk–"

"Wait, Fran! Tell Bill I'll call him back. Then you go home. Don't come back in until you hear from me. It's dangerous for you to be there."

A beat of silence, then Fran said, "Okay, I'll tell him. Be careful, boss." She disconnected.

Rob took the phone off speaker and called his partner. Dolph could hear a faint voice shouting, "What the hell's going on, Rob?"

"It's complicated, Bill, and confidential. If anybody asks where I am, tell them I'm out of town on business, and you're not sure where I am or when I'll be back."

Rob listened for a moment. "I can't tell you just yet. I'll stay in touch." He disconnected.

Dolph swung into a parking lot and drove over to a trash can in front of a strip shopping center. "Toss that phone." Rob leaned out his window and obliged.

They drove for several more blocks before Dolph pulled into another parking lot and put the car in park. He called Skip and filled him in. "I'm thinking Rob needs to stay out of sight. We'll watch the front entrance of Mac's Place from the car, in case unwanted guests show up. Meet us at the Burger King on York Road at 12:30. I have a present for you before you go to meet Judith."

Dolph disconnected just as Rob was opening his mouth to protest. "I need to be there in case she tries to arrest him."

"I doubt that's going to happen but if she's got enough to arrest him, you're not going to be able to stop her."

"But he can't let her take him in," Rob said.

"He won't."

"How's he going to stop her?"

Dolph glanced sideways at him. "Best you not know the details, counselor."

"Shit," Rob said. "Thus the vest."

Dolph didn't answer him.

At twelve-thirty, Rose pulled in beside Dolph's car in the Burger King lot. She lowered her window. "Only one guy watching at Kate's office. Lilly kept an eye on him while we went out the back. She's headed for Mac's Place to check things out."

Dolph got out, motioning to Skip to join him. He walked toward the back of the car. "These guys are getting bolder, going into Rob's office like that."

Skip nodded, his mouth set in a grim line. "They had minimal coverage outside our offices Saturday and Kate's building today, but they have two men go *in* to Rob's office. They're trying to neutralize the insurance policy before they come after us more aggressively."

"That's my take on it." Dolph opened the trunk. "I bought these when BCPD was getting rid of old gear. Bigger one should fit you. Hopefully your jacket will go over it."

Skip frowned at the clunky vest. Before he could voice an

objection, Dolph said, "I got a bad feeling about this meet, son, with you sitting in a public place. But if you don't show, Judith will be chasing you again. It'll make me and Kate feel better if you're wearing this." He figured the desire to ease Kate's worrying would probably do the trick.

It did. Skip shrugged his surrender and took off his windbreaker to don the vest. The jacket was big enough to go over it. Skip deposited his snub-nose .38 in one pocket and a disposable cell in the other.

They walked back over to Rose's car. "We're riding with Rob and Dolph," Skip told Kate. "You're staying outside in the car."

She began to protest. He raised a hand. "Darlin', if this goes south, having to protect you would just make things more difficult. I'm wearing a bullet-proof vest Dolph gave me."

Rose handed Dolph a two-way radio. "I'm going in the back first and check things out. Then I'll be in the back hall. Lilly will be in the alley. You need to get out quick, Skip, you come our way."

"I think I need to go in with you initially," Dolph said to Skip. "Make sure Judith's the only cop there."

At five after one, Dolph pulled up across the street from Mac's Place. He and Skip waited for the all-clear from Rose, then they entered the front door of the restaurant. Both were scanning for familiar faces as they headed for the booth toward the back, where Judith sat talking on her cell phone. She disconnected as they approached.

"Hey, Judith," Dolph said. "I'm on a case so I can't stay. Just wanted to stop by and say hi."

Judith narrowed her eyes at him.

"Sue and I'd like you to come for dinner some time soon. I'll give you a call to set it up."

"That'd be good, Dolph. I'll look forward to it." Her voice was neutral but her expression was still suspicious. She knew him too well.

Back at the car, Dolph radioed Rose and Lilly. "Tall black guy in workman's clothes at the bar is a homicide detective. He's a bit of a ladies' man. You want to go in and chat him up, Lilly?

Be on hand if you're needed."

"What does that mean?" Kate's anxious voice came from the backseat. "Why would Judith have another detective there, and undercover?"

"Not sure. Could just be a precaution."

"It'll be fine," Rob said. "Skip knows how to handle himself."

"He'll be fine," Dolph echoed as he flipped the switch on his police scanner. His eyes were continuously moving up and down the street.

~~~~~~~~

After they had ordered their food, Judith said, "Looks like you're wearing protection."

Skip had been expecting some comment about the vest. He told her the honest truth. "Dolph insisted. This case I'm working has gotten a bit dangerous."

"Looks weird, keeping your jacket on inside."

"It'd look weirder if I took it off. So any new leads on your case?"

"Yes and no. Interviewed Browning. He denied he sent his wife any wine and he's alibied for Friday afternoon. So it wasn't him who met with Jamal Johnson. Of course, he could have hired somebody else to do it."

"That would be his style," Skip said. "Whose prints were on the bottle?"

"The boy's, Janice Browning's and the concierge's."

Skip cocked an eyebrow. "Nobody else?"

Judith shook her head. They both knew the significance of that. Someone had intentionally wiped their own prints off the bottle, and along with them the prints of all the personnel at the bottling plant, distributor, and wine store.

"Janice Browning's death has officially been ruled a homicide," Judith said.

Out of the corner of his eye, Skip saw Lilly come in and take a seat at the bar. She ordered something and then started talking to the black guy next to her. The man's work clothes were a bit too clean and crisply ironed.

Undercover cop. What the hell does that mean?

Their food arrived. Skip took a bite of his sandwich, then returned it to his plate, letting his right hand drop into his lap. "So you said, 'yes and no' regarding leads? Richard's the no part. What's the yes part?"

"I'll get to that in a minute. Tell me again about your meeting with the kid on Saturday."

Skip ran through it again while Judith poked at her salad.

"And that's the last time you saw him, shortly after eleven when he ran away from you?"

"Yes." Skip took another bite of his sandwich for form's sake. Again he dropped his hand below the tabletop, letting it rest on his jacket pocket.

"You didn't go looking for him again later, maybe to see if you could get more information out of him?"

"No."

"We had another witness come forward. Says he saw a guy meeting your description in that alley a little before one o'clock. Said the guy was shaking a black kid's arm and yelling."

"Wasn't me." Skip slid his hand into his jacket pocket while trying not to move his upper arm.

"Where were you around one that day?"

Crap! That was the only window of time on Saturday that he'd been alone, headed for Westminster to dump the GPS device. "Don't remember exactly, but I was with Dolph or one of my operatives most of the day. What was the time of death?"

"M.E. says between eleven-thirty and two, but he also found a contusion on the back of the boy's head that he says happened at least a half hour before the kid was killed. Too much swelling to have occurred just before the heart stopped."

Skip winced at the mental image of Jamal's eager face turning to horror as someone struck him from behind. "So they knocked him out, and then came back later to finish him off."

"Yeah, but you're the only person we got witnesses saying was there." Judith sounded regretful.

Skip's cell phone rang. He pulled it out with his left hand and hit the button to answer it. "Get out of there, son. The BOLO's on again, for murder now."

Judith's hand was creeping toward her purse.

"Don't move, Judith. I've got a gun on you under the table." Skip glanced over to the bar and caught Lilly's eye. He gestured with his head. He flicked his eyes back to Judith, who was sitting very still across from him, her hands where he could see them.

He glanced again at Lilly. She had stood up and had her hand in her own jacket pocket. The black man next to her suddenly sat up straighter, his eyes wide.

Shit! Now his operative would be facing assault with a deadly against a police officer.

He quickly brought his eyes back to Judith. "Thanks," he said into the phone, then pocketed it.

"Don't do this, Canfield. I'm going to try to clear you, but I can't help if you've got resisting arrest charges against you as well."

"Sorry, Judith. It's a bit more complicated than that. Because of this other case I'm working, if you put me in a cage, even for a little while, I'm a dead man. They'll get somebody inside to kill me."

"We'll keep you separated from the other inmates. We would anyway since you're a former cop."

Skip shook his head. "These guys are good enough, they'd get somebody in posing as a guard or janitor, food service. They'd find a way."

"You're not going to shoot me, Skip. You're a good guy. You couldn't shoot an innocent person, a police officer at that."

Skip wasn't about to let on that she was right. "You don't want to bet your life on that, do you? Put both hands on the table and sit real still, and we'll both live to talk another day about why I had to do this."

When she'd complied, he reached over with his left hand and scooped up her purse. Without taking his eyes off her, he made a come-here gesture with his head toward Lilly. He slid out of the booth, his gun now back in his pocket with his hand firmly attached to it.

Lilly had taken the other detective by his arm, as if she were walking him over to introduce him to a friend.

"Have a seat, detective. Hands on the table, please," Skip said quietly. "You got his piece, Lilly?"

"Both of them."

"We got more eyes in here," Skip bluffed in a low voice. "You two stay put for ten minutes. Our people see you move or hear sirens before then and it ain't gonna be pretty. Your purse and weapons will be where you can find them, once we're away from here." In a normal voice, he said, "Enjoy your lunch, folks."

He motioned toward the doorway to the back hall, then followed Lilly out, walking backward facing the room. In the hall, he grabbed Judith's gun out of her purse and tossed the purse to Rose. Then he and Lilly ran for the back door.

He heard Rose call out across the restaurant, "Somebody drop their purse in the hall?"

CHAPTER TWENTY-THREE

Kate's heart was in her throat. It just barely registered when Rob took her hand in his. Leaning around him, she stared out the car's window at the front of the restaurant.

Rose came out and walked briskly down the street toward her car. Sirens wailed in the distance.

Dolph's two-way radio, sitting on the passenger's seat, made a crackling noise. Rose's voice, a bit tinny, came out of it. "Skip got out clean. Take off, Dolph. Judith sees you, she may decide to arrest you for obstructing justice."

He pulled away from the curb. Two police cruisers, sirens blaring, lights flashing, raced toward them from three blocks away. Dolph turned onto the next cross street. The cruisers blasted through the intersection behind them.

"Keep quiet. I'm going to call Judith," he said. After punching in her cell number, he put the phone on speaker and dropped it in his lap.

"Hey, Judith. How'd your meet with Skip go? Was he able to help–"

"Your boy pulled a gun on me," Judith yelled over the blare of a siren.

"He did?" A corner of Kate's anxious brain registered that Dolph was a good actor. He'd sounded genuinely surprised.

"What part of the day were you with him last Saturday?" Judith yelled.

Dolph paused, then said, "All day, from ten-thirty on."

"I don't believe you, Dolph. You said before most of the day, not all. Canfield killed that kid."

Kate gasped. Rob squeezed her hand.

"Maybe didn't mean to," Judith yelled over the background noise on her end. "Maybe he was just trying to scare the kid and something went wrong. But now he's making the whole mess worse. Resisting arrest, assault of a police officer. The charges are stacking up. You gotta convince him to turn himself in, Dolph, before he gets himself killed."

Kate was biting her lower lip. She saw Dolph looking intently into the rearview mirror as he made another turn. She realized he was watching for tails.

"I'll try to catch up with him and convey the message. I'm in the middle of something right now but I can meet up with you in about an hour. I might be able to shed some light on all this for you."

The sirens stopped, leaving an eerie silence. Judith sighed loud enough Kate and Rob could hear her in the backseat. "Come to the station in an hour. I'll be waiting."

Dolph disconnected. "I think they must've lost him. Give him a call."

Kate rummaged through her purse for a phone she hadn't used yet, to be sure it was untraceable. She called the number of the throwaway Skip was using that day, then put her phone on speaker and held it out between the front seats. She almost burst into tears when Skip answered.

"You need to ditch Lilly's truck," Dolph said. "They've got a BOLO on it now."

Kate was surprised he could make out the rumblings coming from the police band radio.

"We're walking away from it now," Skip said. "The detectives' guns are under the seat. I called Rose to pick us up."

"What'd Judith say, son? Why are you a prime suspect again?"

"They've got another wit who's saying I was in that alley with Jamal at one o'clock, in the middle of the TOD window."

Dolph muttered a curse under his breath. "I've got a meeting with her in an hour. I'll see what I can do to keep her off our tail."

"Be careful. You can't afford to be in a cage either."

"It's gonna be a bit crowded in Rose's car but I need you all to take my passengers from me before I go meet her."

"Take them to the other safe house for the time being. We'll all meet back at the shack later. I'd just as soon get out of town now. They may put a BOLO on Rose's car too."

"Good point," Dolph said.

"I love you, Skip," Kate said.

"Love you too, darlin'. Try not to worry."

She snorted as she disconnected. "Yeah, right."

~~~~~~~~

Dolph dropped Rob off behind the new safe house in Catonsville, so he could go through the backyard and wait for Kate to let him in once she'd fetched the key. Best not to let the neighbors see a whole slew of people coming and going, Dolph had pointed out.

It took some effort for Rob to hoist his bulk over the four-foot wooden fence around the yard. He was dropping to the ground on the other side when the back door of the house opened. Kate waved him inside.

Rob sat down at an oval table that divided the house's kitchen from an adjacent family room. Kate was pacing back and forth between the two rooms.

He took a moment to catch his breath, then he pulled out the phone he'd been using for the daily calls to his five colleagues holding the insurance policy packets.

Kate came over and sat across from him as he was completing the fourth call. "Are you sure we should be keeping the ambassador's secret at this point?" he asked her.

"No, I'm not. But I'm also not sure this would all end if we blew the whistle on him. Delgado doesn't seem to be willing to leave even the slightest loose thread dangling."

"Good point," Rob said.

"I sure hope the Secret Service got our messages and they catch up with these thugs soon," Kate said. "I'm not sure how much more of this I can take."

Rob searched his brain for something to say to reassure her, but he came up empty.

He punched a speed-dial number on the phone, then repeated the same message for the fifth time. "It's Rob Franklin checking in. Please hold the package for another day. Thank you."

At least if we all get killed, these guys will tell the police who's responsible. Then for the first time in his legal career, Rob realized how unimportant justice is to the victim. *We'll all still be dead.*

~~~~~~~~

"I owe you big time, Lilly," Skip said. They were in Rose's car on Route 50 going through Annapolis, a mile or so from the Bay Bridge. "I'll find a way to get you out of any charges."

"We'll deal with that later," Lilly said. "The bottom line is you can't be in a cage. That's life or death. Everything else pales by comparison."

A phone rang in Skip's pants pocket. He shifted in his seat to get it out. It was the number he'd given to Sid Pierce.

"Yeah, Sid."

"I'm out walking and a couple *Hiss*-panics just drove by. Stopped and asked me if this here was the road to Middletown, Delaware. I pointed them toward the turn off, real neighborly-like. But they drove on past it."

"Thanks, Sid. Get inside and lock your doors."

"Doin' that as we speak."

Skip punched in Manny's number. The signal was intermittent.

"That...Skip...s happen..."

"Get out now! Can you hear me? Go!"

"Got...call you when...clear."

Skip disconnected and started praying.

~~~~~~~~

The guards burst into the cabin, startling Sue who was watching a talk show on the small TV. "You two take Skip's SUV." Manny tossed the keys to Claude. "There's a track through the woods that comes out further down in the field. I'll try to draw them off, then meet you in town by the Acme. If I'm not there five minutes after you get there, leave without me."

Manny waited until Claude had turned Skip's truck off into the woods. Then he jumped into Dolph's car and raced toward the paved road. Halfway there, he hit the brake as a dark sedan turned into the lane.

Veering off into the cornfield in the opposite direction from the way Claude and Sue had gone, Manny prayed that the car could handle the rough terrain.

He risked a quick glance in the mirror. The sedan was still moving down the lane. Then they must have seen him. The car turned into the field.

"Good," Manny muttered as he floored it. The car bounced across rows of corn stubble, fish-tailing occasionally on muddy patches. He looked in the mirror again. The sedan was gaining on him.

The cornfield ended at a paved side street. As Manny drew nearer he realized there was a large ditch between the field and the road. It was half full from last night's rain. He slowed, allowing the sedan to get closer. Then he raced toward the ditch. At the last second he swung to his right, his back wheel coming within inches of the slippery edge. He wrestled with the steering wheel to get the car headed straight again, along the edge of the field.

As Manny had hoped, the driver of the other car had been too focused on watching him to notice the terrain ahead. He didn't start to turn soon enough. Manny watched in his mirror as the sedan's front end swung around, and the driver's side of the car slid over the edge and down into the ditch. The engine roared. Spinning wheels threw mud and slimy water into the air.

Grinning, Manny drove as fast as he dared around the perimeter of the field. At the entrance to the dirt lane, he swung left and then out onto the main road.

He glanced in the mirror. Two dark-haired men in suits ran into the street a hundred yards back. Manny laughed out loud and hit the gas pedal.

He called Claude and then Skip. "Everybody's out and away clean," he reported to his boss.

"You need to ditch my truck. There's a BOLO on it again."

"We'll leave it at that shopping center in Chestertown." Manny disconnected, then smacked the heel of his hand against the steering wheel. Damn, this job could be exhilarating at times.

~~~~~~~~~

Skip's call caught Dolph as he was climbing out of his car in front of the police station. The younger man filled him in on the latest development on the Eastern Shore, reassuring him that Sue was safe.

"You all get to the new safe house now," Dolph said. "I'll pick up some groceries after I meet with Judith."

"At least we'll have real beds to sleep in tonight," Skip said, then disconnected.

After they were settled in the interrogation room Dolph had insisted on–one he knew was sound-proof with no one-way mirror–he asked his former partner to swear there was no recording device in the room or on her person.

"Oh come on, Dolph. You're acting like we're in some grade-B spy movie," Judith snapped at him.

"That's actually pretty close to the mark. Skip and his wife have gotten themselves into something, through no fault of their own. They have some information about an ambassador of a third world country, information that no one's supposed to know. Someone's been trying to kill them, and anyone else they might've told. That's why Skip can't risk being in a jail cell, even for a few hours. They killed that boy, Jamal, and set him up for it."

"Who the hell are 'they,' Dolph?"

"I wish we knew. It's more than a little complicated. But things are in the works to stop whoever's doing this. If you'll back off from chasing Skip, we'll hand you a solve in the boy's murder."

"You've got to be kidding. The man held a gun on me, resisted arrest–"

"Now did you actually tell him he was under arrest?"

"We hadn't quite gotten that far when he pulled his gun, but–"

"Did you actually see his gun?"

"He said he had it aimed at me under the table."

Dolph just looked at her for a beat. "You really can't make those charges stick."

"I bet I could. And what about that gal, who mysteriously showed up and held a gun on my partner?"

"Now I didn't hear about that. What gal?"

"Oh cut the crap, Dolph. You're in this up to your ears. I know damn well you came in to case the place. You sicced the girl on Dan."

Dolph decided it was time to change tactics. "Let me ask you a question. Would your two witnesses, by any chance, be Hispanic?"

Judith stared at him, eyes narrowed. "And what if they are?"

"And they gave you names and addresses?"

"Of course."

"Have you checked them out?"

"I called them both back to verify their stories."

"Did you check out their addresses?"

Judith stared at him again. "Not yet," she finally answered. "I've been busy chasing Canfield."

"Check 'em out. I'll be real shocked if they're legit." Dolph stood up. "These guys aren't interested in seeing Skip convicted. They just want him temporarily where they can take him out and make it look like a jailhouse killing." He turned toward the door.

"Now wait just a damned minute, Dolph." Judith jumped to her feet. "You can't waltz in here and tell me you know something about my case, and then get up and leave. Who's behind all this?"

Dolph turned back toward her. "I can't tell you yet. And I'd advise against you trying to figure it out." There was a hard edge to his voice now. "These guys are ruthless, and they don't give a shit about that gold badge you carry. They'll kill you if they think you know too much, and make it look like an accident or a mugging. Anything that'll keep it from being investigated."

"Are you trying to tell me they're more powerful than the police?" Judith said.

"That's exactly what I'm telling you. Check out your witnesses. They'll be bogus. Then back off and wait for me to get back to you. I don't want you hurt, Judith."

Dolph turned and left the room.

~~~~~~~~

Rose dropped Lilly and Skip one block over from the new safe house. They had decided it best that she park several blocks away, just in case there was a BOLO on her car now.

When Kate let them in the back door, the look on her face tore at Skip's heart. It was a mix of anger, fear and relief. She opened her mouth but he gathered her to him before she could say anything. "It's alright, darlin'. Everybody's safe."

With her face pressed against his Kevlar-covered chest, her voice was muffled. "You told me she wouldn't try to arrest you."

"I didn't know these assholes were going to produce another bogus witness."

He held her until he felt the tension start to ease out of her body. Then he stepped back to shrug out of his jacket.

He had just finished filling Kate and Rob in on what had happened on the Eastern Shore when Rose arrived. Lilly let her in.

"We're running out of vehicles," Rose said as she stepped through the door.

"We can get my car, or Liz's," Rob said. "They're at Kate's house."

"Liz's. It blends in better." Rose glanced at her watch. "We'll wait 'til tomorrow. Let the dust settle some."

Skip had shed the Kevlar vest. His shirt was plastered to his body with sweat. "I'd forgotten how damned uncomfortable those things are." He held the wet shirt away from his skin and waved his other hand in front of his nose. "And our spare clothes are on the Eastern Shore."

"Ah but we've got a washing machine and dryer here," Kate said. "I'll wash your shirt while you take a shower."

"Shower? As in hot water and real walls around you?" Skip asked, exaggerated wonder in his voice.

Kate chuckled and led the way down the hall to the bedrooms. "Come on. I'll show you the way to Nirvana."

In the master bedroom, Skip laid his gun on the nightstand.

He unbuckled his belt and stripped off the offending shirt. Kate walked over and wrapped her arms around him, snuggling her cheek against his bare chest. He left the belt dangling and drew her tight against him, burying his face in her hair.

Suddenly he was overwhelmed with the need to make love to her. Every moment seemed so precious. "You think anyone would notice if we didn't surface for a while?"

Kate's breath tickled his skin as she answered, "They'll notice but they won't mind."

He closed his eyes, letting the warmth of her body soak into his own. He felt his muscles begin to relax. "I'm not too smelly?"

"Never."

His hand moved to lift her chin so he could claim her mouth. Her lips parted, inviting him in. By the time they surfaced for air, he'd removed her blouse and she'd unzipped his jeans. He picked her up and gently deposited her on the bed. Her slacks joined his jeans on the floor.

He stretched out beside her, head propped up on one elbow, and drank in the sight of her. Kate snuggled up against him and put her hand on his cheek. "I love you," she whispered.

Skip started to reply but the words caught in his throat. It scared him witless that one or the other of them might not live through another day. He struggled to push aside the fear, to concentrate on loving her.

Starting at her neck, he kissed and nibbled his way south, relishing the little gasps and moans. Hands fisted in his hair, she arched her back. He rose over her, staring into her eyes, turned dark indigo with passion. Dropping onto his elbows, he kissed her again, swallowing her moan as he entered her.

He felt the familiar and almost unbearably intense sensation of melting into her body. A small corner of his mind realized that parts of himself that had been dark and cold for several days were now filling with a sweet warmth.

The fear dissipated, replaced by a fierce determination to savor every moment they had left, whether it was another hour or several decades. Inherent in an experience as wonderful as the love he and Kate shared was the painful reality that someday it would come to an end. One could succumb to the pain in advance by worrying about that reality. Or one could glory in the joy of the moment.

He experienced all this in a matter of seconds, less as conscious thought than as a visceral feeling that something profound had shifted in his world, in his being.

He lowered his lips to hers again as they moved together, waves of pure pleasure breaking over them. When the sensations mellowed out into a warm glow, he rolled over on his side and gathered her up in his arms.

She tucked her head under his chin. He stroked her curls for a few minutes.

"You know that Serenity Prayer my daddy used to recite?" he whispered. Her head nodded against his chest. "I think I'm gonna rephrase it. Control what you can, accept what you can't, and enjoy the hell outta life in the meantime."

She pulled back slightly so she could look up at him. "Amen." She smiled, then snuggled against him again.

He tightened his arms around her. Silently he prayed that God would either protect them or allow them to die together.

A profound sense of peace enveloped him. He suspected that was God's answer.

CHAPTER TWENTY-FOUR

Despite being on guard duty half the night, Lilly and Rose were both up by six. Rose got the coffee maker going while Lilly located mugs and spoons. Rob came out of one of the bedrooms, his nose high in the air, sniffing. Rose flashed him a grin and pointed toward the now-full pot.

They sat down at the table with their coffee. Lilly took a sip and groaned in pleasure.

Rob chuckled. "Beats the hell out of that instant swill we had at the cabin, doesn't it?" He breathed in the fragrant steam from his own cup.

"You rested enough to take Rob to get his wife's car?" Rose asked Lilly.

"Sure."

Rose took a healthy swig from her mug, then got up to make breakfast for them. By the time the others surfaced, Lilly and Rob were in Sue's car, headed to Kate and Skip's house where Liz's Camry had been sitting for the past few days.

Rob was wishing he'd brought a second cup of coffee with him. He had a niggling feeling that he'd forgotten something, but his brain wasn't awake enough to figure out what. Suddenly it dawned on him. He checked his pants' pockets. Sure enough he'd left his disposable phones back at the house.

He patted his jacket pockets. Wait, he had one after all.

He took it out and held it up. "Were you given any of these?"

Lilly glanced over. "Yeah. I've only got a couple left."

"Let me have one."

She took one hand off the wheel to fish a phone out of the front pocket of her jeans.

It took Rob a few minutes of playing with the phones to figure out how to program speed-dial numbers into them. He handed hers back to her. "Mine's now number one on your phone and vice versa. We're getting low on these though. So we should avoid calling each other unless we have to."

Lilly nodded. "You drive your wife's car around Towson for a while. I'll follow you. When I'm sure nobody's tailing us, I'll flash my lights instead of calling. If you see me turn off, I've spotted a tail and I'm trying to draw him off of you. That's when I might have to call you, once I've dumped the tail."

"Sounds like a plan." Rob slipped his own phone back into his jacket pocket.

Once again nobody seemed to be watching the house. Lilly went over Liz's car with Dolph's debugging device. When she pronounced it clean, Rob climbed in.

They had only gone a few blocks when he glanced up in his rearview mirror. Lilly was turning right. The car following her also turned right.

Rob drove on down York Road in the beginnings of rush-hour traffic. Three blocks later, he realized the black Taurus behind him looked disturbingly familiar.

~~~~~~~~

Skip had just donned his freshly laundered shirt and walked into the living room when Rose yelled, "Lilly's lost Rob."

Dolph jumped up from the table where he'd been surfing the web on his laptop. "My car." He bolted for the kitchen door.

"How'd she lose him?" Skip called back over his shoulder as they raced across the backyard.

"She drew off a tail. His phone must've fallen out of his pocket. She tried to call him. It rang from the floor of her car."

Skip glanced back at Rose, and then skidded to a stop. Kate was bringing up the rear. "You need to–"

Kate cut him off. "I've got Liz's car phone number."

Skip grabbed her hand. They ran for Dolph's car the next

block over.

Kate and Rose scrambled into the back as Skip jumped into the passenger seat. Dolph started the engine and took off.

Kate turned on her regular phone just long enough to retrieve Liz's car phone number. She punched it into a throwaway cell and put it on speaker.

It rang once, then they heard Rob's scared voice. "Hello?"

"Where are you?" Dolph yelled.

"Not sure exactly. A few blocks from York Road. I've got a tail. I've been trying to lose him."

Kate held the phone out between the front seats so they could all hear better.

"Get back to York Road as soon as you safely can," Skip said. "The car following you, what's it look like?"

"Black Taurus. I think it's the one that was outside my building yesterday."

"Do you know where the sixth precinct police station is?"

"Yeah."

"Head in that direction as soon as you can."

Skip pulled out one of his own throwaways. "What's Judith's cell number?" He punched in the number Dolph rattled off.

"Ander–"

"This is Skip Canfield. Rob Franklin's in danger. He and his bodyguard got separated. He's being followed by some of the bad–"

"Where are you, Canfield? You need to turn yourself in."

"Damn it, Judith! Listen! If these guys get their hands on Rob not only will he die but five other people will be in serious danger. He's headed toward the police station in a dark blue Camry. Car following him is a black Taurus. If you catch the driver of that car, he might lead us to who's trying to kill us."

Dolph had turned onto the Baltimore Beltway. He laid on his horn as he wove in and out of the heavy morning traffic.

"I shouldn't have sent him. I should've gone," Rose muttered from the backseat as she punched in Lilly's number on her phone.

"I'm on York Road again." Rob's voice was a little steadier. "About five blocks from Bosley Avenue."

"North on York," Rose barked into her phone. "Five blocks from Bosley."

Skip repeated Rob's location to Judith, then said, "Damn, I think my battery's dying." He turned his phone off so it couldn't be traced.

He reached back and gave Kate's shoulder a squeeze. Her knuckles were white where she was gripping her phone.

Rose was still muttering to herself. Her eyes were wide, her face pale. Skip had never seen her quite so scared.

"I think I see Lilly coming up behind the Taurus," Rob's voice came from the phone.

"Does the guy know you've spotted him?" Skip asked.

"Not sure. I'm turning onto Bosley now."

Dolph veered off the Beltway onto the Towson exit, then pulled over to the shoulder and slammed on the brakes. "Out, Skip."

He jumped out. Dolph took off. Skip watched as the car careened around the corner at the end of the ramp, just seconds before the light turned red.

~~~~~~~~~

With a heavy hand on the horn, Dolph plowed a path through Towson's rush-hour traffic. As he approached the police station on Susquehanna Avenue, they saw chaos up ahead. The Camry was sitting in the middle of the road. Cars coming the opposite way were forced to creep around the driver's door hanging open into their lane. The Taurus was effectively blocked in, but so was Lilly, in Sue's car behind it.

Two uniformed officers approached the Taurus. One rapped on the passenger's window, one hand on his gun butt. The second officer headed around the back of the car to the driver's side.

The passenger door flew open. A dark blur took off down the sidewalk, the uniform right behind. Lilly jumped out and bolted after them.

An impatient driver inched forward in the opposite lane. His bumper nudged the Camry's door shut. The driver accelerated.

The instant he was past, the Taurus cut over into that lane.

The officer approaching the driver's door jumped back to avoid being run over. The Taurus veered around the Camry and took off.

The occupants of Dolph's car piled out. They ran for the police station.

Rob was standing just inside the doors. Judith Anderson stood next to him.

Kate threw her arms around him. The next moment, he was dragging her out of the way when Lilly and a uniformed officer pushed through the doors, a struggling Hispanic man between them.

Judith nodded to the uniform. He yanked hard on his prisoner's arm. The man settled down and allowed himself to be led away.

Judith stepped over to Lilly and slapped handcuffs on one of her wrists. "Lilly Pendleton, you're under arrest for assaulting a police officer with a deadly weapon." She started reciting the Miranda warning as she cuffed the other wrist.

"Somebody got a phone?" Rob asked. Kate handed him the one still in her hand.

"Don't say anything until Maribeth Benson shows up," Rob told Lilly as he punched in his office number. "She'll try to get you out on bail today."

Dolph grabbed Judith's arm. "Don't put her in a cell unless you want her death on your conscience. These guys chasing Rob tends to prove my story, don't you think?"

Judith pulled her arm loose. "Get away from me, Dolph, before I arrest the lot of you for obstruction of justice."

"I mean it, Judith. Don't let *anybody* get near her."

She shoved him aside and started to lead her prisoner away.

"I'm sorry I screwed up," Lilly said over her shoulder, a stricken look on her face. "I–"

Judith pushed her through the door into the back of the station.

~~~~~~~~

One of Skip's two remaining phones rang.

"Where are you?" Rose said.

"Parking lot behind the Lexus dealer. Is Rob okay?"

"Yeah. Be there in ten."

Skip stared at the phone for a beat after disconnecting. That was cryptic, even for Rose.

When she arrived in Sue's car, Skip said, "Move over, partner. Lemme drive."

Rose looked resistant for a moment, but then got out without saying anything and walked around the car.

Skip settled into the driver's seat, shoving it as far back as it would go. "They catch the guys in the Taurus?"

"One of them. Driver got away. Anderson arrested Lilly."

"Shit."

"Rob's got somebody arranging bail."

Skip gripped the steering wheel. *Have to figure out a way to make things right for her when this is over.*

He glanced over at Rose. She was staring morosely out the window.

Great! My operative's locked up because of me and my partner's doubting herself.

They were halfway back to Catonsville before Rose spoke again. "I shouldn't have sent him."

Thank you Lord, she's gonna talk about it!

Hiding his relief, he shrugged. "Natural thing to do since it was his wife's car."

"You know damn well I shouldn't have sent him. I should've gone myself."

"Hindsight's twenty-twenty. Besides, the general doesn't leave the command center to run an errand."

Rose shot him a startled look. "The general?"

Skip grinned. His eyes on the road, he said, "Don't let it go to your head. But yeah, in this situation, you're the natural one to lead us. And you're doing a great job, by the way."

Rose stared out her window again. "I should've sent Claude or Manny."

"Shoulda, woulda, coulda. Damn it, Rose, will you stop with the guilt. I feel guilty. Kate feels guilty. Lilly feels guilty. We're fuckin' drowning in guilt here."

Rose turned and stared at him for a beat. Then she flashed

a quick grin. "You left Dolph out. I think he's feeling guilty for scaring the crap outta Sue."

Skip threw his head back and laughed.

CHAPTER TWENTY-FIVE

When Kate let Skip and Rose in the back door of the Catonsville safe house, Dolph was sitting at the table, checking news sites on his laptop.

Kate was holding a steaming mug. "Sue found some herbal tea in a cabinet. Thought it might settle our nerves. You want some?"

Rose shuddered.

Dolph snickered and returned his attention to the online version of the *Washington Post*. He was ignoring the cup sitting at his elbow. A small headline caught his eye. He sat up straighter. "Whoa, Nellie, what have we here? Short article in the *Post*. The president of Colombia has postponed his state visit, citing poor health."

"Yeah, wouldn't exactly be good for his health to get assassinated," Kate said.

Dolph read the article out loud. It didn't give many details.

"So we can assume the feds stopped the assassination plot," Skip said. "How do we find out if Delgado's been neutralized? That's not likely to make it into the news."

"I think it's time to call the FBI," Rob said. "I need another phone."

Kate dug around in the bottom of her purse. She finally came up with one and handed it to him. He went into the living room to make the call.

"I want to call Judith," Dolph said. "See if she got anything out of her prisoner."

Rose frowned. "We're getting really low on phones, but,

yeah, do it."

When his former partner answered, Dolph said, "I know I'm not your favorite person right now, but I'd appreciate it if you'd tell me what your prisoner had to say."

Judith sighed heavily into the phone. "He didn't say anything. Made his phone call. Lawyer showed up claiming the guy has diplomatic immunity. Checked it out with the State Department. Had to let him go."

"Shit!"

"My sentiments exactly."

"Lemme guess. Colombian embassy."

After a long pause, Judith said, "Yeah."

"So you believe me now?"

Another sigh. "I believe these people are after you all. Doesn't get Canfield off the hook though, especially since there are additional charges."

Dolph reined in his temper. "Your witnesses who claimed they saw Skip with Jamal, did they check out?"

Another long pause, then, "One apparently lives in the administration offices of a shopping center, the other on a vacant lot."

"Without those wits, you don't have much of a case. How about you drop the charges?"

"How about you bring your boy in?" Judith asked in a tired voice.

"No can do. Not until we know it's safe." Dolph disconnected, then dropped the phone to the floor and smashed it with his heel.

Rob came back into the kitchen to share the results of his own call. "Took awhile to get through to somebody on the case. Finally talked to Special Agent Timothy Billings, who of course wanted me to come in and meet with him, tell him where I was, et cetera. I interrupted and asked if Delgado had been arrested or otherwise neutralized as a threat to myself, my friends and family." Rob paused for breath. "Delgado's on the run. They don't know if he's back in Colombia or still in the States but both countries' law enforcement agencies are looking for him."

"So is it safe for us to go home or not?" Sue asked.

"I asked the agent that. He said, 'Maybe, maybe not.'"

Kate threw her hands in the air. "That's a big help."

"They're not sure they've rooted out all of Delgado's contacts and sympathizers from the embassy staff."

"But if the feds and the Colombian government are on to him," Dolph said. "Then we're no longer a threat. We don't know any more than is already common knowledge."

"Except maybe the ambassador's secret," Kate said. "Did this FBI agent indicate they knew who Garcia really is?"

Rob shook his head. "I think Garcia's still in good standing with his government and ours. They're letting him take credit for foiling the assassination attempt."

"When did Delgado take off?" Skip asked.

"Sometime yesterday."

"So why were these dudes following you this morning?"

"I posed that question to the agent," Rob said. "He didn't have a good answer. Said he'd check into it. I'm supposed to call him back tomorrow."

"That call needs to be from a location far away from here," Dolph said. "At this point, I'm not sure I even trust the FBI."

"How about Towson? I have to appear in court to ask for that continuance."

Several heads were shaking. "Too dangerous," Rose said. "They can find out from the court docket that you'll be there."

"One isn't allowed to phone it in," Rob said.

"Twice now they've double-teamed to try to get you," Skip said, "when they're obviously shorthanded. These guys want you bad and if they get their hands on you, they'll torture you to get the names of the people you sent the packets to."

Rob blanched. "I'll get an associate to request the continuance."

Kate too had paled. "That damned insurance policy has backfired on us."

Dolph was scratching his head. "This makes no sense. If Delgado's plot has been exposed than why the hell would anybody still be after us?"

"Maybe he didn't bother to tell his flunkies 'never mind'

before he took off," Rose said.

Skip turned to Kate. "We're going to have to tell the ambassador's secret. We're never going to be safe until it's out."

Before Kate could answer, Dolph jumped in. "That may stop the danger, but it doesn't clear you of that boy's murder." He'd promised Judith a solve. If they couldn't produce another solid suspect, what would she do?

"Are we safe for today?" Kate asked.

"As safe as we can get," Rose said.

"Then let's see what this FBI agent tells us tomorrow."

"And if it's not good news?" Skip asked.

Kate took a deep breath. "Then we tell the ambassador's secret. This has got to end."

Let's hope it doesn't end with Skip on trial for murder. Dolph opted not to voice that thought.

~~~~~~~~~

The next morning, Rob walked into the kitchen, drawn by the fragrance of freshly-brewed coffee. He'd already had his normal quota, but he was bored and restless after twenty-four hours cooped up in this house. And he hadn't slept well last night.

I miss you, Lizzie!

A phone rang in his pocket. His stomach clenched when he read the caller ID–*Maribeth Benson*–even though he'd been waiting for her call.

"I've got two messages for you," Maribeth said without preamble. "One is from Judge Crawford. She wants to see documentation of your illness when you appear before her next month."

"She wants a doctor's note? What is this, high school?"

"She was not happy. She expressed... *skepticism* might be the best word, when I couldn't tell her the nature of your illness."

"Okay. I'll deal with that when the time comes," Rob said. "What's the other message?"

"I have in my hand an envelope, fancy stationery, handed to me by a guy in the courtroom as I was packing up my papers to leave."

"Lemme guess. Guy was Hispanic. Envelope's addressed to me."

The others, scattered around the family room and kitchen, suddenly sat up straighter. All eyes were on him, listening to his end of the conversation.

"Right on both counts," Maribeth said. "Do you want me to open it and read it to you?"

Rob debated for a second. He suspected the sender had been circumspect about what he'd committed to paper. "Yes."

He heard paper rustling. "It says, 'Dear Friend, I will be departing for an extended trip within the next forty-eight hours. Shortly thereafter, you will receive an indication that concerns for your safety and that of our mutual friends can be put to rest. I deeply regret the disruption to your lives caused by recent events.' It's signed 'Your Concerned Friend.'"

Rob grabbed a notepad and pen from the kitchen counter. "Read it to me again, please." He wrote down the exact words, repeating them out loud for the benefit of the others. After thanking Maribeth, he reluctantly dropped the phone to the floor and stepped on it.

Rob looked at Rose and Skip. "Now what?"

"We need to call Mac," Rose said. "Get his input."

~~~~~~~~

Kate's head was spinning as Rose placed the call and filled Mac in. Could it be as simple as the ambassador saying all clear, and they could go home? Then the "forty-eight hour" part sunk in.

After Rob had read the words of the note to Mac, Skip said, "What do you think this means. And what, if anything, should we do about it?"

"Lemme think about that for a minute," Mac said. "Meantime, two small fry want to talk to their mama and daddy."

Silence for a beat, then a tentative "Mommy?"

Kate's chest ached at the sound of her daughter's voice. "Hi, sweetie. Are you having fun with Aunt Liz and Uncle Rob's mom?"

"Yeah... She said to call her Grandma Franklin. Is that okay?"

"Of course. Are you and Billy being good?"

"Yeah. Is Daddy there?"

"Right here, Pumkin."

"When are you coming to get us?" Edie's voice was plaintive.

Skip's Adam's apple bobbed. "Soon, Pumkin. Real soon."

Kate swallowed hard herself.

Billy's voice was clamoring in the background, "Lemme talk to 'em."

"We love you, Sweetie. Put your brother on, okay." She figured the little boy would have a meltdown otherwise.

"Love you too, Mommy."

Edie's voice was replaced by Billy's. "Mommy, you gotta see Grandma Franklin's house. She says it was built before she was born, and she's really old."

The group around the table stifled snickers. Kate said, "Billy, it's not nice to point out how old someone is."

"Why not? You tell people all the time that I'm four."

Kate smiled at the phone. "True, but once people get to be adults they don't like to be reminded of their age."

"So why is Grandma Franklin's house so interesting?" Skip asked.

"It's got torrents, Daddy!"

Rob chuckled. "Do you mean turrets, Billy?"

"Yeah. Like towers on a castle. And the rooms inside of 'em are round. No corners. They're awesome!"

"Yes, they are awesome," Rob said. "One of those rooms was my bedroom when I was just a little older than you are."

"Really? You think Grandma Franklin'd let me sleep in there?"

"That's up to her and Uncle Mac," Kate said. "You behave now and do what they tell you, okay?"

"Say goodbye, Billy. I gotta talk to your folks again," Mac said in the background, his voice a lot gentler than his usual growl.

"Bye, Uncle Rob. Bye, Daddy and Mommy."

"Goodbye, Billy," the group chorused.

Mac came back on the line. "Ambassador's leaving the country. The question is whether he's gonna spill his little secret so you're no longer at risk."

"I would assume that's what he means," Rob said.

"Maybe," Mac said. "Or maybe he's assuming once he's gone nobody'll care anymore that you know his secret."

"'Cause he's assuming that when he's no longer the ambassador he's of no use to Delgado's crowd," Rose said.

"They may even want the secret to come out," Skip said, "to convince *el Presidente* he needs to be harder on the rebels, that even his own administration has been infiltrated by them."

"Or to just plain discredit the current administration," Rose said.

"That's a helluva lot of assumptions," Mac growled from the phone.

"I agree," Dolph said. "And I don't like assumptions any better than coincidences."

"Can we stay safe for another forty-eight hours?" Kate asked.

"Should be able to," Rose said. "But if he's the one behind all this, we're letting a murderer get away."

"I don't think he is... a murderer, I mean." Kate paused, trying to put words to what her gut was telling her. "If the assassination plot's been stopped without his secret coming out, then why leave the country? I think he's trying to get us out of this mess."

Mac snorted. "Or he's just plain savin' his own hide. Figures it'll come out eventually, like when Delgado's caught."

"Or," Skip said, "he's trying to keep us quiet long enough to track us down."

Kate raised her hand in a stop gesture. "I'm not condemning the man to death. We've kept his secret this long and we're safe here." She heard the sharpness in her voice and paused to take a breath. "We tell his secret once he's gone."

After a beat of silence, Dolph said, "Still doesn't solve the problem of the charges against Skip."

"Yeah, but it'll be safe then for me to turn myself in and try to make amends to Judith."

"Who do we tell? Agent Billings?" Rob asked.

"FBI's not gonna announce it to the world," Mac said from the phone. "It needs to be public knowledge for you all to be safe."

"Ask Judith to call a press conference?" Kate said.

Dolph shook his head. "She can't talk to the media without her lieutenant's permission. He's gonna go up the chain of command. The police chief makes a call to the State Department, and they hush it up."

"Damn!" Skip said. "Here we've been focused all along on should we or shouldn't we tell the secret. Now we can't figure out who the hell to tell it *to*."

"How about this," Rob said, "we tell everybody, all at once. We send out an e-mail to the *Washington Post*, the *Baltimore Sun*, the major networks, the CIA, the FBI, Judith, the President of the United States, our Congressional representatives. Anybody and everybody who might care."

"Oughta work," Mac said.

"I'll start getting together a list of e-mail addresses," Dolph said.

"Uh, Mac, can I talk to Liz for a minute?" Rob asked.

"Yeah. Lemme go relieve her of small fry duty."

Rose picked up the cell and hit the button to take it out of speaker mode, then handed it to Rob. He took it gratefully and headed for the privacy of a bedroom.

It suddenly dawned on Kate that this was Wednesday, and she had a problem. She'd scheduled her depressed client for a session the next day, hoping at the time that this whole mess would be resolved by then.

She told the others she needed to go to her office the next morning. Skip was shaking his head before she'd even finished her sentence. "No way, darlin'. It's too dangerous at this point to go anywhere near the house or either of our offices."

Kate hesitated. She couldn't just not show up. The woman would be devastated if she thought her therapist had abandoned her. "I at least need to call my clients."

"I should check our messages at the agency," Rose said. "And Rob needs to call that FBI agent. I'm thinking the three of us go someplace random, a good ways from here. We need to get more phones, too."

Skip still didn't look happy. "What vehicle you going to take? The driver of that Taurus got a real good look at Liz's car yesterday. And they know your car for sure. Plus the cops may stop you if you take it."

"I've got an idea," Dolph said. "We could trade license plates with a neighbor's car. People don't look at their own plates. It'd be days, maybe weeks before the switch would be noticed."

Rose flashed him a quick smile. "Good thinking. My car and Liz's. Do it."

Dolph headed for the door to the garage to find a screwdriver.

"Just don't get caught," Skip called after him.

"Oh, goody, now we can add theft to our list of crimes," Kate muttered under her breath.

~~~~~~~

As Rose followed Rob and Manny, in Liz's car, around the beltway, she occupied her mind by making a mental list of the vehicles they'd need to retrieve when this was all over. Skip's Expedition was still on the Eastern Shore. Lilly's truck had been abandoned on a side street in Towson. Kate's crumpled car was at Janice's building, if it hadn't been towed by now. Was that all of them? Where the hell had they left Claude's car?

She was trying to distract herself from thinking about Skip and the Randolphs back at the house with just one guard. She'd considered calling in more of the agency's people but had decided against it. Most of their guys were ex-cops who still monitored the police radio frequency. They would have heard the BOLO on their boss by now. She didn't want to risk one of them turning Skip in if they knew where he was.

Manny took the Pikesville exit. Rose followed him into the first shopping center parking lot they came to. They'd brought both cars so Kate and Rob could make their calls in private but at the same time. She didn't want to be away from the safe house any longer than necessary.

Rose got out and walked over to where Manny was standing next to Liz's car. Rob was in the passenger's seat on the phone. "Keep a sharp eye out," she told Manny. She knew the instruction was unnecessary but it made her feel better to say it out loud.

Rob lowered his window. "Billings gave me some mumbo jumbo but basically he doesn't know any more than he did yesterday. I need to call my five guys."

"Give me the phone you used to call the FBI," Rose said. "I might as well use it to check messages, before we destroy it."

It took a few minutes for Rose to work her way through the backlog on the agency's voicemail. As she listened to the last message, she sucked in her breath. *Damn it!* She called another number. No answer.

She motioned Manny over. "I need you to check on something for me." By the time she'd given him his instructions, the others had finished their calls.

Rose walked back to her car. "Rob's riding with us," she told Kate. "Manny's running an errand for me. Everything okay with your client?"

"Yeah. She's feeling better. I've arranged for her to call a colleague if she starts feeling shaky again. She's the only one in crisis at the moment so I'm not going to call the others. They'll just be confused and annoyed when they show up and find my office locked."

"Good. The fewer calls, the better," Rose said. "There's a Best Buy up the road where we can get phones."

They had completed that errand and were almost back to the safe house when Manny called her. "She's not home. Her neighbor said she took her to get her truck last night. Wall's thin between their apartments. Old lady says she can usually hear Lilly moving around in there. She doesn't think she's been home today at all."

Rose resisted the urge to bang her head against the steering wheel. "Thanks. Come on back." She debated about telling Kate and Rob what was going on, but decided to wait. She really didn't want to explain the sorry mess twice.

At the house, she waited until Rob had given his brief report on his call to the FBI.

Then she told them. "We've got a new development. Lilly left a message at the agency last night. Said she knew she'd screwed up and would have to regain our trust, so she was going to, quote, 'make the problem go away, once and for all.'"

"Not good," Dolph muttered.

Rose repeated what Manny had found out from the neighbor.

"What the hell does she think she's doing?" Skip said.

Rose shrugged. "I don't know but she's likely to get herself killed. If we aren't able to reach her by tomorrow morning, Dolph and I'll go look for her."

"Where will you look?" Skip asked.

"That's the part I haven't figured out yet."

CHAPTER TWENTY-SIX

Dolph and Rose set out early the next morning. Once they were far enough away from the safe house, Rose called Lilly's apartment, hoping to hear a groggy voice cussing her out for calling so early.

That didn't happen. After five rings, it went to voicemail. No answer on her cell phone either.

Twenty minutes later, they were banging on her door. A plump, gray-haired woman stuck her head out of the apartment next door. "She never came home last night."

"Are you sure, ma'am?" Rose asked.

"Most definitely. I don't sleep much these days, and when I do, I don't sleep sound. I'd have heard her if she'd come in."

Rose walked over to the woman and offered her hand. "Rose Hernandez. Lilly works for me and my partner. This is Dolph Randolph, our associate."

"Your partner the big buff guy Lilly talks about?"

"Yes, ma'am. Would you happen to have a key to her apartment?"

The older woman looked Rose up and down, then gave Dolph the same perusal. "I can let you in, but I go with you."

Rose hesitated before nodding. She hoped the woman wouldn't end up seeing her neighbor's dead body.

But the small apartment was empty. It had the feeling places get when no one's been around to stir the air for a while. A quick search turned up no clue as to where Lilly might be.

They thanked the woman and Rose gave her a card with a throwaway cell number written on it. "Please don't give that number to anyone else, but if you see or hear from Lilly, call me."

"Guess we're driving to Washington?" Dolph said when they were out on the sidewalk in front of the building.

"Yeah," Rose said through clenched teeth. She wasn't sure which was stronger, her anxiety that one of her people might be in trouble or her fury at the damned woman for making a messy situation a whole lot more complicated.

Unable to think of any better approach, they walked up to the gate of the Colombian embassy and rang the bell. A torrent of Spanish interspersed with static spewed from the speaker next to the button.

Rose asked to see the ambassador. She was told that this was not possible without an appointment. The disembodied voice asked for her name.

"Maybe not," Rose muttered under her breath. No way was she going to identify herself and then wait patiently for the killer to come and get them. She asked instead that the ambassador be informed that she had an important message from a concerned friend.

The voice told her the ambassador was not available.

Dolph had been looking around nervously while she was conversing with the gatepost. "Let's look for her truck," he said.

Rose nodded.

It took them awhile to find it, parked several blocks from the embassy. They approached with caution and peered inside. It was empty, but something was tucked under the driver's side windshield wiper.

Rose scanned the area. No one suspicious looking, just people walking on the sidewalks minding their own business. But she'd bet big bucks someone was watching the truck, if for no other reason than to make sure the message was received by the desired party.

She plucked the cream-colored envelope from under the wiper. "Let's get out of here." Back at her car, she pulled away from the curb while Dolph was still scanning for bugs.

"Clean."

Rose passed him the envelope. She wanted to know what was

in it, but she wanted to put some distance between them and the Colombian embassy even more. She wound through the labyrinth of streets in Washington, her eyes flitting between the traffic ahead of her, the rearview mirror and Dolph. He was skimming whatever was written on the sheet of expensive stationery, and cursing under his breath.

She didn't like the look on his face. "Damn it! Read it to me."

He cleared his throat. "'Regrettably, a young woman in your employ has paid me a visit. I have detained her while I complete the arrangements for my trip. I assure you I have no desire to harm her. However, since you persist in interfering in my business, I feel the need for an insurance policy of my own. If you do not wish her harmed, Mrs. Huntington and Mr. Canfield must come alone to Pier 3 of the Hendricks Marina in Essex tomorrow at nine p.m. They will be detained only as long as necessary for me to make my departure. The details of this arrangement must remain confidential. In exchange for your silence and cooperation, I will provide the evidence needed to clear Mr. Canfield of complicity in the death of the young *negre*.' There's no signature."

This time the urge to bang her head on the steering wheel was much stronger.

The others descended on them as soon as they came in the back door. Rose gestured toward the table. "Sit down, gang."

Still standing herself, she read the note out loud.

They sat in stunned silence for several seconds, staring at her. Then Skip jumped up and paced across the family room and back. "Shit, shit, shit! What the hell was she thinking?"

Rose shrugged one shoulder. She wasn't sure much thinking had been involved. "We've got two issues here. How far are we willing to go to save her from her own stupidity? And how much are we willing to risk to get this evidence he's talking about to clear you?"

"Assuming," Dolph said, "this is on the up-and-up."

Kate nodded. "There's no guarantee that he'll let her go once we show up as substitute hostages."

"I've been racking my brain to think of a way to get in that embassy," Rose said.

"Unlikely. That place is a fortress." Skip dropped back into his chair. "And they might not even have her at the embassy itself." He scrubbed his hand over his face.

His eyes darted toward Kate, then back to Rose. He cleared his throat. "I owe her. She risked a lot by pulling a gun on that cop, to keep me from being arrested. I need to go to that marina tomorrow."

Rose had figured he would feel that way. She braced for the explosion.

Kate crossed her arms and glared at Skip. "So how would getting yourself killed now pay her back for saving your hide before?"

"I'm sorry, Kate, but I can't just hide out here and let them hurt her, or worse. Not to mention the other carrot the ambassador's dangling."

Rob leaned forward. "I don't think Judith can make the murder charge stick."

"Maybe not, but I might do time for the other charges, and my PI license, all of our licenses, would be in jeopardy. You might even end up in trouble with the bar association, for harboring a fugitive."

Kate narrowed her eyes at her husband. "Let's get something straight here. If anybody goes—and I'm *not* agreeing to that *yet*—but if we do this, we both go. That's what the note's demanding."

"Garcia's culture's big on *machismo*. He won't be surprised if I come alone."

Kate shoved her chair back and stood up. "Skip, I need to speak with you." Hands on hips, she turned and stomped toward the master bedroom.

Skip expelled a long sigh.

"Go talk to her, son," Dolph said. "We'll start hashing out logistics."

Skip squared his broad shoulders, then stood up and headed down the hall.

Once he was out of earshot, Dolph turned to the others. "I

think we should assume this is a trap."

"We can also assume Kate will win their argument." Rose pulled out her phone to call Mac. "So let's work on how to keep them safe, and get Lilly back."

~~~~~~~~

Kate was sitting on the side of the bed, arms crossed over her chest. Her mouth was set in a thin angry line, but tears trickled down her cheeks.

Skip sat beside her and put an arm around her unyielding shoulders. With the other hand, he gently turned her face toward him. "I have to do this, darlin'. I wish I didn't but I do."

"Not *I*, Skip. *We*. What happened to Thelma and Louise going over the cliff together?"

Skip was thinking one should watch what they ask for when talking to God. He played the motherhood card. "One of us has to survive this. Edie and Billy need at least one parent."

Fresh tears pooled in her eyes. "Skip, I don't know if I can do it again, be the strong widow for the sake of my children. Once in a lifetime may be all I had in me." She bit her lower lip as one of the tears broke loose.

He brushed the wetness from her cheek with his fingertips, while he desperately searched for another argument.

Kate took his hand and held it against her pounding heart. "Bottom line, the note says we both have to show up. There's no point in one of us risking our life when that may not accomplish anything."

Skip stared at her, his thoughts in turmoil. Then he pulled her against him. The ache in his chest was almost unbearable as he heard his daughter's plaintive voice in his head, *When are you coming to get us?*

Maybe never, Pumkin. He choked back a sob.

They clung to each other for several minutes. "We're assuming the worst case here," he finally said into her hair. "We'll have plenty of back-up. We'll be okay."

Kate nodded against his chest.

He lifted her chin and kissed her tenderly. She deepened the kiss. After a minute, she pulled back and whispered, "Change what you can, accept what you can't and enjoy the hell out of life in the meantime."

He hadn't intended to make love to her. The others were waiting. But when he looked into her eyes... "Dear God, I love you," he said, his voice raw with emotion, as he eased her back onto the bed.

CHAPTER TWENTY-SEVEN

While the Canfields were fighting and making up, the others, in consultation with Mac, had decided that Essex and Catonsville were too far apart. Dolph found the address for the Hendricks Marina online and located a motel nearby. That would be their base for the operation.

It had also been decided that Kate and Skip would wear the Kevlar vests. Their light-colored jackets would be too visible at night, however. Sue had been dispatched with Claude and some cash to buy dark jackets loose enough to cover the vests.

Manny had asked to be included in the operation. Rose hated the idea of leaving Sue and Rob with just one guard. But then again, Kate and Skip would definitely be at much more risk.

When they finally surfaced, Rose filled them in on the plan. Over dinner, for which none of them had much appetite, they ironed out the details.

"Dolph and I are your back-up," Rose said. "We take my car, even though it'll be tight." Both her car and Skip's truck had been custom built for them a few years ago. She wanted the advantage the bullet-proof glass and steel plates in the doors would give them should they end up in a car chase with the bad guys. "Manny will stay with the car, keep it running in case we need to leave fast."

"Wish we had one of those tracking devices like these assholes keep putting on our cars," Kate said. "So you all could follow if the ambassador tries to take us elsewhere."

Dolph's eyes lit up. "Actually, we do. It's in my glove box. I ordered it along with the debugging scanner, but I haven't had a chance to test it yet."

Despite the tension of the situation, Rose almost laughed out loud. Dolph did so love his gadgets.

Skip turned to his wife. "Please hear me out, darlin'. We're in this together but I've been thinking that this *machismo* man is going to expect me to show up first and check things out. Make sure it's safe before I allow my wife to be present."

"He's right," Rob said before Kate could protest.

Dolph nodded his agreement. "Skip's got to go down that pier first, but we'll be as close as we can get. I'll set things up with Judith. See if she can get the Coast Guard on alert as well. I'll have to give her the general area at least. Rob, you'll call her with the exact location of the marina if we haven't checked in by a certain time."

~~~~~~~~

When Dolph's former partner answered her cell phone the next morning, she let out a long-suffering sigh.

"Why Judith, you don't sound all that thrilled to hear from me. My heart is broken."

"I'd like to be breaking something else of yours about now."

"Now is that any way to treat the man who's gonna solve your murder case?"

"Which one? I've got three of them at the moment."

"By nine tonight we'll have the name of Jamal's murderer," Dolph said with far more confidence than he felt. "But we need you to organize the cavalry for us, in case things go wrong."

Judith was silent for a moment. "This better not be bullshit or I *am* gonna track you down and break some body parts you're probably fond of."

"No bullshit. I need you to have some people in the Essex area, near the water, by nine." He gave her an intersection five blocks from the marina. "And the Coast Guard needs to be alerted that some criminals may attempt to flee from that area by boat, *with* hostages. Rob Franklin will call you with the exact location, if things go south."

"And where will Canfield be during this operation?" Judith's sarcastic tone implied she didn't expect an honest answer.

But Dolph gave her one. "Right in the middle of it. If you get nothing else out of this, you'll have him. But you gotta promise to do this our way. A lot of lives are at stake. Innocent lives. His wife's for one, and mine and Sue's. If you flood the area with cop cars and try to find him, you'll scare off our quarry at best, and get a bunch of us killed at worst."

She sighed again. "He's really gonna turn himself in this time?" She still sounded skeptical.

"Judith, sweetheart, if we have to call you, he'll be totally thrilled to see you because you'll be saving his hide at that point."

"And if things go right?"

"He'll turn himself in if you still want him to, but we should have the real killer for you at that point. And no matter how it goes down, the risk of someone trying to kill him in jail will be gone by tomorrow. At that point, he'll be willing to come in and help you get the mess straightened out. You really don't have much of a case against him. Your witnesses are phantoms and he'd reported the murder weapon stolen before the crime."

"I still want a sit-down in an interrogation room with your boy," she said.

"You'll get it, one way or the other."

"Okay. I'll set it up. I'll have to notify the City since that's close to the harbor, and maybe bring in the Transportation Authority's Marine Unit. Lord, what a jurisdictional nightmare. I'd better get that sit-down out of this, Dolph."

"You will." After disconnecting Dolph stared sightlessly at the phone, praying that *his boy* would live long enough to face Judith across a table in an interrogation room.

~~~~~~~~

The Super 8 Motel wasn't exactly hopping on a Thursday afternoon. They were able to get two adjoining rooms.

Skip held the transmitter of Dolph's tracking device in his hand, trying to decide the best place to hide it. It was roughly the size and shape of a book of matches. He leaned over and slipped it into the side of his sneaker. Yup, that would work.

"That works," Rose echoed his thought. She was staring at the screen on the receiver, that looked like a cell phone with an oversized antenna. "Give it to me."

He fished it out again and handed it to her. She passed it to Manny. "Take this for a ride. We'll see how well it works and for how far. Then we'll check out that marina, while it's still daylight."

Rose turned back to Skip. "Meantime, you nap." She pointed at Kate and Dolph. "You too. You all need to be on your toes tonight."

"When are you going to nap, Rose?" Dolph asked.

She gave him a teasing grin. "Don't need much rest. I'm not as old as you."

"Ouch." Skip chuckled. "She gets mean when she's in charge."

Rose narrowed her eyes at him. "*Am* I in charge?"

"Yes," he said, his tone now serious. He knew she was the one most likely to be able to keep her cool.

"Good, 'cause when we're in the middle of this, there won't be time to convene a committee meeting. This is a military operation and everyone's safety depends on discipline." Her eyes flicked from his face to Kate's. "The point may come when one of you is in danger, and the other one may not be able to think straight. So you do what I say, even if it's to run in the opposite direction. And if I tell you to stay put, you better be where I left you when I come back."

She looked at Dolph, then back at them. "So who's in charge?"

"You are," Dolph said. Kate nodded.

Rose put her hands on her hips and scowled, but Skip had caught the impish glint in her eye.

"I can't *hear* you! Who's in charge?"

Kate snickered. "You are," she and Dolph chorused.

Rose turned her scowl on Skip.

He stood at attention. "Yes, ma'am. You are in charge, ma'am." He gave the Army private impersonation his best shot, but he was having trouble keeping a straight face.

She flashed him a megawatt grin.

~~~~~~~~

At eight-twenty, Rose's overcrowded car was cruising the streets near the Hendricks Marina. After sundown on an October weeknight was not a time when boaters were visiting their boats. The waterfront area was deserted.

Squeezed between her husband and Dolph in the back seat, Kate was trying to get her pounding heart under control by giving herself a silent pep talk. It wasn't working.

"Doesn't look like they've posted any lookouts," Rose finally said. She pulled over and parked two blocks from the marina.

Rose reached up to switch off the overhead light so it wouldn't come on when they opened the doors. They climbed out of the car as noiselessly as possible. Manny slid across into the driver's seat.

As she'd been instructed, Kate eased her car door closed until she heard the soft click. Then she took a deep breath and joined Rose and the others at the trunk. She and Skip donned the Kevlar vests, then zipped their dark jackets over them.

Skip put his .38 in his jacket pocket. He leaned over and touched the small bulge in the side of his shoe.

Dolph was also patting his bulging pockets with one hand, no doubt making sure he had everything essential. A two-way radio–the partner of the one in Manny's possession–was in his other hand.

Rose nodded and the four of them moved silently toward the marina. They crept single-file along the dark side of the marina's main building, Dolph bringing up the rear. As they reached the corner facing the water, Kate almost ran into Rose. In the dark shadows, she could just barely see Rose's raised hand, signaling for them to wait.

By comparison the moonlight shining over the water was quite bright. A lawn sloped away from them toward the water where a wooden boardwalk stretched across the width of the property. Several piers extended out from it, with dark, silent boats moored in most of the slips. At the end of the third pier from the left was the only boat showing any signs of life.

A light shone from it, silhouetting a dark figure moving around inside the cabin.

"Moves like a woman," Skip whispered.

"Ambassador's wife," Rose whispered back.

Another dark form was moving in the open cockpit at the back of the boat.

Skip's hand found Kate's and squeezed it. Rose nodded and he moved past Kate and started across the lawn.

Dolph stepped up behind her. Kate felt the reassuring warmth of his hand on her shoulder. She realized she was holding her breath and let it out with a soft whoosh.

They watched the figures on the boat.

Just as Skip reached the boardwalk, the light went out in the cabin. He was halfway down the third pier when there was a flicker of movement at the top of the boat. For the briefest of moments, the moonlight outlined a thin silhouette. "Someone's on the upper bridge now," Rose whispered.

Skip had stopped, facing the back of the boat. The figure in the cockpit stood up. It looked like the right height and shape to be the ambassador. The two men faced each other, apparently conversing.

Suddenly Skip wobbled, then fell forward into the boat. The man in the cockpit jumped back. A male voice shouted, "Raul!"

Kate's heart leapt into her throat. Tears blurred her vision. She fumbled with the radio Dolph thrust into her hands but managed not to drop it.

He was stripping off his jacket. "I'm going in the water, if that's okay with you, Rose. See if I can get on board."

"Do it," Rose said.

Dolph handed the jacket to Kate. "Take good care of that. It has the GPS receiver in it."

"I'm gonna try to get on from the boat next door," Rose said. "Stay here, Kate. Call Rob."

The latter order was hardly necessary. Kate was already juggling Dolph's things into one hand so she could pull out her phone.

Rose moved off across the lawn, slipping from shadow to shadow. Dolph had pulled a plastic bag from his pants' pocket while he was kicking off his shoes. He thrust his gun into the bag and stuffed it back in his pocket. He took off toward the boardwalk.

Kate punched the speed dial number she'd programmed into the phone earlier. Her heart beat erratically. It was taking forever for the call to go through. She made herself take a deep breath.

Come on!

Finally she heard Rob's voice. "Hello."

"Call Jud–" Pain shot through Kate's skull. The moonlit scene before her went black.

CHAPTER TWENTY-EIGHT

"Kate! What's going on?" Rob hissed into the phone.

A deep, heavily accented voice answered him. "Do nothing, Mr. Franklin, if you wish to see your friends alive again. No harm will come to them if you keep your five colleagues informed that they are also to do nothing. You will be contacted in twenty-four hours with the location where you will find your friends. By that time the ambassador and his wife will be safely on their way and you may do whatever you wish."

"Who is this?" Rob demanded. "Let me talk to Kate." He heard only silence.

He hit end, then punched the speed-dial number for the police detective.

"Ander–"

"Hendricks Marina. 895 Hilltop Road. Hurry! They're in trouble."

"Got it."

Rob collapsed onto the chair next to Sue at the tiny table in the motel room. Sue took his big hand in both of hers. Rob opened his mouth to say something reassuring but nothing came out. Fear had closed his throat.

"Our Father who art in heaven...," Sue began. Rob joined in.

~~~~~~~~

The boat slips had narrow finger piers between them. By jumping from boat to finger pier to boat, Rose had made it to the boat next to her target. She heard heavy footsteps on the boardwalk. Cautiously peering around the boat's cabin, she saw the silhouette of a man rounding the corner onto the pier. His face was caught in the moonlight for an instant. *The ambassador's driver.* Rose crouched further down.

As he moved past her hiding place, she realized he was carrying a bundle over his shoulder. She had a sick feeling in her gut. The bundle was the shape of a body.

The boat's engine started as the man lowered his burden into the cockpit. He leaped in after it.

Rose dropped to the finger pier, then dove for the railing of the ambassador's boat as it began moving slowly from its slip.

~~~~~~~~~

The water hadn't been as cold as Dolph had feared, thanks to a mild autumn. Head just barely above the surface, he was moving along the side of the boat furthest from the marina, looking for a boarding ladder. When the engine roared to life, he pushed off the side of the boat with his feet, back-stroking madly away to keep from being sucked into the churning propellers.

The boat started moving. He swam as fast as he could to the end of the pier. There he did find a ladder. His wet feet slapped the boards as he raced along the pier, then tore across the lawn.

Kate was gone. Dolph pulled a waterproof penlight out of his pocket and shone it around. His jacket, radio and Kate's cell phone were scattered on the ground. He grabbed the radio and keyed the button. "Right side of the main building. Fast!"

"Roger," Manny replied.

Dolph pulled his jacket on over his dripping clothes and searched for his shoes while he punched Rob's number on the phone.

"Hello." Rob's voice sounded far away, and scared.

"You call Judith?"

"She's on the way."

"They're headed out into the bay. Hang on." Manny had come around the corner of the building, gun extended in both hands. "We need a boat," Dolph yelled to him.

"I'll find us a fast one." Manny took off for the piers.

Dolph raced after him. "I'm leaving the line open," he huffed into the phone. "Hopefully we won't lose the signal over the water." He put the phone in his jacket pocket.

Manny had stopped next to a slip containing a long sleek boat. He jumped aboard and disappeared inside its small cabin. By the time Dolph caught up and released the lines from the cleats on the pier, Manny had the boat hot-wired. He came up through the hatch opening and slid behind the wheel as Dolph jumped into the cockpit.

Manny maneuvered the boat out of the slip. "Hang on!" He shoved the throttle forward. Walls of water rose on either side as he brought the boat up onto a plane.

Dolph dug the phone and tracking device receiver out of his pockets while he caught his breath. He shouted the coordinates showing on the tiny screen of the receiver into the phone.

"They're headed east, toward the shipping channel," he yelled over the roaring engine.

~~~~~~~~~

Kate woke to total darkness. A splitting headache was her only assurance that she was indeed awake. She struggled to get her bearings. She was lying face down. Something hard dug into her stomach. She tried to bring her arms forward to push herself up. She couldn't move them. It took her groggy mind a few seconds to realize her hands were tied behind her back. She couldn't move her feet either.

Why wasn't she gagged? The thrumming of an engine and the slap of water against fiberglass hull gave her the answer. Her captors didn't care if she screamed. She was on a boat, out on the water somewhere.

She started to shake her head to clear it. Pain shot through her skull, just as she recognized the naggingly familiar scent coming from the warm lumpy surface under her. She heard a low groan and the lumpy surface shifted.

"Skip," she hissed in the direction where his ear should be. He groaned again. Kate wiggled, trying to roll off of him. She managed to slide to one side so his tied hands were no longer jammed into her stomach. She moved her head around in the darkness until she found his cheek.

"Skip, wake up!" she whispered.

He moaned, then muttered, "Where are we?"

"Best guess is the floor of a boat headed out to sea," Kate said, trying to keep the fear out of her voice. "Are you okay? What happened?"

He moved his head and collided with her nose. "I was standing on the pier. Garcia was saying something to me. Felt something sting my arm. Then my legs just went numb under me and I was falling."

"Stun gun?"

Skip's head shook slightly against her cheek. "Most likely a dart from a tranquilizer gun. How'd they get you?"

"Rose and Dolph took off to try to get onto the boat, told me to stay by the building and call Rob. Last thing I remember is punching his number on my phone."

"He'll call Judith anyway, when we don't check in," Skip whispered. "We just have to stall Garcia until the cops arrive."

"Rose was jumping from boat to boat and Dolph went in the water. One or both of them may have managed to get on board."

They fell silent for a moment. Then Skip said, "We need to stay calm."

Kate was surprised to discover that she was calm. The clinical detachment that served her well when her clients were in crisis had kicked in. Nonetheless, she touched her lips to his cheek, drawing comfort from the contact. He turned his head and kissed her hard.

They were blinded by a bright light. A deep, heavily-accented voice sneered, "Look at de lovebirds."

"Shut up, Raul," Garcia's more cultured voice responded. "Untie their feet."

Rough hands yanked at Kate's ankles and she looked up into cold dark eyes. Raul moved on to untie the rope around Skip's ankles. Then he grabbed her and hoisted her up. She stumbled, wincing as blood rushed back into her feet.

Garcia took her by the arm. They were in a small sleeping cabin. Raul leaned down to drag Skip to his feet.

Garcia nudged Kate ahead of him out the door and across a spacious living room. A sliding glass door led to the cockpit.

Once out in the open, Raul shoved Skip toward a bench at

the back of the cockpit. Skip tripped over something on the deck, swayed, then caught his balance. The ambassador led Kate around the obstacle and over to sit next to her husband.

Garcia nodded and Raul climbed the ladder to the flying bridge.

~~~~~~~~

As Skip's eyes adjusted to the relative darkness, relieved only by the moonlight, he realized Garcia was holding a gun on them. Moonlight glinted off the mother-of-pearl handle.

The son-of-a-bitch is pointing my *gun at us.*

"This grieves me deeply, Mrs. Huntington, to put you through this," Garcia said to Kate. "I assure you that you and your husband will come to no harm as long as you cooperate. We just need time to get out of the country."

Skip didn't like the sound of that. Where the hell was he taking them?

"This boat's not seaworthy enough to go out into the ocean."

"Of course not," Garcia said. "We'll put in to harbor further south. We have passports and airline tickets in our new names. I have put money away through the years, for just such an emergency. My family and I will live comfortably overseas for the rest of our lives."

Kate nudged his shoulder with her own. Skip followed her gaze to the bundle of cloth he'd tripped over. It wasn't the rolled-up tarp he'd assumed it was. Lilly lay on the deck, bound hands and feet. She wasn't moving.

Anger surged through him. Did these bastards kill her? Wait, she's probably alive. They wouldn't bother to tie up a corpse. He took a deep breath and brought his mind back to the task of stalling for time.

"Did you know we are expecting a child?" the ambassador was saying.

The question seemed to be aimed at Kate. "Congratulations," she said in a strained voice.

"What are you going to do with us?" Skip demanded.

"Raul has found a small uninhabited island on the map. It is not far from here. We will leave you there with food and water. Once we have a sufficient head start, I will call your friends and tell them your location."

Skip was half tempted to believe him. It was a plausible plan. But he was still going to look for an opening to overpower their captors. Of course the fact that his hands were tied behind his back was a small problem.

He wiggled his hands. Some sensation was returning to them. It felt like he might be able to work the rope loose, given enough time.

Garcia was shaking his head, the moonlight reflecting off the shiny black of his hair. "This was all so unnecessary. It is regrettable that you chose, Mr. Canfield, to send the young woman to investigate."

"She came on her own. She was just trying to help." Skip's mind belatedly registered that the engine had stopped. They were drifting in the water.

"And now you are here, instead of waiting for me to contact you as I said I would in my letter to Mr. Franklin."

"What do you mean, Garcia? Your second note told us to come here."

"What second note? I only sent one note, Mr. Canfield." The ambassador's expression in the moonlight seemed genuinely confused.

~~~~~~~~~

The coordinates on the tiny screen said they were getting closer to their quarry. Dolph read them into the phone. Its signal was starting to break up but he heard Rob repeat the information to Sue, who was on another phone with Judith.

Manny had slowed to an idle. Dolph couldn't hear the other boat's engine. Looking across the water, he thought he made out a dark lump ahead.

Manny shut off the engine. "Tell Rob we've found them," he said in a low voice, as they continued to drift toward the dark lump.

Dolph was about to tell him that the phone signal was gone when the roar of a gunshot surged across the water.

CHAPTER TWENTY-NINE

Kate froze. Skip stiffened beside her. For a horrible instant, she thought he had been shot. Then the ambassador's look of confusion deepened as he slowly pitched forward.

The elegant woman from the newspaper picture stepped out of the shadow of the cabin doorway. An impressive-looking pistol was in her hand. She looked down at her husband sprawled at her feet. "Juan, you were such a fool."

Raul climbed down from the bridge, stepped over his boss's body and started to move past the woman. She put a hand on his arm. "*¡Apurate, mi querido!*" He nodded and went into the cabin.

"They're lovers," Skip whispered to Kate. Louder he said, "Are we at the island, *Señora*? We won't give you any trouble."

The elegant woman let out a not very elegant snort. "I'm afraid Juan's plan has been aborted. I have no intention of living in obscurity for the rest of my life, unable to contact my family or return to my homeland. Instead I will take my poor husband's remains home–the ambassador cut down by an American assassin. After a period of mourning, I will campaign for the presidency of my country. We will stir the masses into a frenzy of hatred for the country they thought was their ally. As a widow I will get much sympathy. Once I am elected, we will crush the rebels and restore my country to its glory. We will no longer be a puppet of the United States."

A swell caught the boat, making it rock. *Señora* Garcia staggered. She grabbed for the ladder to the bridge to steady herself as the boat rocked again.

Kate could feel Skip's shoulder moving against hers. *He's trying to get his hands free*. She wiggled her own. The rope cut painfully into her wrists.

"What about the disgrace when it comes out that your husband used to be one of those rebels?" Skip said. "That won't go over very well with your conservative friends."

She saw a flash of white teeth as *Señora* Garcia smiled. It was not a pleasant smile. A shiver ran down Kate's spine.

"Ah, that hideous rumor will be exposed as yet another American plot when my countrymen learn that the person spreading it is my husband's murderer."

"You can try to discredit me that way," Skip said. "But our friends will come forward with the truth."

The woman laughed. "That is who I am speaking of. I will swear that I saw *Señor* Franklin leave my husband's study just after I heard a shot. I ran in to find my beloved Juan dead on the floor. You, *Señor* Canfield, will already be dead, along with your meddling wife."

He shook his head. "Won't work. The medical examiner and crime scene analysts will be able to tell your husband died elsewhere, and earlier than you're claiming."

"The embassy is Colombian territory. We will not allow Americans to examine our ambassador."

"Then Rob will never be convicted of killing him," Kate said.

"I don't care if the American legal system believes me. All that matters is that the Colombian people believe me. If *Señor* Franklin is allowed to go free, that will just inflame them more."

"The truth will still come out," Kate said. "Too many people know about your husband's past now."

The white teeth flashed again in the moonlight. "Ah, but you see, *Señora* Huntington, *you* are the only person who can link my husband to *Señor* Dawson. And you will be dead, killed while fleeing the country with your fugitive husband. My people will view the claims of these others as a vicious rumor. Yet another strike against the Americans. Not only do they murder our ambassador, they then spread lies about him."

Raul came out of the cabin and spoke to his lover in Spanish. "What does he mean?" Skip said. "What automatic starter?" Kate was not reassured by his tone.

"You will be having an unfortunate accident, *Señor* Canfield. The boat was rented in your name. A typed letter has been sent to your business partner confessing that you did kill *el negre* and you and your wife are leaving the country to escape punishment. You plead with your partner to care for your young children. The note is quite touching."

Above the woman's head, Kate caught the glint of moonlight reflecting off a familiar silky black bun. She could just make out the silhouette of a compact female figure climbing over the railing of the flying bridge.

Kate quickly dropped her gaze and schooled her face into a neutral expression.

"But you are amateur sailors," *Señora* Garcia said, as Raul started up the ladder again to the bridge. "You do not realize that gas fumes can build up in the bilge. So when you start the engine..."

The woman let out an exaggerated sigh. "A pity, people will say. Such a shame that *Señor* Canfield lost his temper and it led to the destruction of himself and his wife."

Kate grit her teeth. *The bitch is enjoying herself!*

"Once Raul has set up the starter so that it can be activated by radio signal, we will be departing in the dingy."

"What about Lilly?" Skip pointed his chin toward the immobile body on the deck.

Señora Garcia waved a hand in the air. "I don't care what the authorities conclude when they find her body, *if* they find it. We will be long gone by then."

The boat swayed again and she clutched for the ladder rail.

Skip wiggled against Kate's shoulder. "Please, let us have a last kiss, *Señora, por favor.*"

What? He wants to kiss? Now?

"Of course." The woman gestured with the gun.

Skip turned to Kate. As his lips touched hers, he whispered

against them, "When I make a move, hit the deck. If you understand, pull back and say my name."

She froze for a second. Rose's words echoed in her head, *There won't be time to convene a committee meeting.* She broke the kiss and gasped, "Oh, Skip."

Bright lights flashed across the water. A voice boomed through a megaphone. "Police. Drop the gun!"

The woman raised the pistol instead and pointed it at Kate's head. "Leave us alone or she dies!"

Skip sprang up between them and Kate dove for the deck, twisting and ducking her shoulder as she'd been taught in *aikido*. The gun roared over her head. She fell on top of Lilly and felt the air whoosh out of the young woman's lungs. Kate's body continued in its roll. She landed on her back, as helpless as an overturned turtle, the Kevlar vest crushing her tied hands against the deck.

Above her, *Señora* Garcia was backing away, her gun pointed at Skip's chest as he lunged across the cockpit toward her.

Kate planted a foot on the edge of the bench and shoved, scissoring her body around. She aimed a kick at the woman's knee and felt a satisfying pop.

Señora Garcia screamed. Her hands flew up in the air. The gun roared again. Arms flailing, the woman fell backward and disappeared.

Skip teetered off balance, his momentum still carrying him forward, no way to grab for support. Kate watched in horror as he followed their would-be killer over the railing.

"Help!" she screamed. "Somebody help him! His hands are tied."

She heard several splashes.

Her mind went numb.

Men and women in uniform were pouring onboard from the Coast Guard cutter and the police boat now flanking the cabin cruiser. A Coast Guard officer lifted Kate to her feet.

She scrambled toward the side of the boat, but the young man grabbed her arm. "Whoa, we don't need you in the drink too. Hold still, please, and I'll get your hands free." He started working on the knots at her wrists.

Holding still was easier said than done. She was shivering uncontrollably and gasping for air. It took her a moment to realize she was sobbing.

She didn't know if the bullets had hit her husband but she did know that people who fell into the Chesapeake's deep shipping channel, even in broad daylight, were sometimes not found again. Not until their bodies washed ashore.

CHAPTER THIRTY

Skip kicked with all his might. The vest that had saved his life just seconds ago was now dragging him to his death. He tried again and again to yank his hands apart, hoping the water would make the ropes slippery. A part of his mind registered the sting of brackish water soaking through to where he'd ripped the skin off his wrists.

Blood is even better.

He yanked again and felt something give. One hand pulled loose.

He tore open the front of his jacket and struggled to get out of it as his lungs threatened to explode. He fumbled with the straps on the sides of the vest, his fingers numb from poor circulation and the cold water. He desperately wanted to open his mouth, to breathe.

He needed to breathe.

~~~~~~~

The same young man who had untied her had lifted Kate over the railing and handed her off to another officer on the Coast Guard cutter. She was huddled in a blanket on a bench, shivering and praying. *Please, God! Please, God!*

As if she were viewing a movie from a great distance, she watched Garcia's dripping wife being helped on board by the diver who had rescued her.

Please, God! Please, God!

The woman's feet no sooner hit the deck than Judith Anderson spun her around and cuffed her. Blatantly ignoring the woman's bleating about diplomatic immunity, Judith started reciting the Miranda warning.

Please, God! Please, God!

A shout came from the water. Kate jumped up and raced to the railing. The dark water was crisscrossed with spotlights.

"We've got him," Dolph's voice floated up from below, accompanied by coughing and retching sounds. One of the spotlights veered in that direction, lighting up the water's surface. Sandwiched between Dolph and Rose, both treading water, was Skip's pale face, dark hair plastered across his forehead. His mouth moved but Kate couldn't hear him.

"He's okay," Rose's voice conveyed the message.

Kate hung onto the railing as her knees gave out.

~~~~~~~~

A young Guardsman reached down to help Skip up the last few steps of the ladder. He stood on the deck, wobbling a bit. Kate threw her arms around him, almost knocking him over. He held her tight against his heaving chest and closed his eyes.

Gentle hands guided them to a bench. Skip pulled Kate onto his lap. They clung to each other. Someone draped a blanket over his shoulders and tuck it around both of them.

A female voice said, "Please, sir, let me examine you."

Skip raised his head slightly and shook it. The raw wounds on his wrists stung like hell. His throat ached from swallowing and then coughing up the brackish water. Now that the adrenaline was wearing off he could feel the pain in his chest where at least one of the bullets had hit the vest. It hurt every time he dragged in a breath. He suspected he had a broken rib or two.

But he croaked out, "I'm okay."

He buried his face in his wife's curls.

~~~~~~~~

Kate heard footsteps and felt a presence standing over them. She looked up. Detective Anderson was accompanied by a uniformed Baltimore City officer.

"We have some questions." Judith's voice was gentle.

Kate slid off Skip's lap to sit beside him on the bench. The Coast Guard medic hurried over with another blanket and her first aid kit. Kate gratefully took the blanket.

Again Skip said, "I'm okay. Thanks." His voice sounded like a file against metal.

Judith introduced her companion as Sergeant Armstrong. The sergeant stood at parade rest. Judith crouched down in front of them. "Dolph filled us in. What happened on the boat?"

Skip started to answer but Kate put a finger against his still blue-tinged lips. "Garcia's wife shot him," she said. "She and the driver, Raul What's-His-Name, are lovers."

"Raul's the guy we found knocked out up on the bridge?" Judith asked.

"Yeah. Rose got him," Skip whispered.

"Dear God!" Kate jumped up. "Tell them not to start the boat's engine. They were letting fumes build up in–"

Judith held up her hand. "The Coast Guard turned on the bilge fan, but to be on the safe side, they're towing the boat in. Is this Raul the guy the FBI's been looking for, Delgado?"

"No." Kate sank back down next to Skip. "Delgado's a cousin or something to Mrs. Garcia. He was part of their original plan, to assassinate the Colombian president during his state visit. The revised plan was to take the ambassador's body back to the embassy and blame his death on Rob Franklin, so anything he said would be discredited. Then Mrs. Garcia was going to use the murder of her husband to rally Colombians against America and the current regime, and get herself elected president. They set it up to look like we were fleeing the country. They were going to blow up the boat, with us on it."

The City officer spoke for the first time. "They're both claiming diplomatic immunity."

Horrified, Kate stared up at him. "You can't just let them go."

Judith shook her head. "No, but we'll have to turn them over to their government. We won't be able to try them for their crimes here."

"The Colombian government will probably treat them worse than we would," Skip rasped out. "Is Lilly okay?"

"Unconscious, but stable. The Coast Guard medic thinks she was drugged. The police boat's taking her ashore." Judith stood up and put a hand on Skip's shoulder. "I've radioed ahead, cancelled the BOLO on you."

"What about the other charges?" Kate asked.

"What other charges?" Judith said with a small grin.

"Against Lilly too?" Skip rasped.

Judith looked at the City cop. He took the hint and walked away. "Charges against her may be tougher to make go away, but I'll talk to Dan."

She paused, then added, "There's another piece to the puzzle you may not know about. Did you hear that Senator Robinson was killed during an apparent robbery in his home in Reisterstown?"

Skip had a stunned look on his face. "When?"

"Last Wednesday evening. In his study."

Kate was confused. She looked from one to the other of them.

"Janice sent me to Robinson's house," Skip started to explain, then paused to clear his throat. "To get something. When I brought it back to her, that's when I saw the newspaper on her desk, with the picture of the ambassador and his wife."

"What was the something you got from the senator?" Judith asked.

Skip shook his head. "Confidential. Not related."

Judith gave him a hard stare. He shook his head again.

She shrugged. "Set up at the senator's house smelled. There was a note pad on his desk. Lab determined that a page had been torn off. Impressions on the page below it indicated it had 'Janice Browning' and 'Colombian ambassador, Garcia' written on it. None of that made sense until after my talk with Dolph the other day."

"That's why you were willing to go along with this craziness tonight," Skip said in a raspy whisper. "You'd put two and two together."

Kate was still totally lost. "Excuse me. The cold must be numbing my brain."

"They didn't go after Janice just because she was staying with us..." Skip's voice gave out completely.

"She'd probably asked the senator to check out the

ambassador," Judith said, "and Mrs. Garcia's men had her phone bugged."

Kate digested that for a moment. "So they might have just been watching us up to that point, but then they figured we were telling people–"

She felt a bump. The boat had docked at the marina. She looked over the railing behind their bench. Rob and Sue were on the pier below, waiting for them.

It dawned on Kate that they could go home, that she would be sleeping in her own bed tonight. And tomorrow Mac would bring the kids home. She almost burst into tears.

The Coast Guard captain helped his passengers down a set of steps onto the pier.

Rob swallowed Kate up in a bear hug. "Let's never do this again," he whispered in her ear. He snagged Rose, who was sporting a blanket shawl, as she tried to maneuver past them. She only gave token resistance when Rob dragged her into a three-way hug. Skip stepped up behind the two women and wrapped long arms around them.

Judith and Dolph were the last to disembark.

Dolph held out his arms. The blanket slid from his damp shoulders.

Sue ignored the open arms and grabbed him by a cold ear instead. "Retired, huh?"

CHAPTER THIRTY-ONE

Kate was incredibly nervous. Outgoing person that she was, she did not normally get nervous just because she was meeting someone new. But then again this wasn't just any someone she was about to meet.

She rubbed a sweaty palm on her skirt. Skip reached over and took her hand.

Kate said a silent prayer for the souls of Miller, Janice, Jamal and Senator Robinson. She added Juan Garcia to the list. Her eyes filled.

She blinked hard, then once again rehearsed in her head the words she'd prepared. She hoped she wouldn't get tongue-tied.

Rob was sitting on her other side in the small waiting room. Liz was beside him. The Randolphs, with Mac and Rose, were across the room. Rob circled his arm around Kate's shoulders. "Deep breath. You'll do fine," he whispered. Skip squeezed her hand just as the door opened.

"Come this way, please," the woman standing in the doorway said.

They filed after her, down a short hallway and through a room containing several desks. Trying not to gawk, they entered the Oval Office.

The President stood behind his desk, smiling, as they trooped in. The woman nudged them into a line, then left the room.

The President went down the line, listening carefully as a thirty-something aide gave a quick and not always completely accurate summary of each person's role in foiling the plot to undermine the United States' relationship with an ally and assassinate that ally's leader. The President shook each person's hand and expressed his gratitude. His words were tailored to each of them.

When he got to Skip, the President said, "Your bravery is remarkable, Mr. Canfield. I don't know that I could have rushed a woman holding a gun, even if I was wearing a bullet-proof vest."

"Mr. President, there is no bravery greater than yours," Skip replied. "Only the very brave or the very crazy are willing to be President of the United States."

The President threw back his head and laughed. "If those are my only two choices, Mr. Canfield, then I accept your compliment."

The President stepped to his left and his aide began his spiel. Kate looked up into the face of the leader of her country. She reached out her hand and he took it.

Interrupting the aide, Kate said, "Mr. President, there is someone else who deserves to be honored as much as we do. His name was Miller Dawson and he served his country in so many ways. He was an operative for the CIA, a soldier in Desert Storm and an employee of the National Security Agency. The coroner's report says that he suffered a heart attack that precipitated a fatal fall, but he was killed because he recognized Ambassador Garcia at a cocktail party."

Kate swallowed hard. "He left a widow, and two children who deserve to know that their father was a hero. Mr. President, I ask that you please give Miller Dawson a Purple Heart posthumously."

The aide cleared his throat, then whispered in his boss's ear. With a nod, the President returned his attention to Kate. "I'm not sure that he would be eligible for a Purple Heart."

Kate's heart sank.

The President enveloped her hand in both of his. "Would the Presidential Medal of Freedom do instead?"

~~~~~~◇~~~~~~

Author's Notes

If you enjoyed this book, please take just a moment to post a short review on Amazon and/or other retailers. Reviews help to keep the series going by promoting sales that provide the funds for cover art, editing and formatting. You can find the links to these retailers at http://misteriopress.com/misterio-press-bookstore/#kassandra-lamb

Just a few quick comments and expressions of gratitude, and then I will share with you a peek at the next two Kate Huntington mysteries.

As Kate points out to Miller, the therapist is not responsible for the client's success in therapy, the client is. Most of my clients worked extremely hard in therapy to put to rest the traumatic events that were holding them back in life, and most achieved most or all of their goals. But a smaller group did more than just put the past behind them. They totally transformed themselves and their lives. The fictional character, Miller Dawson, is meant to exemplify and honor those clients.

I always saw my role as that of tour guide on a very critical and difficult journey. I walked the path with my clients—mostly beside them, sometimes a little ahead leading them—and always trying very hard to point out the road signs (options), roadblocks and potholes. I felt then and still feel today that it was a great privilege to be a part of their healing process.

If only we could put a country into therapy. Poor Colombia has been torn by violence and unrest for decades. I tried very hard to research the history and politics of the country and portray them accurately. Hopefully any errors are minimal. There is now, theoretically, peace between the left-wing rebels, right-wing paramilitary groups and the government. The current regime is trying to maintain that peace and make some efforts to help the poor, but bribery, corruption, unemployment and poverty are still rampant.

Despite that dismal backdrop, the Colombian people are

known for their open and friendly nature, which speaks to the resiliency of the human spirit. I personally know two immigrants from Colombia and they are delightful individuals.

On a lighter note, I want to thank the many wonderful people who helped me make this book happen. I will be eternally grateful to Angi, my good friend and primary beta reader, who handed it back saying, "It's got the potential to be the best one yet, but it needs a lot of work;" to my other betas, Gina, Sue and Ralph, who helped me make it better and better, and then better still; to *misterio press* author, Catie Rhodes, for her thorough and incredibly valuable critique and to my editor, Marcy Kennedy, both of whom not only helped me put a final polish on this book but helped me become a better writer; and last but not least, to *misterio press* author, K.B. Owens, who did the final read-through and proofread to make sure my revisions made sense.

Also a big thank you to all the wonderful people who support me in my writing endeavors, especially the members of my Facebook writers' group, WANA1011, and my fellow authors at *misterio press*. A special thanks to my friend and partner at *misterio*, Shannon Esposito, who has talked me off the ledge more than once during this writing journey. And I'd better not forget my long-suffering husband who proofreads my manuscripts and puts up with my writerly ways (like staying up until 3 a.m.) Kisses and hugs, sweetie!

And now without further ado, a preview of Books 6 and 7...

ZERO HERO
A Kate Huntington Mystery (# 6)

First responder Peter Jamieson saved many lives on 9/11, including several children. For the next ten years, the reserved firefighter pursued the only career he had ever wanted.

Then on the tenth anniversary of 9/11, the media replays the videos again and again–the smoke against the blue sky, the towers coming down, the aftermath at Ground Zero... and Pete starts having nightmares and flashbacks. His world quickly spirals out of control as he turns to drugs and alcohol in an attempt to block the images and feelings. He hits bottom when he is suspended from the job he loves.

Seventeen months later, Pete is slowly recovering the life he once had when the insurance companies cut him off.

Psychotherapist Kate Huntington is afraid that her lawyer friend, Rob Franklin, has lost his professional objectivity with regard to Pete's case. Are the *pro bono* client's symptoms stirring up Rob's memories of his own past struggles with PTSD? When she meets Pete, she soon finds herself sucked in as well. How can they not do everything possible to help this man who risked his life to save others?

Pete's circumstances go from bad to worse when he is accused of murdering his best friend and former drug dealer. As Kate and her private detective husband try to clear him, they find themselves caught up in a lot more than they bargained for–drug dealers, pimps, and the Mafia. Can they save Pete from the system, and himself? And keep themselves and their friends alive in the process?

FATAL FORTY-EIGHT
A Kate Huntington Mystery (#7)

Kate's former boss, Sally Ford, is retiring. The new man in her life, Charles Tolliver, has convinced her to turn over the reins of The Trauma Recovery Center to others and spend her golden years with him.

But instead of many golden years, she may only have forty-eight hours. On the evening of her retirement party, she is kidnapped by a serial killer.

Normally the disappearance of an adult would be handled by a different department, but Lieutenant Judith Anderson of the Baltimore County Police Department realizes the MO is similar to a rash of kidnappings/murders that occurred in New Haven, Connecticut the previous year. When Kate and her P.I. husband insist on being part of the investigation, Judith's hesitation is brief. A woman's life is at stake and there is no time to lose.

Unfortunately the pair of FBI agents who arrive from New Haven have mixed emotions about civilian involvement. The middle-aged male agent is happy to have Kate's assistance as he fine-tunes his psychological profile of the 'unsub' the press hads dubbed the Forty-Eight Hour Killer. But the voluptuous, young female agent believes in doing things by the book.

As she locks horns out in the field with Skip, misunderstandings abound back at headquarters. But there's no time for these innuendoes and jealousies. Sally has less than forty-eight hours to live.

About the Author

Kassandra Lamb was a psychotherapist for over two decades, specializing in trauma recovery. She has also taught psychopathology at Towson University and at other colleges. Now retired, she devotes the majority of her time to her other greatest passion, writing. The magic portal to the world of Kate and her friends (i.e., Kassandra's computer) is located in Florida, where Kass's husband and dog catch occasional glimpses of her.

She has completed six books in the Kate Huntington series and two Kate on Vacation novellas. She is currently working on book seven.

You can read and see more about Kassandra and the Kate Huntington series (including photo galleries) at http://kassandralamb.com. Please sign up for the newsletter to get updates regarding future releases and other interesting tidbits about the series.

Kassandra blogs at http://misteriopress.com about psychology, relationships, and a variety of other topics. Please check it out.

She also hangs out on Facebook (https://www.facebook.com/kassandralambauthor), on Twitter @KassandraLamb, and on Pinterest (http://www.pinterest.com/kassandralamb/) or you can contact her at lambkassandra3@gmail.com.

At misterio press, we take pride in producing top quality books for our readers. All manuscripts are proofread several times, but proofreaders are human. If you discover any errors in this book, please e-mail the author at lambkassandra3@gmail.com. Thank you!

Look for these other great *misterio press* titles

Karma's A Bitch (Pet Psychic Mysteries)
by Shannon Esposito
Maui Widow Waltz (Islands of Aloha Mysteries)
by JoAnn Bassett
The Metaphysical Detective (Riga Hayworth Mysteries)
by Kirsten Weiss
Dangerous and Unseemly (Concordia Wells Mysteries)
by K.B. Owen
Murder, Honey (Carol Sabala Mysteries)
by Vinnie Hansen

www.ingramcontent.com/pod-product-compliance
Lightning Source LLC
Chambersburg PA
CBHW031252170626
46807CB00001B/109